Moishe Fantasy

By Paul Chow

Tammy
This is a time before
you. I hope tragic
like this doesn't happen
any more. If your dad
were alive, I would certainly
like to hear this story

Paul Chow
Oct. 15 2011

This book is a work of fiction. Names and characters are either products of the author's imagination or are used fictitiously.

MOISHE FANTASY. Copyright © 2010 Paul Chow

ISBN: 1453611738
EAN-13: 9781453611739

Manufactured in the United States of America.

Acknowledgments

I wouldn't be able to tell this story without the help and encouragement from my friends. Tony Chu and C. Y. Lee suggested the background, Juno Lu helped me collect material from Shanghai, Teh-han Chow set the opening style, Vera Chow listened and offered opinions to my ever-changing stories, Wen Tan advised on the music and suggested the title, Susan Tuan offered criticism and corrected some of my grammatical mistakes, Jo Fergerson edited the 1st draft, Alma Vactor and Iris Shah edited the later drafts, Helen Giedt proofread and offered encouragement and Jennifer Chiu put the final touch on the manuscript and put it to press.

Moishe Fantasy

CHAPTER ONE

The bearded man in the black suit looked nervous. He was holding on tightly to an overhead sling in a jam-packed tramcar. His stiff body swayed passively to the rocking motion of the tram. His free hand moved nervously back and forth from the side pocket of his pants to the breast pocket of his stylish suit. The suit was meticulously bespoken, made from finely woven Shetland mohair with the last ebony sleeve button undone. It was obvious that the man was not used to dressing up even though his suit clung to his body like a glove. His mind was somewhere else. From time to time he pulled out a pocket watch. He mechanically put it to his ear before taking a look at it and then returning it to his waist pocket.

The man's free hanging hand suddenly shot up like a dozing crocodile snapping on a crane that had intruded into its space. The tram jerked. It stopped. The door swung open. The man rushed out of the tramcar, dragging behind him a skinny boy whose twiggy wrist was tightly clamped in the crocodile's jaw.

The door was quickly shut and the tram moved on, leaving just the man and the little boy in an otherwise deserted street. The man looked down in extreme anger. Next to the dangling chain of his pocket watch, he saw two wide-open eyes on a pale dirty face staring at him. Their expression was of surprise and curiosity rather than fear and remorse. That infuriated the man even more. Livid with rage, he raised up his free hand. Like a bolt of lightning, it came down on the dirty little face. The tiny head jerked back like the tip of a cracking whip. The impact tore the little hand out of the man's grip. The small bony body flew out and fell onto the cobblestones. Lying there, the two round eyes were still fixed on the man.

The man was breathing heavily. If he had not acted in time, he thought, that dirty little thief would not have just taken his pocket watch but could also have stolen the lives of his entire family! He couldn't imagine what would have come upon them. The more he thought about it the angrier he became. He walked up to the little urchin who was still lying motionless on the cobblestones. In exasperation he lifted up the shoe that he had meticulously polished before coming out and aimed it at the small pile of bones.

But instead of delivering the apocalyptic punishment, the shoe hesitated in midair. Then it dropped back down on the stone pavement.

What could that accomplish? He could bet anything that this little bugger would go right back to picking another pocket and, after that, to snatching another purse. That was the only way these *Untermensch* knew how to keep themselves alive. These lazy low intelligent creatures were like flies in the ghetto and cancers in a body. The only way to get rid of flies was to exterminate their entire species from the source, the city's cesspools. Swatting one or two could never solve the problem. Besides, why should he appoint himself the policeman to clean up the trash for the entire society? It was not worth dirtying his polished shoe. He had more urgent matters to attend to. The man turned around and hastened away in disgust.

On his way he walked past a pawnshop. He peeped into the window. The place was stacked with all kinds of odd things like a poor man's museum, nothing expensive. He wouldn't be surprised to find his pocket watch among them if he had not caught that little creeping hand in his pocket. Nothing in particular caught his attention except a violin. But this was not the time to browse. He hurried on.

2

Paul Chow

The bearded man came to the end of the street. He looked at the large enamel street sign displayed high up on the corner of the building - "Beethoven Platz". He pulled out a piece of paper from his pocket. After checking with what was written on the paper, he resumed his journey slowly until he came to the third house.

He stopped in front of a maroon colored door. He checked the number with that on the piece of paper in his hand and then looked around. He could not believe that there was not a soul in the entire street. He put the piece of paper back into his pocket and straightened his back. He pulled on his coattail. He had not dressed up like this for so long that he couldn't even remember when the last time was. He touched his tie before walking up the doorsteps. When he reached the top of the stairs, he took a deep breath. Then he lifted the heavy doorknocker.

He knocked. There was no answer.

He waited for a few seconds before knocking again. When he still did not get any response, he hesitantly tried the doorknob. To his surprise, it opened. He entered cautiously and found himself in a tall foyer. There was no one there except a few angels in white gowns surrounded by many cherubs with red cheeks looking down at him in silence from the ceiling dome.

"May I help you?" a voice in a foreign accent startled the intruder. He quickly turned toward the voice. In the meantime, his hand reached into the inside pocket of his coat and pulled out a piece of paper. He had no idea where this man had come from. He bent his body forward as much as he could and lowered his head toward the man as he had seen people in pictures do to the Buddha in an Oriental temple. He was told that this was how these people greeted each other instead of shaking hands; they considered body touching rude. How civilized! The man did not acknowledge his greeting, obviously a low ranking official who was not familiar with manners. He handed the man the piece of paper with both hands, according

3

to the custom that he had been told. But the cultureless man took it from his hands with just one hand. After taking a quick glance at the paper, the man opened one of the doors.

"Follow me," he said and led his visitor into an inner room.

Inside the room there was a man in a suit sitting behind a large oak desk. The obviously lower ranking official handed with both hands the piece of paper to the man sitting behind the desk. The two men exchanged some words, incomprehensible to the visitor. Then the man behind the desk stood up and stretched out a hand.

"Please sit down," he said after shaking the visitor's hand. "May I see your passport?"

"Passport? I... I don't have one," the visitor answered in embarrassment.

"What kind of identification do you have then?"

"Just this..." the visitor's trembling hand fumbled a little while in his coat pocket and took out a card that was crumbled from being carried around and yellowed from age.

The man behind the desk took a quick glance at the card without taking it from the visitor's hand and said, "That's good enough for me. How many are there in your party?"

"Three. Just my wife, my child and I. But I don't have their papers with me. I'll..."

"That's all right."

"I can go back to fetch them."

"It's not necessary. It certainly is not worth your effort to make an extra trip for them. They will soon be worthless to you anyway. Just give me their names." Saying this, the officer pulled out a sheet of paper and wrote down all the names the visitor gave him. After that, he carefully put a big round seal on the paper. The seal was the color of a lamb's fresh blood. It was as big as the brand on a lamb. After making sure that it was dry, he folded it and put it in an envelope. He handed the envelope to the visitor and said,

"Don't let anyone see it until you get to your destination.

What I am doing is against the policies of your government and mine. I have circumvented all the red tape. If I get into trouble, so will you."

"Sir, you are so kind!"

"That word *kind* is too heavy. This is my duty. I am just a messenger."

"May God bless you, Mr. ... how should I address you, sir?"

"You don't need to know my name. You will never see my face or hear my name again. Go tell your people that the door to this office will remain open for them as long as I am here and don't get caught."

"What will happen to you if you get caught?" the visitor was unable to hide his curiosity.

"I don't know," the man behind the desk chuckled as he answered. "But that's my worry, not yours."

"But this is too good to be true. Without a name, people may think it is a hoax. They may not believe me."

"My name is written next to the red seal."

"How do you pronounce it?"

"Heh Fengshan. My official title is under the name. They can check on it. Customs will admit you with no questions asked when you reach your destination. But I don't know how you are going to get there from here," he chuckled again, not as light heartedly as the first time. "That will be your worry. You had better go now. You must have a lot of things to take care of before you leave. May your god bless you."

The bearded man hurried out of the building and traced his way back to the main street. After making a few more turns, he came to a busy street that was lined with shops. Ordinarily Vienna was never short of shoppers. But on this day, there were only a few pedestrians. As he walked down the street, he scanned the signs hanging over his head along the sidewalk. He soon spotted the sign that he was looking for. He pushed open the door underneath the sign and was immediately blinded by the glittering of so many precious stones in the display cases surrounding him. The man paid no attention to any of them. He walked straight up to the counter. He reached his hand into his inner coat pocket and took out a small package. He put it on the counter and unfolded the wrapping. Without wasting any time he asked the man behind the counter,

"How much can you give me for this?"

The jeweler bent his head down toward the counter. His eyes suddenly opened wide. In front of him was a string of at least 50 brilliant cut-diamonds of about 3/4 of a carat apiece. He picked the string up and held it against the light. Their sparkle and color paled all the stones under his display counter. Then he reached into his pocket and pulled out a magnifying monocle. He stuck it onto one of his eye sockets as he brought the object in his hand into a stronger light. After thoroughly inspecting every stone on the string, the man took out a pad and wrote a number on it.

Bastard! The bearded man thought to himself in disgust. But what came out of his mouth was quite different.

"I'll take it."

He knew he was taken. Ordinarily he would never have bought or traded anything without bargaining. But this was not the time and he was not in the mood. To him time was a luxury commodity.

He counted the stack of money the jeweler had taken out of his safe and put it on the counter. He separated the bills into several smaller stacks. After hiding them in different pockets in his inner clothes, he walked to the store door. He did not go out. He opened it just enough to poke his head out. He looked in both directions to make sure that there were no suspicious people hanging around. Then he hurriedly stepped into the street.

His hastening paces carried him out of the business district and into a street lined with big graceful shady trees. On both sides stood a row of huge mansions. As he walked down the abandoned street, he heard some footsteps following him. He stopped and turned around abruptly to look. There was not even a single shadow moving in the dusk of the setting sun. No loiterer was allowed in this part of town, not even stray cats or gutter rats. But as soon as he resumed walking, the footsteps came back again. After several stops, he realized how silly he was. They must be the echoes of the sounds his heels made on the cobblestones. A twist of a smile of relief and embarrassment appeared momentarily at the corners of the man's mouth. He hurried on.

He came to a black door. He rang the bell. He was immediately admitted into the building. Once inside, he knew that he was in a safe haven. Whoever was following him was now shut outside of that huge black door.

The man was no stranger to this place. During the past years, he had visited it at least three or four times a year. Every time he came, he would spend at least half an hour, sometimes an hour, taking the measurements of the man of the house and showing him samples of materials for his new suits.

With his hat tightly clutched in his hands, the tailor waited nervously in the foyer. He did not wait very long before a man came down a wide curved marble stairs in his smoking jacket.

The man seemed to be in a hurry. He looked impatient. He spent less than five minutes with his tailor this time. After having counted the stack of money the tailor handed to him, he took out his pocket book and wrote something in it.

"Your name will be on the list," the man said. "There are three of you, right?"

"Yes, sir. My wife, my..."

"Never mind giving me their names. I'll just say three under your name," saying that he finished writing. He tore off a page of what he had just written from the pocket book and handed it to the tailor. "It'll be taken care of. Show this to whomever is in charge." Then he stretched out his hand and said, "I guess this is it. I don't imagine we will ever see each other again. Let me wish you the best of luck! Good-bye, my friend. I will certainly miss your exquisite workmanship."

"Sir, you can't realize how much you have helped me and my family. We may not see each other again, but I will forever remember your kindness. May God bless you."

The man in the black suit came out of the mansion feeling much relieved. He did not hear the echoes of his own heels following him any longer. He still had some money left in his pocket. He pulled out his pocket watch and put it to his ear. He shook it and listened to it again. After repeating this several times, he took a last look and then hurriedly traced his steps back to the busy street where he remembered seeing the pawnshop.

The man had no trouble finding the place. He went in and saw that the violin was still there. From where he stood, he could tell that it was cheaply made. He asked the price. The money left in his pocket was more than enough to cover it. Without taking a close look at it or attempting to bargain, he counted out what the pawnshop owner asked. If he had bargained, he could have at least knocked the price down to half. Who would want to buy that cheap instrument for such an exorbitant price? The tailor realized that all these people: the jeweler, his friend, this pawnshop owner and even a pickpocket, were taking advantage of the predicament of his people at this time. But what would he do with the extra money he saved?

As soon as he stepped out of the pawnshop, that eerie feeling came back to him again. He felt that someone was following him. But what did he care? He had neither the necklace nor the money on him any more. All he had was his old pocket watch that did not work most of the time and a cheap fiddle under his arm.

Rabi came into the apartment and was surprised to find that the dining table was covered with the lace tablecloth, which was only seen on special occasions. Displayed on it were his wife's best silverware and china.

"Whom are we expecting for dinner, Mama?" he shouted aloud.

"No one," his wife answered from the kitchen.

"Then why all this fancy stuff on the table?"

"What do you want me to do with them? Pack them up and take them with us or leave them to the swine?"

His wife's words hit him with a chilly reality. He remembered what he had gone out for. His buoyant spirit was instantly deflated.

Trying to cover up his embarrassment and insensitivity, the tailor asked, "Do you have everything packed?"

"Do you realize how long you have been gone? I could have packed and repacked twice during that time. I made matzos. I even gave... Moishe... a haircut. Go take a look."

"Why didn't you wait for me? I told you that I would give the haircut."

"If I waited for you for everything, we would never be able to get out of this place."

"How did... uh... he take it?"

"Dinner is ready. Go wash up."

The family sat down at the table, Mr. and Mrs. Rabi at the two ends of the fully set table and the boy with a fresh haircut between them. Considering that she had never done it before, the tailor must admit, his wife gave a pretty good haircut. Then Mrs. Rabi stood up to do the lighting of the candles.

"Papa, why does Mama light the candles? This is not Friday," the boy, who was still sulking about the haircut his mother had given him, asked in a high-pitched pre-puberty voice.

"Because this is a special night," the tailor said.

"How special?"

"We may have to wait for a long time before we can do this again."

"How come no one at school mentioned it?"

"It is for our family only."

"Will anything bad happen to us?"

"I don't know."

"What will happen to my friends at school?"

"I can't tell."

"Why not?"

"Only God knows. It could be something bad. It could be something good. Tell you what, later on when I get so old and senile that I cannot remember anything any more, I want you to remind me of tonight and tell me everyday why this day is so special."

"Why is this day so special?"

"You will find out by..."

The tailor stopped in the middle of his sentence and stood up from his chair. His wife froze in alarm with her eyes fixed on her husband. The tailor left the table and tiptoed toward the front door. When he reached the door, he stopped. Then Mrs. Rabi felt the fire burning her fingers. She shook it out as the tailor slowly brought his hand to the doorknob. The tailor waited while his family was watching him at a total loss. Then with the swiftness of swatting a fly, he pulled open the door.

There, sitting on the doorsteps, was a little boy.

So that was what had been giving him the spooky feeling in the street!

"What are you doing here at my doorsteps?" the tailor shouted in anger at the top of his lungs. "Have you been following me?"

The boy did not answer. Two big eyes peered out of an expressionless face. They looked somewhat familiar to the tailor.

"What do you want?" Rabi asked in irritation.

The boy remained silent.

"Go away!"

The boy did not move. The man walked up to the kid. He tried to push the thin body off the step with the tip of his shoe. Through the leather of his shoes he could feel the shaking of the small body. Certainly, he remembered that bony body! He knew it.

"I say go away!"

Seeing nothing move, he lifted up his foot and drew it back. It hesitated. Then slowly it set back down to the ground.

"All right," the tailor said. There was more food on the table than his family could consume. It would be thrown away anyway. He gave in. "Come in. But don't you dare to touch anything in the house. I let you off easy last time. If you take even a toothpick, I'll send you right to the Gestapo. Food is all you will get. I want you to leave immediately after you finish eating and never come back again. You hear me?"

The boy did not answer. But the long lashes above the two big brown eyes blinked as his head bowed down.

The tailor's wife came to the door and said, "Come with me, dear." She took the boy by the hand and led him to the bathroom. "You must wash your hands before eating. Look at them. How on earth did you get so dirty?" After washing, she sat him at the table across from her own child.

The two boys stared at each other with wide-open eyes. Neither had any expression on his face. Their hair was cut in the same way. Their feet were dangling from their chairs to the same height from the floor. They looked about the same age.

"This is Moishe," said Mrs. Rabi. "What's your name?"

"Lenduai."

Rabi was surprised to hear the boy speak! He even had a name! Rabi had assumed all along that the boy was deaf and dumb. His wife sure had a way with kids. That showed what women could do that men could not. The tailor shook his head as he walked to the china display cabinet and got two yarmulkes out from the drawer. By that time, his wife had already finished lighting the candles. After putting a yarmulke on the head of each boy, he sat down and recited aloud,

"*Baruch Ata Adonay...*"

The new boy at the table was not listening to the tailor's prayer. The pile of food in front of his eyes was too tempting. The display of the glittering silver ware, the fancy china and the lighted candles blinded his eyes. He had never seen so many luxuries before in all his life. Then with saliva welling up in his mouth he watched the lady of the house putting heaps of food on a plate and handing it to him. Through the candlesticks and piles of meat and bread he could see the other boy across the table. The boy stared back at him. In curiosity and discomfort he raised his hand to touch the yarmulke on his head. The other boy did the same, seemingly with the same stimuli. A grin appeared on his face. The other boy grinned back. Then the other boy picked up his fork. The new boy hesitated and did the same awkwardly. Moishe took a forkful of food. Lenduai followed. Then like a fire caught on a dry bush, suddenly both hands of the street boy were in the food on his plate. The fork went back on the table. The boy across the table was flabbergasted. How many days had this boy not eaten?

Neither Mr. nor Mrs. Rabi was paying any attention to the two boys. They were preoccupied with the exchange between themselves.

"Did you get it, Papa?" Mrs. Rabi asked.

"Yes," the man said.

"Let me take a look."

The tailor handed his wife the piece of paper he had gotten from his rich customer in the big mansion. Though he did not show her the paper with the big round seal, which he got from this man called Heh Fengshan. He could never forget that name. The man even pronounced the *H* aspirated as in Hebrew. The man told him not to show it to *anybody.*

"*Banchina di S.,*" the tailor's wife read aloud syllable by syllable. "*Baségio.* What does that mean?"

"I don't know."

"Did you ask him?"

"He is an important man. He was in such a hurry to dismiss me that he did not even write all our names down in his pocket book. I didn't want to be rude."

"Vous es de mer mit dear?" the tailor's wife raised her voice in Yiddish. *"What's so rude about asking him to explain what he had written? How difficult is it to say you don't understand? You paid for it. You did not steal it. He took the money, didn't he? Well, it is a business transaction, not a charity!"*

"I was thinking..."

"What was there to think about?"

"It did not make any sense."

"Now you tell me! You mean you have given him all that money, I'm sure many times more than it's worth, and all you got is something that you think does not make any sense? He sure cut you up as... as the merchant of Venice!"

"That's the place," a high-pitched voice made the tailor and his wife stop talking and turn their heads. They were confronted by two small faces, one with a fresh haircut and one with a face smeared with food. They both stared at the tailor's wife with blank looks.

"What did you just say?" Mrs. Rabi asked, not addressing either one in particular.

"The pier," the boy from the street tried to swallow the food in his mouth and answer at the same time.

"What pier?" Mrs. Rabi asked, pointing to the piece of paper in her hand. The boy nodded. She quickly pressed further, "Is this *Banchina di... a* pier?"

"It's in Venice."

"How do you know?"

"Lots of big ships dock there."

Mrs. Rabi turned to her husband and said, "I guess that makes sense, doesn't it, Papa?" Then immediately to the boy she asked, "How do you know?"

"Everybody could see them."

"Where?"

"In Venice."

"You have been to Venice?" Mrs. Rabi asked in disbelief.

"Many times."

"Don't joke with me, boy!" Mrs. Rabi sensed a tone of bragging in the boy's voice.

"It's two blocks from the old church."

"What church?"

"San Sebastiano."

"You sure?"

"It's across the bridge."

"What bridge?"

"A brick bridge over the canal."

"Papa, go check on the train schedule to Venice," Mrs. Rabi said anxiously.

"But we can't go by train," her husband said.

"Why not?"

"They check IDs at all the train stops and the borders. And there must be over a dozen checkpoints to go through between here and Venice."

"Then how can we get there?"

"I don't know."

"What shall we do?"

"..." The tailor spread out his hands and opened his mouth. But no sound came out of it.

"You can go with the caravan," another unsolicited answer came out of the mouth that was full of food.

"Caravan?" the puzzled Mrs. Rabi turned to the boy and asked.

"The caravan never crosses any border," the boy explained.

"What caravan?"

"Ours."

"Who are you?"

"Roma."

A twinkle of hope lighted momentarily in the tailor's eyes. But it disappeared as fast as it appeared. In apprehension the tailor asked,

"Why do you think your people will take us?"

"I can go ask," the boy said.

"But they are Gypsies!" Mrs. Rabi turned to her husband and warned in Yiddish, *"These Gypsies..."*

"I know. I know. But what choice do we have, Mama? Haven't you heard the rumors?"

"Yes, yes, I know. But they cannot be after everybody. There are so many of us. They are just after the strong men to work for them. Neither you nor me can fit in."

"Then tell me why were there old people, men as well as women, being rounded up?"

"They are undesirable people, a burden to society."

"How do you know we are not also considered one of those undesirable people?"

"They are Polish."

"A Jew is a Jew. These swine don't give a damn whether you are Polish or Hungarian for that matter."

"Look at the Jews in Germany. Some of them act just like the swine," The tailor's wife scoffed.

"They consider themselves German. They have tried very hard to assimilate. They think they are better than the rest of us. You wait. They'll get it too sooner or later."

"Don't be so pessimistic, Papa! We abide by the law. We have paid taxes. Even if it meant us, they must be doing it just for some political reasons. It is not going to bring us great harm."

"Then why are we doing this?"

"Just in case..."

"I don't think these people are joking. I heard that they are building special camps somewhere."

"Rumor, rumor, rumor! What for?"

"I don't know. For us perhaps."

"So we get rounded up. It's going to be just a matter of money and time. No politician will refuse money and no politics can last as long as our history. We have come a long way and survived all kinds of persecutions. Look, we are still here. You wait, the policy will change."

"How do you know it won't change for the worse?"

"What's our choice then?" asked Mrs. Rabi.

"We can stay here and wait for them to round us up; or we can go by train and have them apprehend us sooner, if not at the station then at the border; or we can take a chance and gamble our lives with the Gypsies."

"What if they sold us out at the checkpoint? Who knows what these Gypsies will do?"

"What's the difference between that and being apprehended at the border if we went by train? You think the latter is more civilized? Besides, why would they sell us out? Look, the Gypsies are in worse shape than the Jews. The Germans treat them like they are stray dogs. They don't even issue them IDs. At least we have IDs and names."

"Is that supposed to be better or worse?"

"Look, like the boy said, they travel from one country to another without being stopped. The boy is right. They must have a way to avoid going through the checkpoints."

"Whatever you say, Papa," Mrs. Rabi finally gave in. She turned to the Gypsy boy, who could not understand a word of what the couple had been arguing about, and asked, "Tell me, Lenduai, what do you mean that the caravan never crosses any border?"

"I have never seen what borders look like."

"How often do you travel with the caravan?"

"Every time it moves."

"How often does it move?"

"All the time."

"What do you mean all the time? How many times a year?"

"I don't know. I guess whenever the season changes."

"You travel on regular roads?"

"Sometimes, sometimes not. Most of the time through woods, prairies and dry creeks, whichever way we can avoid the militiamen."

"Let me ask you this. What makes you think your people will take us?"

"I can go ask the King."

"The King?"

"The chief."

"We have money. We can pay."

"I don't think he will accept any money from friends."

"Friends?"

"I mean, you know, not just a stranger on the street."

"But he does not know us."

"I know you."

"Well, everybody needs money. So does the King. Otherwise why do you people...?"

"Steal?" The tailor's wife was relieved that the Gypsy boy had taken the word out of her mouth. Even hearing it made her feel disgusted.

"I don't mean... I mean..."

"We don't steal from friends. We steal from strangers only."

"When is the caravan going to leave?" the tailor's wife was glad to hear her husband coming to bail her out of her embarrassment.

"Tomorrow."

"Early in the morning?"

"Not very early."

"When?"

"Whenever the King feels like it."

"When are you going back to your camp?"

"You want me to go now?"

"No, no, not now. Why don't you finish eating first?" said the tailor as his wife was dishing out more food onto the boy's

17

plate. "You can sleep here tonight."

"Here?"

"You can sleep on that couch in the living room. We'll go to the camp with you early tomorrow morning."

Rabi did not go to bed when his wife and his boy retired upstairs. He went to the kitchen and put a kettle on the stove. While waiting for the water to boil, he went back to the dining room. He pushed everything on the dining table to one end and spread out a stack of newspapers on the other end. Then he took out the fiddle that he had bought from the pawnshop and went into the kitchen. The Gypsy boy became curious. He followed the tailor.

The tailor tightened the strings as tight as he could. Instead of tuning it, he placed the joint between the fiddle's neck and its body over the steam that was shooting out of the spout of the kettle. A little while later, the strings suddenly sent out a crashing sound and bundled up. The neck popped up like the neck on a dead chicken with all the strings curled around it like feathers around the chicken's neck. The tailor pulled it apart from the body of the violin as if he were pulling the sleeve off a coat after cutting all the threads.

"Cheap stuff!" he mumbled to himself as he put the disassembled instrument on the dining table.

Then he went to the bottom of the china display cabinet and pulled out an old leather box. Out of the box appeared a fiddle the color of autumn leaves. The Gypsy boy's sleepy eyes opened up.

The tailor did the same to the second violin as he did to the first one, but with much more care. It took him longer this time to sever its neck from the body. Then he took out a can of glue and heated it as he stirred. Back to the table, he carefully glued the fiddlehead separated from the pawnshop violin to the resonance box of the one he had taken out of the leather box. After letting the glue dry for a while, he held the finished product at arm's length and inspected it with great satisfaction.

Paul Chow

"How does it look?" he asked his attentive audience.

"Uh,..."

"You better not say good. It is supposed to look cheap."

"What are you going to do with the rest of these?" the boy seemed to be more interested in the disassembled parts on the table than the finished product in the tailor's hand.

"Just throw them away, I guess. Look at that cheap resonance box and its shoddy workmanship. It is worthless."

"The King may like it."

"You think so?"

"I am sure."

"Didn't you say the King wouldn't accept any payment? Do you think he will accept a gift?"

"He goes crazy whenever he sees a fiddle."

CHAPTER TWO

The rolling landscape outside the city was covered with tall graceful trees. The foot travelers followed the trail that ran along the stream. It wound through one woods after another. The air was so crisp that Rabi could almost hear Strauss' music playing with the running of the stream and the singing of the birds.

Soon before the travelers' eyes, a thin strand of blue smoke rose in the distance amidst the morning mist that permeated the woods. Streaks of light that squeezed through the bare branches painted the misty veil into many bleached stripes of bright ribbons. After a few hundred yards, a clearing opened up in front of them.

There were five wagons parked around a smothered but still smoking campfire. The wagons had no resemblance to any vehicle seen on the city streets. They looked like some kind of produce hoppers, covered with patched awnings. Their weathered and unpainted timbers matched the color of the donkeys that were hitched to them. However, they were mostly hidden under colorful laundry and cooking utensils. People at the camp were busy packing their wagons. No one noticed the approach of the foot travelers except the man sitting by the heap of smoking cinders. His hair was grayish black, his beard all white and his skin dark brown. His face was rough and stiff, incapable of producing any expression. Across one of his bearded cheeks was a big long scar, which was knotted and bare. Hanging in his mouth was an old pipe, burned on one end and chewed on the other end.

"Who are these people, Lenduai?" a deep voice crept out between the pipe and the cracks of a set of tobacco-stained teeth.

"These are my friends, Uncle," answered the little Gypsy boy with pious respect.

"What do they want?"

"They want to go to Venice."

"Why do you bring them here?"

"They can't take any chance on the train."

"Why not?"

"They're afraid that they'll be detained at the border by the Gestapo."

"Oh, you mean they are...?"

"What?"

"You mean they want to travel with us?"

"Yes, Uncle."

"Is that kid your friend?" asked the King pointing to Moishe.

"Yes, Uncle."

"He looks like a fine boy," the King said. The long scar on his face curved up in the shape of a Persian dagger. Was that supposed to be a smile? "Take good care of him, Lenduai." Then turning to the new comers, the elderly Gypsy said, "Then you are our friends too."

"Our name is Rabi," said the tailor figuring that it was better not to keep any secret from these people. There was a long way ahead of them. If the Gypsy held some grudges against his ethnicity, he would rather have him tell them right away. He did not want to be thrown out in the middle of nowhere. He wouldn't know where to go then. "We are Jews."

"Jews, Christians, Muslims. It makes no difference to me. They are the phony distinctions you Christians made up for yourselves."

"We are Jews, not Christians," corrected the tailor.

"You read the same Bible and pray to the same God, don't you?"

"Well, that's about it. But there is..."

"Isn't God what Religion is all about? Then you are the same to me. We only make a distinction between friends and strangers. We treat all our friends as our family members. The rest are all strangers. Pile your stuff onto that wagon over there." After giving his authoritative command, the old Gypsy squinted his eyes and scrutinized his new "family members" up and down and one by one. Then he said, "Those clothes on you won't do. Lenduai, go find some decent clothes for our friends to change into so that they look more like Roma."

"We don't know how to thank you, sir," the tailor said.

"Don't you SIR me!" the Gypsy's voice sounded as if he was insulted.

"I have a small token to express our appre..." the tailor remembered what the Gypsy boy had told him about the King. He presented the black box in his hand to the Gypsy and said, "I mean friendship."

"What have you got in here?" he asked as he took the box from the tailor. When he opened it, he yelled out, "You liar! You call it a small token? Look at that fiddlehead! It must have once belonged to a maestro! Where did you steal this?"

"I did not steal it. I bought it."

"Let's take a look and see how it sounds."

The Gypsy immediately put the violin under his chin and started to tune it up. These Gypsies were so musical. Even the tuning sounded musical. The tuning gradually became melodic. Then the "shoddily made cheap stuff" suddenly came alive and turned into a beautiful soprano. It was a merry tune in a vivace tempo. The bow caressed the strings as a mother's tender hand on her baby. Another moment later, it started to tear on the strings as a hungry lion tearing on a carcass. When the Gypsy stopped playing, Rabi asked,

"You like it?"

"Yes, it sounds better than that old fiddle of mine," said the old man. Then he noticed sparkles in Rabi's eyes. He asked, "You like my music?"

"Yes, I used to play it too."

"Come, let's hear you play." The Gypsy handed the violin to Rabi.

Rabi stretched out his left hand toward the Gypsy. It did not take the fiddle. The Gypsy was stunned by what he saw. Without saying another word, he put the violin back under his chin and started to play again, this time with only his index finger. The Gypsy's finger swiftly slid back and forth from the end of the fingerboard to the top of the bridge like a skilful skater and skipping from one string to another like a flying trapeze. The bow followed. One could not tell whether it was following the rhythm coming out of the fiddle or the swaying of the body. Or was it the body following the bow? An old Gypsy love song rose up with the smoke from the cinders and filled the morning air in the woods. It was beautiful. But it was melancholy. Then came the staccato. The lone finger on the left hand kept in synch with the fast plucking index finger of the player's right hand. After the last note out of the resonating box faded into the smoke, the Gypsy pointed at Rabi's left hand with his bow and said,

"If I can do it with one finger, you can certainly do it! You have two."

He handed the fiddle to Rabi. Challenge or encouragement, how could Rabi refuse such a friendly gesture? He hesitantly put the fiddle under his chin. He looked more like a beginner. All that the instrument produced was the sound on the four open strings. After a little while, the tailor's index finger timidly touched on the G-string. The thick silver-thread-wrapped string reacted with a deep and full volume. The vibrating A went directly from his index finger to his chin and all the bones in his body. It set the tailor's chest in resonance and made his heart beat rapidly. Old bittersweet memories surged up in the tailor's head. The tailor's two fingers suddenly broke loose. They skimmed up and down on the string and then flew over to all the four strings. The fiddle sang out the same love song that the Gypsy had just played, hesitantly here and there but never missing a single note. The fiddle was somewhat shy but it was very expressive and sentimental, more than it had been when it was under the caress of the Gypsy's finger. It brought tears to the old man's eyes. As the song ended, the Gypsy king raised his hand and slapped down hard on the tailor's back. He almost knocked the violin to the ground.

"Son-of-a-gun! You play better than I do!" said the Gypsy. "You play like a pro."

"I used to be one. Then I had that terrible accident," the tailor spread out his left hand that had only two fingers.

"Fight over her?" he cast a lustful look at the woman standing next to the tailor. "Good man!"

"Not exactly."

"What do you do now?"

"I am a tailor. You play very well. Even when I was playing professionally, I couldn't do that well on the harmonics like you do."

"What harmonics?"

"You know, playing with your fingers sliding and barely touching the strings."

"Oh, you mean like this." The Gypsy took the fiddle from the tailor and slid his fingers lightly up and down the strings like four dragonflies skipping water.

"Beautiful! Beautiful!" exclaimed the tailor. "See what I mean?"

"That is without the harmonics, not on the harmonics," the Gypsy corrected the tailor. "You must screen out all the harmonics to get to the very pure sound. Your fingers just ride on the nodes of the standing waves."

"Nodes?"

"Yes, at the depression where the string is not vibrating.

Try it."

"I can't do it as well as you do."

"Rubbish! If I can do it and Moses could do it, then you can do it."

"Moses?"

"Yes, your prophet. I don't mean that boy of yours."

"What does that have to do with Moses?"

"Wasn't that how he played the Red Sea?"

"The Red Sea?"

"Yes, the Red Sea is shaped like a flute. It can accommodate all kinds of waves. Moses played on it to have the waves stand still in bundles and expose the bottom at the nodes."

"But your strings never touch the bottom, I mean the fingerboard."

"Who knows? They may when you combine enough of these nodes together like what your Moses did."

"Moses didn't make it happen. God did."

"Who cares who did it as long as it happened? Now let's see you do it on this fiddle."

The tailor took over the violin and tried it with his index finger. Suddenly a single frequency that sounded as pure as the singing of a lark fill the air.

"See, you are as talented in music as you are in tailoring!" complimented the Gypsy.

"What do you know about tailoring?"

"You did it like fitting a suit to your customer at the first fitting!"

The two men bent over and broke out into a hearty laugh.

Then the Gypsy noticed that tears were streaming down the cheeks of the woman standing next to them. He stopped laughing and asked in dead seriousness,

"What is troubling you, my dear sister?"

"Nothing troubles me. They just gushed up spontaneously. I can't stop them," said Mrs. Rabi, wiping her tears off with her palm. A smile showed under her eyes. "Do you know? This is the first time I have heard my husband touch a violin since he lost his fingers. These are tears of joy. Never mind me, my Lord."

"Lord?" exclaimed the Gypsy, turning around as if he was looking for someone. Seeing no one, he said to the woman, "There are no lords or ladies among Roma, only friends. Rabi, you sure you won't regret later parting with this fine instrument?"

The tailor did not respond to the Gypsy. Instead, he picked up another similar black box lying on top of his luggage. It was made of a piece of old leather chafed here and there. He opened it up and there was another violin.

"You see, I have another one," he said proudly. "Try this one."

The Gypsy picked up the fiddle and inspected it carefully. He tapped on its back like a doctor tapping on the chest of his patient. He peeped into the sound holes like a doctor peeping into his patient's ears. Then he tuned it up and played a few notes. The pupils in his eyes dilated. But instead of finishing what he started to play, he put it down.

"A fine instrument," he said.

"You like it?" the tailor asked.

"Yes."

"It's yours."

"Mine? Oh, no!" the Gypsy shook his head as he took another admiring look at the fiddle in his hand. Then he handed it back to the tailor and said, "I like the other one better. It's got a better-looking fiddlehead. I don't like the fiddlehead on this one." Then he turned toward the wagons and shouted, "Folks, bring out the bread and the wine! Let's share what we have with our new friends before we start off on our long journey!"

While the women were bringing out the food, the two newly acquainted friends continued to share their fun on their fiddles, with much laughter.

The caravan rolled down dirt roads through budding forests, over sprouting prairies, across dry riverbeds and running streams in the open country. Everything was alive. The Rabis had long forgotten what they were there for. They had never realized how beautiful the countryside was. Although their ancestors had lived on this land for many generations, they were all urbanites. None of them had ever been outside the cities. If it had not been for this sad predicament they were in, they would never have discovered the beauty of nature. What irony! A melancholy feeling suddenly swelled up in Rabi's chest.

"Oh, God, just let me stay alive," Rabi yearned in silence. "I wouldn't mind spending the rest of my life among these people. Look at how well Moishe fits in among those kids!"

For Moishe, it was just too good to be true. There was no school, no piano lessons, no scolding and not being told what to do and what not to do. His mother didn't even know what to do among these Gypsy women herself, not to mention telling him what to do. They slept under the stars; they washed in streams; they cooked with wood gathered by the children in the woods... Only going to the toilet posed a problem to the city folks at first. But they soon learned how to squat and how to cover up what they left behind.

"Why cover it up?" Moishe asked. "Isn't this wilderness? No one is going to come walk on it."

"That is the difference between a cat and a dog," he was explained to. "The cats always cover up what they left behind. But the dogs have been domesticated by people too long that they forget how to do it."

Moishe joined the other children of his age running ahead of and around the slow-moving wagons, picking wild flowers and berries and chasing butterflies and hares. But being a new kid on the block, he could not avoid tricks being played on him and insults being hurled at him. Children were cruel.

"Hey, Moishe Pic Pic," a big burly boy said to him one day, pointing to a bundle of twigs on a bare limb of a tall tree. "Do you know what that is on the tree?"

"That's a bird's nest."

"I say it's a squirrel's nest," the big boy challenged, grinning mockingly. Then all the kids laughed in support of his challenge. His spirit exalted. "What do you say, Moishe Pic Pic?"

"Squirrels don't build nests," Moishe said.

"Oh, yeah? Why not?"

"They don't lay eggs."

"How do you know whether there are eggs in that nest or not?"

"Simple, just go take a look."

"You go!"

"Not me."

"What's the matter, Moishe Pic Pic? Don't you city boys know how to climb trees? Scared of height perhaps?"

Moishe could hardly remember seeing any tree in the ghetto where he had spent all ten years of his life, let alone climb a tree. But he knew that he must take the challenge to prove to the other boys that he was not afraid of anything, particularly not to be intimidated by this bully. He looked up the tree. He could not believe it. Just in a matter of seconds, the tree had grown many times taller. His legs started to shake.

"Moishe," he suddenly heard his name called. It was Lenduai. "It's not as bad as it looks. Let me show you how. Just follow me and do exactly what I do."

Before Moishe could figure out what Lenduai was up to, his friend had already climbed onto a lower branch that could be reached easily from the ground.

"See, it's nothing," Lenduai urged in encouragement. "Come on, Moishe."

"Hey," said the burly boy to Lenduai. "I asked that sissy, not you."

"Go bully your cronies, not Moishe and me," retorted Lenduai. "Moishe and I do whatever we like. Moishe, let's show that wimp how to climb a tree. He asked you to do it because he does not have the guts to do it himself."

"Ha, you think you can dare me into doing what you want?" asked the big boy. "Let's first see if that city boy can do it."

"Come on, Moishe," Lenduai urged. "Watch me. Put your hands and feet wherever I put mine. Don't look down."

Moishe climbed up on the branch. Noticing that the boy's legs were shaking, Lenduai whispered to his friend, "It's okay. You don't use your legs to climb anyway. You climb with your hands. You see, the feet cannot grab. They are for supporting your weight once you reach a safe branch. Even if they slip once in a while, it doesn't matter as long as you have your hands holding onto something. That's why monkeys have such long fingers and long strong arms."

"My hands are shaking too," Moishe whispered confidentially to Lenduai.

"It's all right," Lenduai comforted his friend. "You think monkeys' hands don't shake?"

"They are monkeys."

"Our ancestors were also monkeys."

"Who told you that?"

"The King."

"How does he know?"

"He knows everything."

"And he told you that your ancestors were monkeys?"

"Yours too."

"Not mine," Moishe repudiated with scorn.

"What were your ancestors then?"

"Adam and Eve."

"How do you know they were not monkeys? Your god made monkeys first, didn't he?"

"No, they were made out of mud?"

"Who told you?"

"The Bible."

"Oh, yeah? How do you suppose Eve got the apple?"

"So Eve knew how to climb trees," his voice was full of anger. "So what?"

"So can you." Seeing that his friend was worked up, Lenduai started to climb. "Let's go! Make sure that you never let go of your grip before your other hand makes the next firm grip."

Following his friend from one branch to another, Moishe finally got to the nest. He looked at the nest and exclaimed,

"There is no egg!"

Then he looked down. All he could see were faces. All the children in the camp, boys and girls alike, were gathered below to watch him. He could not believe that he had climbed so high. It looked as if he was on top of the Alps. He felt dizzy. Then he heard a whisper in his ear.

"Don't look down!"

It was his friend Lenduai again. He closed his eyes. The feeling went away. In the meantime, he heard a mocking voice shouting from below,

"You believe me now, Moishe Pic Pic? You see, I am always right. There is no egg. It is a squirrel's nest as I told you."

"But there are two chicks," disregarding what his friend had just warned him, Moishe looked down at the boy as he was shouting out the last word. He wanted to see the expression on that bully's face. Strange, he did not feel dizzy any more. He felt so good.

"You're bluffing. Show me the chicks!" said the big boy below.

"They are not to be disturbed. Come up and look at them for yourself!" Moishe felt good that he could talk back. Then he heard his friend's voice, loud enough for everybody down there to hear,

"Don't force that wimpy fatso, Moishe. He looks big. But he's a chicken. He might fall. If he falls, not all the king's horse and men can put him back again."

Moishe heard the crowd down below bursting into loud laughter.

When Moishe came down from the tree, the boys surrounded him like he was a hero and patted him on the shoulder. The girls looked at him with adoring eyes.

"I'll take you to the streets with me when we get to the next city," everyone, boy or girl, fought each other to offer Moishe. He had finally earned full membership among these Gypsy kids.

Moishe was disappointed. The caravan did not stop at any city, not even a village. He never had any opportunity to go into town with the other kids. What the Gypsy boy said to the Rabis turned out to be amazingly correct. There were no borders for Gypsies. The caravan crossed from one country to another without ever running into a single checkpoint or soldier.

What was most amazing about these Gypsies was that they had neither a map nor a compass. They knew their way like the migrating geese. They could always smell the guards and go around them when crossing a border. They could always smell out running water to camp for the night. They knew this land like they knew their palms. The women even claimed that they could see one's past and tell one's future by looking at one's palm.

"What is my future when I get to that far away land where I am going?" Mrs. Rabi asked as she spread out her palms in front of the King's wife. The elderly Gypsy woman picked up Mrs. Rabi's hands and shifted her eyes back and forth from one palm to another. Then with absolute confidence she said,

"You will live a long comfortable life and you will have a daughter."

"In this time of war, who wants more children? One child is more than enough."

"When fate calls upon you, you are not allowed to voice

any opinion," said the woman in dead seriousness. "Your palm does not lie. See, it says right here on this..." the Gypsy suddenly stopped short of finishing what she was saying. Then she changed into the tone of a sympathetic friend. "Think of it this way. When you two get old, your daughter will still be with you while you won't even know where that boy of yours is. He may have run away with a gentile girl or a Gypsy girl, ha, ha, ha, ha! I've heard that Oriental girls are exotic."

The Gypsy family shared with their new friends not only food and drink but also music and friendship. The women taught Mrs. Rabi how to read palms and Taro cards. The Gypsy patriarch and the Jewish tailor played duets on their fiddles to entertain the kids and to make the women dance. At night, after all the women and children had turned in, the two men would continue to sit by the camp fire drinking and smoking. Sometimes they talked, sometimes they let their violins talk and sometimes they just stared at the fire until the last red cinder turned into a piece of black charcoal. Evening after evening, the friendship between them grew until they became so intimate that one could not be seen without the other. At the end, there was nothing the two men would not say to one another. But for the Jewish tailor, there was this one thing that continued to bother him. He did not know how to put it across to his friend. The thing was: although he was aware that his family owed its life to these people, he still could not approve of their moral concepts and life style.

Finally one day the caravan stopped along a small stream in a clearing under a group of shady olive trees.

"My brother, I guess this is where we part," the King said to the tailor. "This is as far as we go. We are going to make camp here for the summer. Tomorrow morning you can follow this road into town. It's a small place. You will have no trouble finding the waterfront. Lenduai, why don't you take our friends there and see that they get safely on board their ship?"

That night was the last night the Rabis spent with their

hosts. The tailor decided that he should tell his Gypsy friend what had been on his mind all this time. He knew he could never repay him for what he and these generous people had done for his family. A sincere word of advice was the only thing he could offer.

"You know," the tailor said. "We Jews used to have our own country, a peaceful and beautiful country. Then one day we were being chased out of our ancestral land. That was a long, long time ago. Ever since then, we have never had a country. We wandered from one place to another, just like your people. We were in Egypt, in Persia, and all over this continent. Eventually we settled down. Wherever we stayed we tried to abide by the rules of the land. That's how we could survive and live harmoniously with the local people. We accepted the country of our residence as our home. Many have assimilated. Why don't your people do the same?"

"Ha, you call that home? What kind of home is it? You accepted them. Did they accept you?"

"Yes, in fact, you can find many Jews doing very well. Many of us are even richer than the gentiles, I mean the indigenes."

"Then why are you here with us?"

"Well, ... Just because we have a bad ruler at a particular time in the history does not mean..."

"Let me tell you, my brother. What you see is not just taking place at this time. It has been going on like this all the time. As long as people live together, there are always some people who want to get on top of others. Why do you think my ancestors left India? These people give themselves all kinds of noble titles to fool the people they rule: maharajas, knights, lords, emperors, presidents, you name it. They call their empires all kinds of fancy names: kingdom, colony, commonwealth, republic, union... What's the difference? They all have the same purpose: to rule. To rob the people is really what it is. These people are parasites. They don't work. They enslave you and tax you. When people realize their schemes, they switch to new games like revolution, independence, crusades or liberation. But nobody likes to be ruled or to play their taxing games. When they run out of games to play, they invent slogans like democracy and freedom in some countries and nationalism and patriotism in other countries. Some even let the people elect their own rulers."

"Where did you learn all these big words?" the tailor was amazed at what he had heard from the mouth of the Gypsy.

"I have lived in all these places. I have seen all their games. I don't play their games. But I watch. You play soccer?"

"No. I like to watch kids play it though."

"You see, you can only watch. You have the freedom to cheer, to yell, to throw your fist or not to watch. But you don't get to play. Government is the same thing. You can cheer or throw your fist at the rulers. You can even elect your own ruler. But you don't get to play. Who's controlling the so-called election? Who are the candidates? Sure, when you don't like the ruler, you can protest and riot, you can make revolution and declare independence. And you have a lot of people killed in the process. Then what? You have a regime change. How would the new regime be run? If you have a democracy, you will elect another ruler among many candidates. You still don't get to play. But you will pay taxes just the same."

"You sound like a learned professor," said the tailor who could not believe to hear all these erudite arguments coming out of the mouth of a Gypsy.

"I may be illiterate, I am not ignorant. It does not require any learning to see their schemes. They all run on the same simple idea: to rule by hook or by crook. Wasn't that madman *elected* the same way, by the people? What do they call that regime? Democratic something?"

"Every community must have rules," Rabi argued. "To live harmoniously in the community, one must abide by some rules. You also rule as the head of your tribe. I believe you must have some rules too."

"The difference is," the Gypsy said. "They force everybody to obey their rules. My rules are for my family only. What I call my family consists of everyone who eats and drinks with us and who chooses to stay with this group and to travel with this group voluntarily, not forced. They can be my blood relatives or they can be my friends like you and Lenduai."

"Isn't Lenduai your nephew? I heard him call you Uncle."

"No, Lenduai is not related to me in any way. Uncle is just our way of addressing elders. Didn't you hear your own son calling me Uncle?"

"It's so nice of you people to adopt him."

"We did not adopt him. He adopted us. We'll take in anyone, you or Lenduai, who wants to join us. But while he is with us, he must obey our rules. The difference between our family and your country is that if a member of our family doesn't like our rules, he doesn't need to start a revolution or call for independence. He can just leave. Do you know how a swarm of bees works?"

"Bees?"

"Yes, bees. When some bees don't like the rule of their queen bee, they don't kill her or start a revolution. They just leave the colony and start their own."

"Doesn't every bee colony have to have a queen?"

"The break-away bees will elect one bee among themselves, mind you, not among the royalty, and start feeding royal jelly to her. She will become the queen. And that's how we Gypsies act in whatever country we're in. We don't believe in forcing other people to live our way. We do not believe in being forced to live their way either. If we don't like the place, political-wise or weather-wise, we just pack up and leave. We don't believe in revolution and killing."

"If you don't believe in killing, why do you all carry knives?"

"That is for self defense. If anyone tries to rob me of my

35

property, I will kill him without thinking twice."

"That is considered a crime by all civilized laws."

"We don't abide by your laws. For a Roma, killing to settle a personal score is honorable. For example, if you touch my wife or any of my daughters, I'll kill you right on the spot. What we loathe is killing the innocent and those we don't have any reason to hate, like you do in your revolutions, crusades and inquisitions."

"You mean if you steal and get caught, it's all right for them to kill you?"

"Come on, no one gets killed for stealing. Everybody steals. What's the difference between things being stolen and things lost? But there is a difference between stealing and robbing. Robbing a person is forcing him against his will. The peasants rob the labor of the bulls and the milk of the cows. The landlords rob the land and the sweat of the peasants. The capitalists rob the lives and livelihood of the workers."

"If a capitalist pays his workers fairly, then you cannot call it robbing."

"What do you call being fair? One mark or ten marks? If he pays you one mark and turns around to sell it for ten marks, do you call that being fair? We don't rob. We just take what's in your pockets."

"How would you feel if someone picked your pocket?"

"If I caught him, I would teach him a lesson. If I did not catch him, I would take my hat off to him. What could be put in anyone's pocket could not worth much, certainly not amounting to life or death. We don't take your livelihood, your land or your life. We Roma are not greedy like you Christians."

"We are Jews, not Christians."

"That is exactly what is wrong with you people. You believe in the same God. Yet in the name of this God you kill each other because you each call yourselves a different name, Catholics, Protestants, Jews, Orthodox, Muslims... Did I leave anyone out?"

Rabi gave up and said good-bye to his friend the next morning.

CHAPTER THREE

The place looked exactly as the Gypsy boy had described it, the church, the bridge, the canal and the ocean-going ships. They were all there.

"There are three of you, right?" asked the officer at the landing of the gangway as he checked the names against the paper in his hand.

"Yes, sir," said the tailor.

"Are you all here?"

"Yes, sir."

"Follow this steward. He will take you to your cabin."

The cabin was just big enough to accommodate two bunks, a sofa and a cubical that was called the toilet. Although the cubical was fully equipped with a flush toilet, a washbasin and a shower, only one person could occupy it at a time. Was this what Rabi had paid for with his wife's diamond necklace? That thief! Among all the thieves and robbers he had encountered: the Gypsy boy, the pawnshop owner and the jeweler and this one, the last one got to be the biggest.

He had been his tailor for over ten years. He thought they were friends. But look at this rusted tin can, so old and so small. He was told that was the only thing available. So he grabbed whatever he could. But here on this very dock, there were posters advertising much larger ships, faster passage and cheaper fares. He definitely got cheated! Perhaps the King was right.

But Rabi had no regrets whatsoever. He would have been willing to pay even more for the peace of mind that he now had.

The passengers all gathered on deck to watch the ship pull away from the dock. Leaning against the railing, Rabi realized that this was his last glance of his homeland - Europe. His homeland? He suddenly recalled what the old Gypsy had asked him, "You call this home? What kind of home is it? You accepted them. Did they accept you?"

The situation back "home" had been getting very tense and uncomfortable. There were all kinds of rumors flying. It had never been like that in all his life. War, he could stand. Discrimination, he could live with. Having his earnings taxed by the government and his pocket picked by the Gypsies, he could understand. But the spooky feeling of the unknown made him lose lots of sleep at night. When he thought about the millions who chose to stay behind to face their unknown destinies, he felt fortunate to be able to stand here on this deck. What was going to happen to them? Rabi did not want to think. Like what the Chinese consul, Heh Fengshan, said, that was not his problem. They had made their choice and he had made his.

He realized that he was not alone. There were several hundred of them on this ship. They all came from different places. Although Rabi did not know a single one of them, he realized that their ancestors had come from the same place and now they were bound by the same fate. No one knew how it would turn out. There was no Moses to lead them this time. Was that what God meant, "free will"? Or was that what the Greeks called "democracy"? Were they making the same mistake that Adam and Eve had made? The difference was that they had all chosen voluntarily with their "free will". No one forced them or talked them into this. They did not have a snake to blame this time.

What was going to happen to them? Would they be better off than those who stayed behind? What had happened to the Jews who stayed behind in Egypt at the time of Moses? The Bible never mentions it. For better or worse, being crowded on this deck gave Rabi a warm feeling of comradeship, the same feeling that he had had when he was among the Gypsies. Perhaps the King was right. Had he adopted the Gypsy philosophy? Had he become a Roma?

Once the ship was out in the open sea, she started to roll and pitch into a strong head wind and a succession of roaring head-on seas. The Rabis had never seen the sea before, except in photographs or paintings. They could never have imagined that the sea could be so alive and the space could be so vast. It boggled their minds. The crowd on deck quickly thinned out. Mrs. Rabi and Moishe hurried back to their cabin. The rich breakfast they had at the Gypsy camp was ready to be emptied out.

The tailor remained on deck to watch the land of modern civilization that he so proudly associated himself with sink beneath the northern horizon behind the ship. He realized for the first time why the Mediterranean Sea was considered the cradle of civilization. In whatever direction you sail, you can always reach the land of some ancient civilization. To the south was the 7000-year old Egyptian civilization; to the east was the 3000-year old Greek civilization; and to the west was the 2000-year old Roman Empire. What made him especially proud was that you could find the footprints of his people everywhere on these lands. But so far none of them had been brave enough to venture out of this Garden of Eden, not even Abraham or Moses. Now for the first time in history, this shipload of Jews was going to venture beyond their Biblical land. Was he sad? What was the outside world like? Would he be able to find any civilization among those people the Christians called *heathens?* Would he or his descendents be able to return to their "homeland" one day? If so, when?

Suddenly, a water mountain taller than any man-made thing he had ever seen in his life rose in front of him. It dwarfed the ship like a camel under a sand dune. Without any warning, the brave little camel dove into it, taking the tailor on its hump. If Rabi had not held on to the railing at the time, he would have fallen flat on his face. As the ship recovered from the dive, her bow scooped up whatever she could from her burial and dumped it on herself. Rabi was drenched from head to toe. Like a drunken sailor, he waddled inboard back to his cabin. He found his family lying there like dead sardines in a can.

In order to take in as many passengers as possible, all the space on board including the first class lounges and saloons had been converted to accommodate more bunks. Meals were served in one common mess hall in steerage with no distinction of classes.

The hot sirocco blowing from the Sahara desert tossed the refugee ship like a toy in a bathtub. It kept most passengers in their bunks. That evening Rabi showed up in an almost empty mess hall. As he was trying to balance his dish of soup in one hand from spilling and to scoop up a spoonful to put into his mouth with the other, he saw someone across from him. This person was not using a spoon. He was balancing the soup dish with both hands next to his mouth, covering his face. When there came a lull, he emptied the dish with a sucking sound like a cow drinking from a trough. Then he put down the dish and revealed his boyish face. God, it was that Gypsy boy!

"How did you get on board, Lenduai?" Rabi asked in great surprise.

"I just walked up the gangway."

"Did anybody stop you?"

"No."

"But they were checking everyone at the gangway against a list when we were boarding."

"I saw this old lady who could hardly walk on flat land. She asked me to help her carry her luggage. When we got to the landing of the gangway, all the officers rushed forward to give her a hand. I left her luggage on the landing and slipped through."

"I was told that every bunk was occupied. People have paid big money for them."

"I am not going to sleep in a bunk."

"Where are you going to sleep then? This is going to be a long voyage."

"I'll find some place. Maybe here in the dining hall? It's nice and warm here. Look, I can sleep on one of these mess tables."

"That is not a good idea. You might get caught."

"What can they do with me, throw me overboard?"

"Well, perhaps not."

When the tailor went back to his cabin and told his wife whom he had seen, his wife said,

"Why didn't you ask him to come stay with us? That poor boy! We could put him in that bunk with Moishe."

"But..."

"Oh, they are just kids."

On the next morning, the sea calmed down somewhat. The whole Rabi family was able to go to the dining hall for breakfast.

"Lenduai!" Moishe was so glad to see his playmate that his seasickness immediately vanished. When he saw the way Lenduai was devouring food, he even got his appetite back.

"Mrs. Rabi and Moishe were asking about you all night," said the tailor to the Gypsy boy. "I came looking for you in the dining hall. You weren't here."

"They lock the doors at night."

"Where did you sleep then?"

"There are a lot of lifeboats. I just crept into one of them."

"Those are for lifesaving in case of a shipwreck. No one is supposed to touch them."

"No one can see me. They are hoisted high above the deck and outside of the railing."

"Why don't you come stay with us?" Mrs. Rabi suggested.

"Mr. Rabi told me that every bunk on board is occupied."

"We have a cabin."

"Oh,..."

"You want to come stay with us?"

"Me?"

"Yes."

"You don't mind?"

"Of course not," the tailor joined in to persuade the Gypsy boy. "Listen, Lenduai, now that you are with us, you are a member of our family, just like with the King."

"You mean...?"

"Yes, but like the King said, each family has its rules. Like the King said, if you chose to stay with us you must observe our rules."

"What rules?"

"There are six hundred and thirteen of them," said the tailor humorously. "But there are only ten most basic ones."

"What are they?"

"For instance, this one says: Thou shalt not steal."

"I don't steal from friends."

"You don't steal from anybody on this ship."

"Are they all your friends, Mr. Rabi?"

"You might say that."

"Then I promise I won't touch their pockets."

Lenduai went with the Rabis to their cabin after breakfast.

"Mr. Rabi sleeps on the sofa," Mrs. Rabi said. "You can share this bunk with Moishe."

The Gypsy boy had slept in stables, in tents, at railroad stations and on the sidewalk, but never in a cabin and never sharing a bed with anybody.

"It looks so crowded," was what he said.

"But you two are small enough to fit in."

"I think I'll stay in my cabin."

"Your cabin?" Moishe asked excitedly.

"The lifeboat."

Moishe's eyes immediately opened up wide.

43

"But isn't it cold and wet out there?" asked Mrs. Rabi.

"It's got a canvas cover."

"Yes, I noticed that," said the tailor. "But I also noticed that they all look so old and are full of holes. Did you get wet when it rained last night?"

"No, I found a corner where there was no hole in the canvas and sat up 'till the rain stopped. It is not so stuffy there."

"Then at least take this blanket with you," Mrs. Rabi said. "Here are some of Moishe's clothes. I made them before coming on this trip. Some of them are still new. Moishe doesn't need all of them. They will keep you warm."

As Lenduai was wondering how rich a family had to be to make new clothes to go on a journey, Moishe was intrigued by the idea of sleeping in a lifeboat. He did not wait for Lenduai's response. He picked up the blanket in his bunk and the clothes his mother handed out.

"Let's go," he said to his friend, "I want to see your cabin."

A little while later, Moishe returned to the cabin and asked his mother if he could go sleep in the lifeboat.

"All alone with that Gypsy boy? No!"

For five days all the refugees on the ship saw was a body of heaving water bound by a flat circular horizon. They had no idea where they were. They could, however, feel the change of climate on their skins. Then early one morning they thought they had awakened in an oven and found that the rolling and pitching had all stopped. Moishe looked out of the porthole and, to his great surprise, he saw solid land paved in cement. Uniformed men were standing guard with rifles on their shoulders. Barefoot men wrapped in white cloth from head to toe, showing only their dark skinned faces, carried loads on their heads. Moishe had never seen people with skins so dark before. When people back home mentioned black people, he always thought they were talking about the Gypsies.

"Where are we, Papa?" Moishe asked with great curiosity as his father came back into the cabin.

"Port Said," Rabi repeated what he had just found out.

"Where is Port Said?"

"In Egypt."

"Can I go ashore?"

"I tried. They stopped me."

"Why?"

"Because I am a Jew."

"What's wrong with being a Jew?"

"The British don't accept Jews on their lands."

"But you just said this is Egypt, Papa."

"Egypt is a colony."

"What is a *colony?*"

"Colony is a country occupied by some foreign country."

"Who occupies Egypt?"

"The British Empire."

"Where is Egypt located?"

"West of where our ancestors came from."

"Where did our ancestors come from?"

"Palestine."

"Is that where we are going?"

"No."

"Then what are we doing here?"

"Getting ready to go through the locks."

"What are locks?"

"Water steps for ships to climb up or down."

"How?"

"You just wait and see."

"Where are we climbing into?"

"The Red Sea."

"Who are those people on the dock?"

"I have already told you. They are British."

"I mean the people in white robes."

"They are the natives of Egypt."

"What are they called?"

"Egyptians. What else?"

"Why are only these white-robed people, I mean Egyptians, working? Why don't the uniformed people work?"

"They are British."

"Why don't the British work?"

"They are the colonialists."

"What are colonialists?"

"They are the rulers of the colony."

"How did they become rulers?"

"They are powerful. They have strong armies. So they go around the world and grab other people's lands to supply their homeland."

"So they are foreigners?"

"Yes."

"Why do they grab other people's lands?"

"Because their own land is poor. They *rob* other people of their wealth." Rabi suddenly realized that he was quoting the word, *rob,* from his friend, the Gypsy King.

"Why don't they work?"

"Because they can *enslave* other people to work for them." There was another word out of the King's mouth, thought Rabi to himself.

"Are they lazy people?" the child asked.

"You can say that. I have never thought of it that way though."

"How did they come?"

"On ships."

"Like ours?"

"Only larger and stronger. And they had guns."

"Were they pirates then?"

"Not exactly. Pirates are sailors who rob other ships on the high seas. When people in a country go by ship to rob other countries, they are called colonialists."

"What's the difference?"

"I guess there is no difference."

"Why call them different names?"

"It sounds better."

"I think *Pirates* sounds better," Moishe said. "*Colonialists* doesn't sound as romantic."

"Because you are a foreigner."

"I thought you said the British are foreigners."

"We are all foreigners."

The tailor had never thought of the world that way. He suddenly felt sorry for the natives. He had never felt that way either. But what could they do? Then he thought of his own people. The Jews were not much better off. They were also suppressed and forced to live in ghettos as second-class citizens in the countries where they were. The difference was the Jews were not forced into their predicament like these people. The Jews chose to go there of their own free will. These people did not have a choice. They have been here for thousands of years. They do not even know what free will means.

The Red Sea was calm like a mirror. Sailing on it was totally different from sailing on the Mediterranean Sea. There was no rolling or pitching. It was like driving on flat land. The dining hall, which had rarely been filled, was fully occupied that evening. The tailor was lucky to find a table for his family. He pulled out of a basket candles and two yarmulkes. As he put the skullcaps on the two boys' heads, Mrs. Rabi lit the candles.

"Is this a special day too, Papa?" Moishe questioned his father in a challenging tone. The memory of the last dinner back in their apartment came back to him vividly. That was when he met Lenduai. Now Lenduai was with them.

"We are now in the Red Sea," the tailor said.

"What's so special about the Red Sea?"

"Remember what you are supposed to ask me at the Passover dinner?"

"Me?"

"Yes," the tailor answered firmly.

Mrs. Rabi took out a package. She unwrapped it and took out a stack of matzos.

"But, Mama, it is not Passover yet."

"This is just as good as any time to remember."

"Where did you get the matzos?"

"I made them before we left home. Remember?"

"But why matzos?"

"Because we were coming on this long journey, we did not know where we could find food on this journey. Matzo is the only bread that will keep and not spoil. In fact that was why the Jews in ancient times carried matzo with them when Moses led them on their long journey out of Egypt."

"You mean out of Port Said, where we were?"

"And all that land you now see to our right," added the father.

"Why did the Jews have to leave Egypt, Papa?"

"Because there was a bad ruler in Egypt who persecuted the Jews."

"What's the name of this ruler?"

"The Pharaoh of Egypt."

"Were the Jews Egyptians?"

"No."

"Were they colonialists?"

"No."

"Then what were they?"

"Slaves."

"Why do we come back to this place now?"

"We are not coming back. We are just passing over."

"Why?"

"Because there is a bad ruler in our homeland who persecutes the Jews."

"Just like the Pharaoh of Egypt?"

"Yes."

"Who's worse?"

"I don't know. That is one more thing you'll have to tell

me when I become old and will not be able to think."

"Where did the Jews in Egypt go?"

"They crossed the Red Sea to that land to our left."

"What is that land called?"

"Sinai."

"Now I remember. The angels came at night and marked their doors with lamb's blood."

Blood? The big red round seal which the Oriental man back home put on that piece of paper suddenly popped into the tailor's head. He could feel the blood running through his vein.

"Did they come on a ship like this?" the boy asked again.

"Uh?" Rabi woke up from his daydream. "No, they walked."

"Across the Red Sea?"

"Yes."

"How can they walk on water?"

"Moses prayed to God and God parted this water and exposed the bottom for them to walk across."

"Did all this water really go away?"

"Otherwise how do you suppose you and I and Mama are here?" As he addressed the curiosity of the child, the tailor suddenly recalled what the Gypsy king had said about Moses playing with the water in the Red Sea, on the nodes just like how the Gypsies played on their fiddles. A smile appeared on his face. He continued, "It did not dry up. It did not go away either. It just got pushed away to the two ends." Then he said to himself amusingly, "Moses sure knew how to play the Red Sea. I wonder on what key."

"Will the Red Sea part for us this time, Papa?"

"It had better not."

"Why?"

"You see, when the Jews left Egypt, the Red Sea was blocking their escape route. Now it is not blocking us. Quite the contrary, it is helping us on our exodus."

"Why do you call our journey an exodus? I thought Exodus

only occurred in the Bible."

"Because just as the Bible says, we are running away from our homeland."

"Where are we going?"

"A land very far away."

"Farther than Sinai?"

"Much farther."

"Farther than Palestine?"

"Much farther."

"Why do we have to go so far away?"

"Because there is no other place for us to go this time. No one will let us into their country."

"What about the British?"

"We were there. You saw it. They did not even let me touch their land with my toes."

"You mean Port Said? What about America?"

"America is the same. They don't want Jews."

"Isn't there any other place on earth where we can go?"

"No."

"Why not?"

"If they are not under the threat of the Third Reich, they are under the control of the British or under their influence. Neither of them likes Jews."

"You mean we are going to be like Noah, having no shore to land on?"

"No, this time we will have a place to land. God promised us."

"Is it written in the Bible?"

"No, but God gave us a sign."

"What sign?"

"The rainbow. Remember?"

"What did the Jews do wrong, Papa?"

"I don't know."

"What's that place called?"

"What place?"

"The place where we are going to."
"The Orient."
"Where is the Orient?"
"On the other side of the globe."
"What is that place like?"
"I don't know. I have never been there."
"Is it like Sinai?"
"You can say that metaphorically."
"What does *metaphorically* mean?"
"I mean similar."
"How do you know they will let us go ashore when we get there?"
"I have a paper that says so."
"Just like the rainbow?"
"No, like the lamb's blood the angels marked on the doors of the Jews in Egypt."
"Who gave you that paper?"
"An Oriental gentleman."
"Is he as powerful as the bad man who forbids us to leave?"
"Uh... I would say more powerful, but in a different way."
"How different?"
"He is... he is... Well, who do you think is more powerful, the one who persecutes the Jews or the one who leads the Jews out of the persecution?"
"You mean Moses?"
"Yes... No... I mean... Well, you can think that way metaphorically."
"Why isn't this Oriental gentleman here with us metaphorically?"
"He must stay in order to keep his office open so that he can sign more papers for more Jews to get out."
"Who are these people who live in that far away place?"
"Orientals."
"Are they Gypsies?"

"I don't think so. But like the Gypsies, they are gentiles. They don't believe in our God."

"If they are not Jews, why do they take us in?"

"I don't know. You'll have to ask them when we get there. Now let's break bread."

As the ship sailed toward the tropics, the weather got hotter and hotter. To make it worse, the captain rationed the water.

One quart per person per day. For drinking only.

All the faucets on board were shut off as soon as the ship left Port Said. What happened was that when bunks were added to take on more passengers, the ship's owner forgot to add more water tanks.

Every morning the passengers lined up on deck to receive their daily water ration. Not everyone had brought bottles. So all kinds of makeshift containers were seen in the water line, umbrellas, raincoats, hats, even shoes. The morale of the refugees, who had been celebrating their fortune in being able to escape the persecution back home, sank rapidly. Shouting, quarreling and fighting were heard and seen on deck everyday. Even cursing of God could be heard occasionally.

One morning as the Rabis were standing in line waiting to get their ration of water, they saw a man hurry by them toward a child who had just had his bottle filled and was struggling to screw on the cap. The man caught up with the child. Suddenly he snatched the bottle from the child. Then in plain view of everyone on deck, he put the neck of the bottle to his mouth and poured the content down his throat. The child started to cry.

The tailor was so enraged by what he had seen. He got out of the line immediately and ran up to the man. He caught him by his shoulder. The man swung around and raised his arms. There was nothing in his hands. Rabi was confused. He looked at the child. The child had stopped crying. The bottle was back in the child's hands. Only it was half empty. The tailor walked over to the child. He put his hand on the child's shoulder and bent over to comfort him.

"What did you say to the kid?" his wife asked him when he got back into the water line.

"I told him I'll fill his bottle with what I'll get in mine."

"What did that man say?"

"Nothing."

"What did you say to him?"

"Nothing."

"Just nothing? What are you thinking, Rabi?"

"He's the rabbi."

"Oy Vey!" cried Mrs. Rabi in shock. "What on earth..."

"Don't be too harsh on him. He is a human being too. Look, these torturous deserts even made God do weird things."

It did not take long for all the cabins to smell like pigsties. That drove all the passengers out on deck. Men and children pulled up their trousers and stripped down to their waists, women flipped up their skirts and unbuttoned their blouses, just short of exposing their breasts. They fought for spots on deck where one could catch the breeze generated by the forward motion of the ship. But moving at 10 knots, it could hardly cool their sweating bodies. What they did not realize was that by exposing more skin to the air, the evaporation rate of their bodies had increased exponentially. They became thirstier. Finally, someone pointed out that the native Egyptians all covered themselves up from head to toe, leaving just their faces, hands and feet exposed.

By the end of the second day on the Red Sea, heat, thirst, suffocation and filth had made Mrs. Rabi's head so delirious that she did not object any more to Moishe's moving into the lifeboat with Lenduai.

It was much cooler there than in the cabin. The canvas cover kept the scorching sun off during the day while the holes in it provided ventilation. The boys guarded their little secret carefully from the rest of the passengers lest it should be swarmed.

At night, Lenduai opened a corner of the canvas and stuck it up with an oar. That not only exposed a full display of stars above their heads but also funneled the headwind of the ship into their "cabin". Moishe was so excited that he couldn't close his eyes on the first night. He had never seen so many stars so bright. Unlike those he had seen in the Gypsy camp, these were bigger and not twinkling. Lying on the floorboard, he could feel a little cool air on his bareback. He listened to the ship's hull cutting through the water. He could hear ships passing in the opposite direction. He could feel the gentle rolling generated by the bow waves of the oncoming vessels and hear the sound of rushing water.

"Are you awake?" Moishe asked in a whisper.

"Yes," answered Lenduai.

"Did you hear that?"

"Yes."

"Where did it come from?"

"I think it's inside our boat."

"Where could it be? The boat is just so big."

"Under us?"

"What could be under us?"

"Let's take a look," suggested the Gypsy boy.

The two boys got up and lifted up the floorboard. Then to their surprise they cried out together in a hushed voice,

"Water!"

There must be at least ten centimeter deep of water in the bilge!

"Where did it come from?" Moishe asked.

Lenduai dipped his finger into the water and then licked it with his tongue. "It's not salty. It must have come through those holes on this canvas cover when we ran into those heavy rainstorms in the Mediterranean."

"Let's scoop it up and take it to our cabin," Moishe suggested.

The Rabis were awakened with a great surprise. Rabi immediately plugged up all the basins in the toilet cubical: the shower pan and the washing bowl. To make sure they would not leak, he sealed them up with wax from the candles left over from the first night they had dinner on the Red Sea. Moishe and Lenduai, in the meantime, ran back and forth between the cabin and the lifeboats with their bottles.

"Let's take a look in the other boats," suggested Lenduai when the boys dried up the bilge in their lifeboat. But the floorboard in the next one was stuck tight. Neither of them could lift it up.

"Let's try to lift it together," suggested Moishe. They untied their belts and looped them on the floorboard through the cracks. Then they both got down on their bare knees in the crowded space, Moishe in front and Lenduai behind him. They pulled. It would not budge. They pulled again. It still did not move.

"This won't work," Lenduai said to his friend, "I'll count. Wait until I count to three. Then pull."

They tried again. Sure enough, the floorboard popped up at the count of three. Lenduai fell down on his back. Moishe's shorts got caught on the sharp edge of the floorboard. He twisted his body to get free... he fell on his knees... they both heard something tearing... Moishe's shorts split open... his head hit the gunwale... his naked crotch landed on Lenduai's face...

"Holy...!" Lenduai yelled out in shock as he pushed away the bare legs over his face. "You...? Why...? I don't believe it!"

Moishe quickly covered her crotch with both hands. She got up, sat on her heels and started crying. Lenduai did not know what to do.

"Are you hurt?" Lenduai asked worriedly when he finally got hold of himself. "Let me take a look."

"Take your hand off me!" after pushing Lenduai's hands away from her crotch, Moishe continued to cry.

"Don't cry," comforted Lenduai, not knowing where to put

his hand that was just rejected. It awkwardly landed on Moishe's shoulder. He then said, "Boys don't cry."

"I am not a boy! Can't you see?" said Moishe. She was disappointed at her friend's insensibility toward her embarrassment.

"But why did you pretend to be a boy all this time?" Lenduai was also disappointed. His only concern at the moment was that he had lost his buddy. He never liked girls. Now he did not know how to treat Moishe.

"Papa did not want me to travel as a girl. So Mama cut my hair."

"She did! When?"

"The night you showed up at the apartment. Didn't you notice?"

"You mean you had long hair before I met you?"

"Yes."

"What happened to it?"

"Mama cut it!"

"How did you look with long hair?"

"What do you think? Just like any girl."

"Uh!" To Lenduai, all girls looked like sissies. Long hair looked messy. "But isn't Moishe a boy's name?"

"That is not my name. They made it up for me."

"Well... You are Moishe as far as I am concerned. Can we pretend that nothing has ever happened?"

"How?"

"If you won't tell, I won't tell. Then no one can tell. We'll keep it just between you and me."

"But look at my shorts! Mama will..."

"Take it off. I'll mend it for you."

"She will notice."

"Then let's exchange shorts. I am wearing your shorts anyway."

After the two friends exchanged shorts, Lenduai took a little box out of his sling-bag. From the box he took out a needle. With barely enough deck light to see the needle, he threaded it and started to sew up the tear. As Moishe watched her friend working on the torn shorts, her mind was on something else. She finally broke the silence,

"Lenduai."

"What?" Lenduai responded without lifting his eyes from his work.

"Will you still play with me?"

"If you will keep being a boy."

For a full minute, not another word was exchanged between the two friends. Lenduai was concentrating on sewing. Moishe watched with disbelief and marvel that the needle could go in and out of the fabric so swiftly under the fingers of that boy. Was this the same boy who encouraged her to climb trees?

"How did you learn to do that," asked Moishe in amazement a little while later.

"How else am I going to take care of this?"

"What I mean is... Oh, never mind!"

Five days after passing through the Suez Canal, the refugee ship finally made port at Assab, at the mouth of the Red Sea from the Indian Ocean. It had taken the steamer as long to sail through the Red Sea as to sail across the Mediterranean. But to the passengers, the latter passage seemed longer and never ending. The Mediterranean was torturous only to those who had weak stomachs. But on the Red Sea there was no escape for anyone. Everyone was baked and dehydrated. They had even forgotten what green vegetation looked like. Their reaction to the first sight of the palm trees rising from the horizon was like that of the people on Noah's ark to the straw the dove brought back from its scouting flight.

The ship's water tanks were refilled and the passengers were quenched. They had a whole day in port to wash and clean up. The deck was filled with laughing adults and frolicking children. Yet, no one except the crew was allowed to go ashore. All they could do was lean against the railing and stare at the shore. Someone got out an accordion and played. Young people danced to the music. Rabi joined in with his violin. After all the practicing with the King, he managed pretty well with his two fingers.

The place looked as desolate as the shores along the banks of the Red Sea. The flag flying on the flagpole was the same Union Jack. The hats on the soldiers guarding the dock were cocked in the same spiteful manner as those on the heads of the soldiers in Port Said. Assab was another colony of the British Empire. The same rules applied. No Jews were allowed. How far did this wicked empire extend? The refugees wondered if the place they were going to was also under British rule. The thought of that made their outlook grim.

The people working on the dock looked much darker than those in Port Said. When perspiration covered their skins they sparkled like coal. "Put us under this sun for a year," Rabi thought to himself. "We will all be as black as these poor souls. Put us under it for a few generations, our babies will be born black. Is this how different races come about, those baked by the sun born black and those buried in snow born white?"

The refugees were glad to get back to sea.

Sailing in the Indian Ocean was uneventful. There was no line for water, no fighting and no quarreling. The best thing was there was always a sea breeze. So the last seven days in crossing turned out to be the most pleasant of the three sailings.

Calicut was an ancient port in Southwest India, much older than any of the seaports in the Indian Ocean. But in present day maritime commerce, its role had been replaced by other modern ports like Calcutta and Bombay. Just because of this, the refugee ship chose Calicut to make port in order to avoid the busy harbor traffic. And because of this, the restocking of the ship's fuel, water and provision would take longer. But what did it matter? The refugees had all the time in the world. They might be swallowed by the sea, but they could never be touched by that madman any more.

The climate in Calicut was tropical, hot and humid. The people had dark skins, a shade between those in Port Said and those in Assab. It was also under the rule of the British Empire. Therefore, no Jews were allowed to go ashore. However, there was no sight of the arrogant British soldiers. The soldiers guarding the ship were all local people, Indians. Their uniforms were the same as those worn by the British guards in the previous colonies. But their thick mustaches and colorful headgear made them look distinctively different.

"Have you seen Lenduai?" Moishe asked her parents. She had been looking for her playmate since the ship docked in the morning. Lenduai did not show up for either breakfast or lunch.

"Where could he be?" When Lenduai did not show up for dinner, not just Moishe, the whole family began to worry. That did not sound like Lenduai. The Gypsy boy liked food so much that he had never missed a single meal. "I have looked everywhere. The ship is just so big."

"Go around once more," Mrs. Rabi urged.

Moishe spent the night in the lifeboat all by herself dozing in and out of sleep. She woke up at every little sound and her worry increased every time. What if Lenduai never showed up again? What could have happened to him? Could he have fallen overboard? Could he have gotten crushed to death in the engine room? What was he doing in the engine room anyway? Could the captain have found out that he had not paid for his passage and put him ashore? Why hadn't her parents reported Lenduai missing? Oh, what a disaster...

In the middle of the night, Moishe was wakened by the ruffling of the canvas cover. Against the dim light from the dock, she saw a shadow climbing into the lifeboat.

"Is that you, Lenduai?" Moishe whispered.

"Yeah," a response came from the shadow.

"Where have you been?" she sat up and asked with great

relief. "I looked everywhere for you. I was worried to death."

"I went ashore."

"Ashore? Why didn't you take me with you?" Moishe showed anger in her tone.

"I had to climb down the mooring line."

"I can do that. I climbed up the tree, didn't I?"

"That's not the point."

"What is the point?"

"No Jew is allowed to go ashore!"

"How did you prove that you were not a Jew?"

"No one asked me."

"Why not?"

"Don't I look like one of them?"

"You are not dark enough."

"They come in different shades. Some of them look like me."

"I could have darkened my face."

"Your mother would have had a fit."

"What about you? You could have gotten caught."

"I know."

"Then why did you do it?"

"I wanted to take a look to see what this place was like."

"Why this place out of all the places we have been to? Why not Port Said? Why not Assab?"

"This was where my ancestors left a thousand years ago to go to Europe," said Lenduai.

"How do you know?"

"They told me."

"Who told you?"

"The King."

The more Moishe thought about it the angrier she became. This was betrayal. Did Lenduai not consider her his friend? Was it because he had found out that she was a girl? What did he have against girls? She turned her head abruptly away from Lenduai and declared, "I won't talk to you any more."

"What did I say wrong?"

"You did not take me ashore with you. I thought we were friends. We do everything together."

"Come, look what I got for you." Lenduai pulled out a string from his pocket. With the dock light shining on it, it looked like foggy ice beads on a tree branch after an ice storm back home. "You like it?"

"What are they?"

"What do they look like to you?"

"Teardrops on a string."

"Yes, they are teardrops from the deep of the sea."

"I don't believe you. How can teardrops stay in water and not be washed away?"

"You are right. So they had to turn solid and then became pearls."

"You are not pulling my legs, are you?"

"Have I ever lied to you? They are the tears of clams at the bottom of the sea."

"You are not joking?"

"I am serious."

"Why do clams cry?"

"Just like you do when sand gets into your eye. The tears are to flush the sand out of your eye. But for a clam, there is water all around it. How can you wash anything in dirty water with more water? So its tears just wrap around the sand and turn it into a pearl."

"You mean there is a speck of sand in every pearl?"

"Yes."

"How can it be so big?"

"It keeps irritating the clam. So the clam keeps crying."

"How long will it cry?"

"Many years and a lot of tears."

"Who told you this?"

"The King," Lenduai said. "Let me put it on your neck."

Lenduai put the necklace on Moishe. A smile finally

appeared on Moishe's face. Turning to her friend she said, "Can you keep a secret?"

"This?" pointing to the necklace on her neck, Lenduai asked.

"No, a real secret."

"What's a real secret?"

"Something you cannot tell ANY one."

"Not even to you?"

"No, not even tell it back to me."

"Why?"

"Because I want to forget it."

"Then why do you want to tell me?"

"So that I don't have to think about it any more."

"What is it about?"

"About me."

"Why do you think I would tell a secret about you to anyone else?"

"I don't know. You swear?"

"I swear on the body of a dead black cat," said the Gypsy boy with dead seriousness.

"I wish I weren't born a Jew."

"All right, what is the secret?"

"I wish I were not born a Jew."

"Is that all?"

"Yes."

"What's wrong with being a Jew?"

"Nothing's wrong. I just wish I were not one. Would you like to be called a Jew?"

"I don't know. I have been called everything but never a Jew. If you don't like being called a Jew, what about Jewish?"

"That sounds a little bit better. I don't know."

"What about Gypsy?"

"That sounds even better. But Papa has always warned me not get too close to the Gypsies."

"But why did he let you come sleep in the lifeboat?"

Paul Chow

"You are different. I suppose Papa doesn't look at you as a Gypsy."

"Then become a Roma."

"Isn't that the same thing?"

"It sounds better, don't you think? What would you like to be if you don't want to be a Jew and your Papa doesn't want you to be with the Gypsies?"

"A normal person."

"What do you call a normal person?"

"One not being picked on, not being laughed at, not being called names, not being asked to leave home, not being... I want to be just like the other kids at home."

"That's easy. Just dress like them."

"But Papa said it is not my looks. He said the Jewishness is in my blood."

"You believe that?"

"What else can I believe?"

"Let's take a look."

"How?"

Lenduai put his hand into his pocket and pulled out a pocketknife. He unfolded a needle-like pick. Then he grabbed Moishe's hand. Before she realized what was going on, she felt a sharp pain on her fingertip.

"Ah!" Moishe let out a loud cry, "Why did you do that for?" She tried to retract her hand. But it was tightly held in Lenduai's strong grip.

"Don't you want to take a look at your blood?" the boy asked as he squeezed out a drop of the girl's blood onto his forearm. Then he pierced his own fingertip and squeezed out a drop onto his forearm next to Moishe's. He said to the girl, "Take a look. Do you see any difference?"

"No," Moishe said after looking at them for a while. Then she saw the Gypsy boy push the two drops of blood together and mix them with his knife.

"What are you doing?" she asked.

63

Moishe Fantasy

"Let's see if they clot."

"What then?"

"If they clot, then we are destined to be together."

"What if they don't clot?"

"Then you are a Jew and I am a Roma."

Moishe bent down her head and blew on the blob of blood on Lenduai's forearm.

"What is that for?" the boy asked.

The girl did not answer. She kept on blowing. When she emptied her lungs, she stopped briefly and said before taking another gulp of air,

"I want it to clot."

No more words were exchanged. Both pairs of eyes were concentrated on the red dot. A full minute later, Lenduai dabbed his finger on the dried blood. Then he stretched his arm out to his friend and said,

"See, it clotted. There is no difference between us. But who is going to look at our blood? They tell people apart by looking at the way they dress. Look, I had always thought that you were a boy until you tore open your pants."

"But somehow people could always tell I am a Jew. They even made me hate myself."

"Just ignore them."

"How?"

"Look at me. I got kicked and slapped all the time. I never let it bother me."

"You are different."

"How so?"

"You are a Gypsy."

Lenduai suddenly became quiet. Then his eyes slowly moved toward the skinny body with a necklace hanging down on a flat naked chest.

"Are your earlobes pierced?" he asked.

"Yes. Why do you ask?"

Without saying another word, Lenduai's hand reached into

his pocket and pulled out a pair of rings larger than Moishe's ears.

"Where did you get these?" the girl asked.

"Never mind." The boy said. "Put them on."

Lenduai looked at the girl before him with two large gold earrings and said,

"If you let your hair grow longer and put on a flowery blouse and a full skirt, you will be able to call yourself a Roma. No one will think that you are a Jew."

The ship left port on the following morning.

The tailor did not question Lenduai when he saw him at breakfast. The way the Gypsy boy was stuffing himself was already attracting too much attention in the dining hall. Rabi did not want to arouse more attention by making known the boy had been missing. It could raise suspicion from the ship's officers. That would be disastrous.

"Come to the cabin with me!" the tailor said to the boy after he had finished eating. Once he had the boy in the cabin with his family, his voice turned stern. "Where did you go? Listen, now that you are a member of my family, I have the right and duty to know what you do and where you are at all times. Where were you yesterday?"

"Ashore."

"Not to mention violating the ship's rules, that is against my rules too. You are not supposed to go anywhere without my permission."

"Yes, Mr. Rabi," said Lenduai. "I got something for you and Mrs. Rabi."

Rabi's anger was calmed by the innocent look on the boy's face. The Gypsy boy took out a package wrapped in a piece of old newspaper in some strange wiggling writing. He unwrapped it. A beautiful silk sari and a colorful silk necktie appeared in front of the Rabis' eyes. The tailor's anger immediately returned.

"You have promised me not to steal again!" he shouted at

the boy.

"They are not my friends."

"I don't care whether they are your friends or not. A promise is a promise. It is strictly between you and me. What else did you steal?"

"Some food."

"Food?" exclaimed the tailor in confusion. Then why did the boy eat this morning like he had not eaten for a whole week? "Where did you hide it?"

"I gave it away."

"Then why did you steal it in the first place?"

"There were so many little kids begging in the streets. They looked like they were starving."

"How did you know they were not faking?"

"You could see their bones under their skin. Their bodies were covered with boils. Flies were clinging to the pus on the boils. They smelled terrible. No way they could have faked it. Some didn't have limbs, some no eyes, some no noses and many without upper lips. They fought over what I handed out. Whatever they got they stuffed into their mouths. Some did not swallow quickly enough. Others came and snatched them out of their mouths. I saw one choke trying to swallow. So I went back to the food stands and took more when people were not looking. No matter how much I gave them, it disappeared right away. I went back to steal more. But there was never enough. I stayed until all the food stands packed up and left the streets."

"Well," the tailor was confused. He did not know what to advise the boy, to obey the Ten Commandments, thou shalt not steal, or to follow one's conscience, to steal and feed the needy. "In any case, you should not have stolen the sari and necktie."

"What do you want me to do with them, Mr. Rabi?"

"We can't accept them."

"You can give them to someone else or throw them into the sea. I can't go back."

"Why don't we keep them for the time being and decide

later what to do with them?" Mrs. Rabi finally suggested.

"What can I do with a tie on a refugee ship?" said the tailor.

"Do anything with it. It's for you," saying that, the Gypsy boy walked out of the cabin. Moishe followed her friend to "their cabin", the lifeboat.

Moishe had been shaking all night. She mumbled in her sleep. Lenduai put his hand on her forehead. It was hot! He woke her up and quickly got her out of the lifeboat. He put her on his back and carried her to the cabin.

The Rabis took her to the ship's doctor.

"He's contracted malaria," the doctor said. "It is from those Indian mosquitoes. Some of our crew members have also contracted it."

"What shall we do?"

"It's all right. He won't give it to others. We are not in port any more. There are no mosquitoes at sea."

"But what shall we do with his fever and shaking?"

"He will get over it when the protozoa in his blood streams go into their dormant stage."

"Will they stay in his blood?"

"Unfortunately yes."

"What will happen?"

"He will have the fever and the chill again when they break out."

"And then?"

"After that they will go into a dormant cycle again."

"You mean he can never get rid of the disease?"

"Oh, yes. We can treat it with this," the doctor took out a bottle of pills and showed it to the Rabis. After giving instruction on how to take the medicine, he said to his patient, "It's called quinine."

"Aren't you going to give some to my boy?"

"Unfortunately we only have enough for our own crew. You can buy them at the next port."

"How long are we going to have to wait 'till we get to the next port? Besides, we are not allowed to go ashore if it is a British port again."

"As a matter of fact, it is a British colony. I can get them for you if you give me the money. Or you can ask any crewmember to get them for you. Just tell them to go to a chemist and ask for QUININE. If you could get ATABRINE, it is even better."

"What shall we do in the meantime?"

"Just make him sweat and drink a lot of water."

"But he has chills and shakes."

"Then put some blankets on him."

With a feeling of great depression the Rabis came out of the ship's clinic. How many more days must Moishe suffer? They returned to their cabin with Moishe still feverish.

"I am cold," cried Moishe, even though the ship was sailing near the Equator. Mrs. Rabi piled all the blankets on her. But it still did not stop her from shivering.

A few minutes later, Lenduai came into the cabin to check on his friend.

"How is Moishe doing?" he asked.

"He's still shaking," said Mrs. Rabi.

"Give him this," Lenduai handed a handful of pills to Mrs. Rabi. "Take them as the ship's doctor instructed."

"What are these?" the tailor's wife asked.

"Quinine."

"Where did you get them?"

"From the doctor."

"How did you get him to give them to you?"

"I did not ask him."

The tailor, who was sitting on his bunk brooding over his desperation, jumped up and exclaimed,

"Don't tell me you stole them!" There was not the slightest

tone of anger in his voice this time, just surprise.

"No," said the Gypsy boy. "Mr. Rabi, I promised you not to steal any more. I just borrowed them from the doctor. Didn't he say that you could ask some crewmember to buy some for you at the next port? You can return them to him then."

"What if he finds out about this before that?"

"He won't."

"How is that?"

"I put some cotton at the bottom of the bottle and left it at the same place. There were still so many in there. He won't even notice it. Besides, didn't he say that once we left India there should be no new cases breaking out? He won't miss them."

The quinine pills worked like a miracle. The fever and the chills were gone. Before long Moishe returned to her activities as if she had never been sick.

For the next week all the shipload of refugees saw was blue water and flying fish. There was not even a single seagull or albatross following them. Either the ship was not moving or the circle that imprisoned them for the past three weeks had followed them wherever they went. Although by this time their bodies had already been conditioned to the constant motion under their feet and the prevailing heat that permeated their skins, their minds were becoming weaker everyday.

On the sixth day after leaving Calicut, the ship made landfall. That brought the entire shipboard population out on deck to greet the beautiful green shoreline. It was Banda Aceh Point at the entrance to the Malacca Strait. However, the ship did not get any closer than necessary to take a bearing from the Banda Aceh Light. She kept her course in the middle of the Strait where the channel was so wide that the shoreline on both sides sank under the horizon. The ship was back on the open sea again.

Moishe Fantasy

The next day mangrove covered shorelines reappeared on both sides of the ship. The never-ending rolling and pitching had stopped. The surface of the sea was as smooth as a sheet of silk on a tailor's table. The only wrinkles on it were those made by the ship's bow as it cut across the water like a pair of scissors. The night air was so still that neither Lenduai nor Moishe could close their eyes. They had the canvas cover of their lifeboat furled to expose the bright stars above them. The shooting fireworks of the red cinders from the last stoking of the furnace had just vanished.

Suddenly a succession of hammering on the ship's hull took the youngsters' eyes away from the sky. They turned to each other with questioning looks. They stuck up their ears in alert. But all they could hear was the sizzling made by the bow cutting through the water. Their sleepy eyes soon closed. They fell asleep.

Then suddenly all the deck lights came on. The foredeck was lit up as bright as daylight. An announcement coming from the ship's loudspeakers woke everybody up. The passengers were given ten minutes to pack up whatever personal effects they could carry with their hands and leave the rest of their belongings in their cabins. The next order through the loudspeakers was to gather on the foredeck. On the foredeck rumors started to fly:

"Are we abandoning ship?"

"Did the ship hit rock?"

"What were those hammering sounds?"

"Is the ship sinking?"

Moishe and Lenduai did not join the passengers. But Moishe became nervous.

"Let's get out, Lenduai," she suggested in a whisper.

"Not so quick," said Lenduai in deep thought. "If the ship is sinking, we are in the right place." Then seeing no one was rushing to the lifeboats and noticing that the ship was still sailing on at full speed through the dark night, the Gypsy boy

70

whispered to Moishe, "Let's keep quiet and stay here for a while to see what comes next."

A little while later, the crew also came out to join the passengers on deck.

Surrounding the gathering on deck was a band of strange looking people leaning against the railing. They were dark in complexion, short in stature, barefoot and naked above the waist. Cutlasses clenched in hands and Mauser pistols tugged under waistbands, they looked distinctively different from anyone the passengers had seen thus far on this voyage, Africans, Indians or Gypsies. They could be natives of Malacca or Sumatra that lined the narrow channel.

A few minutes later, the ship's officers and three bare-footed buccaneers exited from the bridge and came down to the foredeck where the refugees were gathered. The one in front looked just like the rest of the band except that he had a red scarf around his head and was not holding any kind of knife in his hand. A pistol was tucked under his waistband. It was much smaller than the Mausers carried by the others and shiny like a silver spoon. Only its handle was showing. The silver stub was inlaid with pearls, colorful stones and gold. A small band of buccaneers were gathered behind the one with the red headband. As their kingpin walked majestically through the refugees like a general inspecting his troops, his cronies were grabbing and tearing off valuables from the frightened passengers. Besides what were on their necks and wrists, the overnight cases the passengers had been ordered to pack were the primary objects these pirates were after. Common sense told them that they should contain all the passengers' valuables.

But the fortune seekers were greatly disappointed by what they had gathered. The furs and fancy clothes these passengers left behind in their cabins were absolutely no use to the tropical buccaneers. After all, they were refugees, not stylish and luxurious voyagers. It was no use to take hostages either. What kind of ransoms could one collect from refugees? The old and

71

the young hostages could only hinder the mobility of the fortune seekers. The Malacca Strait was busy with traffic. They could always wait a few hours for the next prey.

The two children hiding in the lifeboat could only rely on their ears to tell them what was going on out there. From the shouting of demands of the pirates, the cries of fright of the women and children and the sounds of looting and beating, they could pretty much construct a picture in their minds of what was happening. Then suddenly it became quiet. All they could hear was their own hearts beating rapidly in their chests.

The pirates left in the same way they had come, over the railing and sliding down the ropes hung on the grapples that they had thrown onto the ship when they boarded the ship earlier. Small rowboats were waiting in tow while these men were ransacking the refugee ship.

"I think they are gone," whispered Lenduai.

"Let's go take a look," suggested the girl.

The foredeck was still brightly lit. There were only the passengers huddled in small groups. Lenduai could not see a single suspicious person on deck. He climbed out of the lifeboat and sneaked under the shadows of the lifeboats along the railing towards the ladder. Moishe followed behind.

Suddenly Moishe's shoulder was grabbed by an iron vise from behind. It swung her tiny body around. Facing her was a short barefoot man of dark complexion with a red headband. He mumbled something unintelligible. Then pointing at the string of pearls on Moishe's neck, he demanded it. Moishe took it off and yielded it hesitantly. The man seemed satisfied and walked away. Just as he had one of his legs swung outboard over the railing, Lenduai dashed forward and grabbed onto the necklace in the pirate's hand. The pirate turned around and swung his free hand. It landed squarely on Lenduai's face and knocked the boy onto the deck. The pirate hurriedly brought his other leg over the railing and slid down the rope swiftly to join his men below. Within a few seconds, the pirates and their rowboats disappeared into the dark channel as mysteriously as they had appeared.

The Rabis returned to their cabin to find all their belongings dumped out on deck. Among them was the empty violin box. The tailor did not show any emotion when the pirates took his pocket watch, which had been with him for the most part of his life. But when he saw the empty violin box, he broke down in tears.

The tailor's wife was a practical woman. Instead of lamenting over her loss, she counted her blessing in what the pirates had left her.

"Thank God they left our clothes untouched," she said. "Look, they even left us our fur coats. Don't just stand there, Moishe. Go pick them up and hand them to me. Give me that suitcase."

Lenduai wanted to help. But he did not know how. He just followed his friend as she sorted through the piles and gave whatever she handed him to Mrs. Rabi. Suddenly Moishe yelled out,

"Papa, look what I found!"

There was the violin!

Rabi sighed in relief as he picked up the violin and wiped it with his shirttail. Then he turned to his wife and asked as if he had not seen the mess on the floor until this moment, "Did they take anything?"

"What can they take?" she asked. "My dirty underwear?"

"I mean out on the foredeck, besides your silk sari."

"And my necklace," added Moishe.

"They were stolen goods anyway," said her mother. "Except your father's pocket watch."

"Yeah, I am going to miss it," said the tailor.

"You don't need it anyway."

"Ha..." the tailor quickly changed the subject. "Lenduai, did they take anything from you?"

"I don't have anything for them to take besides the shorts

on me," said the Gypsy boy with a big smile. "But see what I got from them."

"Holy Moses!" exclaimed the tailor in shock while looking at the shiny object in Gypsy's hand. "Where did you get that?"

"I took it from the guy with the red headband."

"You could have gotten yourself killed."

"He won't notice it until he gets into his rowboat."

"What makes you think so?"

"I took it when he was climbing over the railing. In the dark I saw him carrying Moishe's necklace in his mouth. So I figured he must have both of his hands on the rope."

"What are you going to do with it?"

"I have always wanted a pistol."

"You should stop doing that sort of thing, Lenduai. One of these days you will get into real trouble."

"It's a fair exchange. See what they have taken, your pocket watch, Mrs. Rabi's silk sari and Moishe's necklace. I took just this one thing."

"Give it to me!" the tailor ordered.

"But I have always wanted a pistol," the Gypsy boy protested while yielding his newly acquired toy to Rabi.

"I'll keep it in a safe place for you." Saying this, the tailor stuffed the silver pistol under his belt. Then turning to the Gypsy boy he asked, "How do I look?"

The tailor immediately realized how silly he was. He took the pistol out of his belt and looked at it. It was a beautiful piece of jewelry! He wiped it before burying it under the clothes in his suitcase. His hand reached mechanically to his waist. Finding nothing there, he said, "I will sure miss my pocket watch."

Singapore was the cleanest city these Europeans had ever seen. For the first time since they left Europe, they saw faces of light complexion.

"Papa, didn't you say that people who live near the Equator have dark skins?" Moishe asked.

"These people must be Orientals," the tailor said. "Didn't you ask me what the Orientals look like? Well, you are looking at them right now."

"How do you know they are Orientals?"

"Because we are in the Orient now."

"Since when?"

"Since the pirates boarded our ship."

"Can we go ashore?"

"No."

"Why not?"

"Look at that flag?"

"The one with the double cross?"

"What does it tell you?"

"Is it still British?" the girl was not quite sure of her answer. She could not believe that after four weeks of sailing, the ship still could not get out of the domain of this ominous Empire.

"No Jews allowed," added her father.

"How are you going to get the quinine pills to return to the ship's doctor then?"

"Ask Lenduai to buy some for us."

"Why can Lenduai go ashore?"

The tailor hesitated for a while. Then in the voice of a philosopher, he said, "Although I have forbidden him to go ashore, to him I am just another fellow human being. The harbor authority says he is free to go because he is not a Jew. God gave him the free will to choose between obeying my order or making reparation of a crime he has committed earlier."

"But he stole those pills for me," the daughter reminded her father.

"I know it was my duty to get those pills for you. But I wasn't given the chance. He had the chance and he made the choice between stealing and letting his friend suffer. This is called 'free will', like the one Adam and Eve faced in eating the apple. Just like Adam and Eve, he must face whatever consequence that comes from his actions. It's between him and his God. Give him this gold coin for the pills in case he decides to go ashore. I don't want him to steal again. If there is any leftover, he may get himself an ice cream."

Ice cream! She hadn't had any for ages. She ran out to look for Lenduai.

Moishe found her friend in the lifeboat.

"How come you are here all by yourself?" she asked.

"Where else can I go?" Lenduai asked.

"Ashore."

"Your Papa told me not to go."

"He gave me this gold coin to get the quinine pills to return to the ship's doctor."

"Did he say I may go ashore?"

"He said it is our decision based on our own consciences," Moishe realized that was not exactly what her father had said. She had given it a little twist. It should not constitute a lie. "Papa said whatever a person does is the person's free will. The person has to eventually settle it with God. He also said if there is any money left, we can treat ourselves to some ice cream."

"But you are a Jew."

"If you don't tell, I won't tell. Then no one can tell."

They waited until dusk when everyone had gone to dinner.

"There is someone standing watch on the bow," said Lenduai. "Let's take the stern."

With Lenduai leading, the two friends climbed onto the hawser that served as the stern line. They immediately encountered their first obstacle, the mouse-stop. With his legs wrapped around the hawser, Lenduai untied the large round disk. He handed it to his friend and said,

"Tie it back on behind you. Not too tight. We will have to untie it again when we return to the ship."

The rest of the trip on the hawser was as smooth as coming

down a slide in a playground.

Early the next morning before anybody got out of bed, Lenduai sneaked into the ship's infirmary and refilled the doctor's bottle with the quinine pills he and Moishe had bought on their shore venture the previous night. On his way out, he passed by the ladders to the bridge. He could not resist the curiosity to go take a look inside. He climbed up the ladders and found the door to the bridge unlocked. There was nobody inside! He went in. There before him was the steering wheel that guided the ship! It was twice his height. He put his hand on it and turned it back and forth pretending that he was piloting the ship through a narrow channel. Behind the bridge there was a room filled with all kinds of instruments that he could not even begin to guess what they were for. He ran his hand over each of them pretending that he was reading them intelligently.

The ship left for sea that evening. As the Rabis watched the ship pulling out of the harbor, Moishe asked, "Papa, what time is it?"

"I don't know," answered the tailor. Then he patted his waist and said, "The pirates took my pocket watch. Remember? I sure miss it."

"You are better off without it," said his wife. "It never kept the right time."

"What do you mean never? It kept good time half of the time."

"Which half?"

"Well,..."

"Then what's the use of knowing the time when you don't know whether it is the right time or not?"

The Rabis returned to their cabin. There was a conspicuous looking box sitting on the tailor's bunk. It was made of wood stained in the color of a violin. It was rectangular in shape, larger than a jewelry box and smaller than a hatbox. It had a lid with a shiny brass latch.

"What is this?" the tailor asked. He lifted it up. It was sort of heavy. Then he tried on the latch. It opened.

"*Oy Vey!*" Rabi cried out.

"What?" asked his wife.

"Look at this!"

It was a shiny brass clock as large as a soup bowl mounted on two concentric brass rings.

"Lenduai!" the tailor instinctively turned to the Gypsy boy and looked him in the eyes as he cried out angrily. "Where did you get this?"

"From the ship's bridge," the Gypsy boy said.

"Do you know what this is?"

"A clock."

"This cannot be just a clock! A clock cannot be so heavy and does not have gimbals. What clock needs to be maintained in level against the ship's motion on these gimbals?"

"It looks like a clock to me."

"Look what time it says."

"Yes, I noticed it. It's not quite working. But I thought you could use it because your pocket watch worked the same way."

"It is working all right. But it is not our time. I bet you it's some kind of instrument for navigation. This is too much! You want to get all of us lost at sea? You want to walk the plank?"

"*Walk the plank?*" the Gypsy boy asked.

"Being thrown overboard, dummy! Get it back to where it belongs this instant before the captain catches you!"

"But didn't you say you miss your pocket watch, Mr. Rabi?"

"You want me to put this in my pocket?"

"You can keep it here in your cabin. They've already got a clock on the bridge."

"Never mind what they have!"

"I saw it on the wall."

"Do as I say."

"But..."
"This minute! Don't argue with me!"

Moishe Fantasy

CHAPTER FOUR

The blue water slowly turned muddy. The rolling and pitching of the ship gradually eased off. A solid line appeared on the southwestern horizon. As the rusty "ark" continued to plod toward that solid line, the hope of the refugees sank into the muddy water that was emptying out over the earth's edge behind them. The earth sure looked square from here. Was this the end of it?

The line turned into a stretch of bleak looking flat land. There were neither the lush green jungles of the tropics nor the waving palm trees of the desert. There was no sign of civilization except a lone white building. Was this the Promised Land? Was this what they had given up their rich European-Judaic culture, subjected themselves to 38 days of imprisonment at sea and sailed half around the world for?

It had cost Rabi all he had, he meant his wife's diamond necklace. With that kind of money, he could have gotten a first class passage on a newer and faster ship in Venice, if he had not been so impatient. Had he been taken? Didn't he consider that gentile a decent man? He had always given him a good price for his suits. He thought of him as his friend rather than just a customer.

After all, was it the right decision to leave the place where their ancestors had settled since the Babylonian Captivity? Should they have stayed with the others? Why couldn't he endure the difficult time like his ancestors? No bad time could last forever.

Oh well, what's done is done. At least this way he had his fate in his own hands, not in the hands of that madman. How it was going to turn out would be the consequence of his own free will. If it turned out bad, there would be no one to blame but himself. Rabi finally concluded that just for the peace of his mind, it was worth every single diamond of his wife's necklace.

The passengers were all out on deck squeezed along the railings. They watched the anchor splash into the muddy pool. Then out of nowhere, appeared a horde of rowboats, which the sailors told them that the local people called *sampans*. They reminded the refugees of Venice, but their appearance was totally the opposite of the *elegant* looking gondolas. Instead of being nicely painted, they looked as if they had been put together with driftwood and straw mats. The boat people, old and young, men and women, children and babies, were all wrapped in rags. Their faces hollow. They wailed like hungry sea lions.

The boat people looked up to the passengers with sad eyes; they joined their hands together as in prayer; they patted their stomachs; they touched their mouths; they lifted up baskets on long bamboo poles swaying toward the ship's deck. Begging was a universal language. It needed no telling. Many passengers hurried back into the dining hall where they were having lunch before the anchor dropped. Luckily the stewards were all out on deck to refresh themselves from the long voyage with the sight of the shore and its people. The dishes were still on the tables uncollected. The passengers quickly gathered all the leftovers they could scoop up. When they returned to the deck, they saw the crew cussing and laughing. They had turned their water hose on the beggar boats. Their cussing in rapid Italian chorused with the wailing of the boat people. Most of the passengers' alms missed the baskets and fell into the muddy water. Men rowed vigorously after them, women scrambled to scoop them out with nets. Kids dove into the muddy water to compete with the hungry sea gulls.

"Is this the place we have tried so hard and waited so long to reach?" Moishe asked her father.

"Think of it this way," said the tailor. "At least we get to practice our *free will.*"

"Like that? With these people?"

"It's up to us. Living with them does not necessarily mean living among them. A society is made up of many strata interdependent of each other. Yet each stratum maintains its own standard of living."

"Is this Shanghai?"

"Not quite. The city is further up."

"Is Shanghai like this?"

"I sure hope not."

Shanghai was still at some distance up the Whampoo River from where the refugee ship was anchored. Whampoo was the last of many tributaries of the grand Yangtze River. The Quarantine officer insisted on holding the ship there indefinitely for observation after he had read the ship's doctor's log on the cases of malaria. A disturbance immediately broke out on deck.

"There has not been a single recurrence since we left Singapore," the passengers grumbled to each other. "Why is he still holding us in the middle of nowhere? Doesn't the schmuck know that the incubation period of the parasites is in hours, not in weeks? What kind of doctor is this man? What ship from Europe does not go through the mosquito belt? By the way, he looks English and speaks with an English accent. Englishman! Did he pick on us because we are Jews?"

Rabi was elected to go talk to the captain. He took Lenduai with him because he figured that the boy had visited the bridge before.

"I am as anxious to dock as you people are," said the Italian captain. "But what can I do? The British run this place."

"British?" the tailor could not believe what he had just heard. "Half a globe away from England and it is still English? I thought Shanghai was in China. I have an official permit from the Chinese Consulate in Vienna to enter this place," said Rabi. He showed the captain the document in his hand. It bore a big red seal and a name in Chinese.

"That paper does not work any longer, Mr. Rabi," the captain glanced at the document and said.

"The Chinese gentleman promised me that I could land. He told me that all I have to do is to show them this paper. See, his name is right here, Heh Fengshan."

"This place is not Chinese any more. It is now occupied by the Japanese. In any case, your document won't work where we are going to dock. The dock is in the British Concession, neither Chinese nor Japanese."

"What is a Concession?" the tailor asked in confusion.

"The British do not own China like they own India and Singapore. But they have many concessions here. Concessions are small pockets of land scattered all around China. They were yielded to the colonialists through treaties signed with China. They could be sections of cities or the entire city. Through these treaties the British also run the Customs and the Postal Service for all of China. They also have the rights to all the inland waterways, mines, railroads..."

"We are not interested in their rights in China," the tailor interrupted. "We only want what was promised to us. We want to go ashore."

"Read this Quarantine paper yourself. It says very clearly here that we must anchor at Woosong outside of the Whampoo River until we are absolutely clear of Malaria."

"How long will it take?"

"As long as the Quarantine officer wishes."

"How far is the dock from here?"

"Quite a ways yet, about 15 nautical miles."

"If we ignored the order, how would they know at the dock that we are quarantined? Look, there are so many ships going in and out of the river. How can they keep track of all of them? How can they distinguish one from another?"

"You think the British are stupid? Although they did not invent bureaucracy, they have certainly managed it very well. The quarantine officer has a carbon copy to bring back to his office. Once he files it, it becomes official. They can check against it in case any question arises at the dock."

"Sir," the Gypsy boy interrupted the conversation between the captain and the tailor. In hesitation, he pulled out a piece of paper from his pocket and handed it to the captain. "Is this what you mean?"

After comparing it with the piece of paper in his hand, the captain asked in astonishment, "Where did you get this?"

"I tore it out of his pad."

"You WHAT?"

"I didn't steal it, sir. He left it open on the doctor's table when he was looking the doctor's log book."

"You... How did you...?"

"Please forgive him, Captain. This is my son," the tailor quickly stepped in to defend the Gypsy boy.

"Your son?" said the captain after switching his eyes back and forth several times between the tailor and the Gypsy boy.

"Yes, sir," said the tailor. He thought if he could give the captain some time, the Italian would eventually come to his senses and take advantage of the situation. So he went on with a lengthy apology, "I will spank him, Captain. The boy likes to play pranks sometimes. You know how boys are. But this time he went too far. He is a good boy though. He has never stolen anything before. I swear to you on the Bible. If he had known it was something valuable, he wouldn't have taken it. He must have thought that it was just a piece of paper and was not worth anything. Am I right, Lenduai? I guess he was just trying to show off to his sister, I mean his brother, I mean... Well, he did not mean any harm. I will discipline him. I promise. I will make him swear that he will never steal again. If there were a way to return it to the British officer, I would certainly make him do so. But come to think of it, doesn't this solve our problem?"

"Yes, but..."

"We don't have to go right away. We can wait until evening. That officer has to go home sometime. He has to eat; he has to sleep; and he has to be with his family. He has so many ships to deal with. He will forget what he had done. He will forget us. And without that piece of carbon..."

"That's not the problem," the captain said. "When we get to the dock, we must show them some kind of quarantine clearance paper in lieu of this one in my hand which clearly says that we are quarantined until cleared."

"Sir," said Lenduai as he pulled out another stack of papers. There were several crumbled sheets with some blue carbon papers in between. He handed all of them to the captain and asked, "Will this work?"

The Italian was dumbfounded by what he saw in his hand. "Where did you get them?" he asked.

"They came off together with the one I just gave you."

After flipping the blank quarantine forms back and forth several times, the captain said,

"But we'll have to fake the officer's signature."

"Well," said the tailor in relief. "I am sure there must be some one among us who can do that."

The fifteen nautical miles of waterway in the Whampoo River was the most exciting and memorable sailing of the entire ten thousand-mile voyage for the refugees, in fact, in their entire lives. As they sailed into the river, they watched the sun set on one branch of the horizon and the night "dawn" on another branch as the city lights were turned on. They had never seen so many different kinds of boats weaving among each other, some with lights and some without, some spitting out black smoke from their big fat funnels painted in different colors and some filling up bagsful of wind in their ragged sails, some in tow and some rowed by hands. They crisscrossed each other and cut heedlessly across the slow plodding refugee ship's bow as if she were not there. The traffic on the Danube, the Rhine, the Seine or the Moldau was no comparison to this. And most amazingly, no one collided with anyone.

As the ship approached the city, tall smokestacks and buildings appeared on the bank to her starboard side. On her port side, the bank remained flat and bleak with fields and dirt mounds. Finally, twinkling in the twilight like a bouquet of jewels, the Bund appeared. That was the bank of the Concession. It was lined with a row of high-rise buildings and a floating carpet of boats on the waterfront. When the ship nudged closer to shore, a broad avenue could be seen beyond the floating carpet and in front of the high-rise buildings. It was jammed with vehicles moving in a sea of people.

The place had a European look but a mysterious feeling. Although halfway around the world, the flags flying on the buildings still bore the double-cross of the Union Jack. The only difference was that Jews were allowed to go ashore.

As soon as the refugees planted their sea legs on solid land, they were immediately immersed into a sea of filth and rags. They were surrounded by walking corpses in all directions. These poor souls looked more pathetic than the boat people on the beggar boats at the estuary of the Whampoo. Not to mention having a deck to sleep on and a straw mat over their heads, the only things these land creatures could claim as their own were the empty rice bowls in their hands and the rags hanging on their skeleton bodies that could not even cover the open wounds on their skin. Their faces were yellow like wax. They looked more miserable than the boil-covered hairless stray dogs that were limping among them to compete for discarded refuse. There was a smell of decadence in the air. The refugees had seen plenty of Gypsies in Europe. But compared with these *Untermensch*, the Gypsies were like a breed of pedigrees.

Finally, the refugees were relieved to see some European faces among hundreds upon hundreds of flat Oriental faces.

Even though they were British, the refugees felt that they were finally among their own kind. Most comforting was that these people were not in uniforms. They were in business suits.

"Nice suits," the tailor's eyes sparkled. "Expensive. But their style is a bit behind the times. I should not have any difficulty in finding work in this place. I'll bring style to this city."

With great apprehension, the refugees followed the instructions given by the British and climbed obediently onto the trucks waiting for them on the dock. It immediately gave them a chill. It reminded them of the German trucks back in their homelands rounding up the Jews for the labor camps. At least the Germans allowed their prisoners to hang on to their luggage. This time they were not allowed to take any of their luggage onto the trucks. But luggage was the last thing they should be worrying about. They were thankful that they were not being shipped to the labor camps.

The trucks weaved and honked through the streets. The streets were crowded with barefoot men pulling *rickshaws,* oversized wheelbarrows in reverse, alongside chauffeur-driven black limousines; carts with wooden wheels pulled by men and animals next to trams on tracks driven by electricity; heavy loads carried on human shoulders as well as on animal backs and on motor trucks; hawkers, beggars and stray dogs competing with each other to make a living in the deafening city noise of honking, clanking, hollering, chanting and grunting.

"Is this the place we have waited so long to reach?" Rabi suddenly remembered what his daughter had asked earlier. Where were the graceful pavilions with shiny colorful ceramic tiles and marble lions guarding their doors as shown in the picture books? Where were the monumental temples with tall wooden columns and decorated roof ridges as embroidered on tapestries? Where were the peaceful pastoral scenes displaying thatched farmhouses and water buffaloes as painted on the fine china teacups? None of the scenes in front of their eyes fit in. The refugees realized that these people also had "free will". Their choice was between pulling a rickshaw and pushing a flat cart. The difference between this and the labor camp was that at the end of the day, those at the labor camp would be fed and these people might not have earned enough for a meal. Was this hellhole what the refugees were getting into? How could they compete with these people, let alone the animals?

How had he answered his daughter? Suddenly Rabi regretted that he had left the home of his ancestors.

The truck stopped in front of a school. Like sheep in a herd, the Rabis followed everybody off the truck. The underworld they had been in a while ago suddenly disappeared. To their amazement, they saw their luggage again. They were waiting at the door to be identified and picked up.

They did not see any students at the school. Unlike the roundups back home, nobody was shouting at them. There were no rifle butts pushing and shoving them. There were no police dogs snarling at them either. Instead, they were greeted with smiles. No rules were laid down for them, only words of welcome. They were even served hot tea! Did the British finally have a change of heart?

The refugees were led into the school auditorium. It was filled with bunks, stacked three high with clean bedding.

"Welcome to Shanghai," said the director of the place, a heavyset German woman with a heavy shade of mustache above her upper lip. "Whether you are German, Polish, Russian, Iraqi or what-not, you are all *Yotahning*. The Chinese cannot differentiate between a *Yotahning* and any other white people, let alone a Viennese Jew and a Baghdad Jew. This camp will be your temporary home before you find some arrangement outside on your own. Pick any bunk you want. Families might want to pick bunks in the same stack or next to each other so that you can put up curtains to have some privacy. You might wonder how it can matter under such depressingly sub-human conditions. But believe me, as time goes on, you will find that a curtain can give you a lot of privacy. Privacy is the last defense you can hold onto. When that is gone, so will your human dignity and you will be reduced to one of those indigent Chinese."

Is that why all the Chinese men urinate on the walls on the streets and kids with split pants crap right on the sidewalks? No human dignity? Talking about curtains, the new arrivals wondered to themselves what could be behind the two large curtains at the far end of the auditorium. It did not take them long to find out. Behind each curtain was a row of short wooden barrels painted in red and shaped like miniature wine barrels. The paints on most of them were peeling.

"The Chinese call them *muodong*. We call them *Le Matin de Shanghai, ha, ha, ha,*" the director chuckled as she was saying the French words with a German accent. "You know, where you do your morning business. Left row for women and right for men. Let us try our best to keep them clean. Please put the lid back on as soon as you finish using it. Otherwise this whole place is going to stink worse than a big pigsty. When you use it, try to cover it with your fatty behind as much as possible. This will keep the smell from getting out of the honey pot. God did not make our fannies round without a reason, ha, ha, ha, ha!" The speaker seemed to be the only one to enjoy her own humor. No one else laughed. They had no idea what she was talking about. "For those of you who do not mind being deprived of privacy and exposed to the smell and the flies and the maggots, there is a public outhouse at the other end of the school compound. It is for the Chinese. You are free to use it. As a matter of fact, you are free to use anything that belongs to the Chinese. But don't let them come into our quarters. They will turn them into Chinese in no time. In the public outhouse, you have to squat. They are just some holes on a floor over an open cesspool separated by short partitions. There is a roof. That's it. There is not even a door."

Moishe Fantasy

On the following morning, the refugees realized what the German woman meant by calling the barrels *"Matin-de-Shanghai"*. A hand-pulled cart carrying two large wooden tanks came to the street early in the morning to collect the night soil from the red barrels. The whole neighborhood was wakened by the chanting of the cart-puller. (The same tune was chanted throughout the entire city so that the residents could recognize it wherever they were.) The residents responded by calling out to each other, *"Muodong! Muodong!"* Soon the smell of the *muodong* or of the *matin* (morning) spread out through the entire neighborhood and permeated into all the houses. There was no escape because all the houses had cracks in their walls, which were made of paper-thin wooden boards or paperboards. At the end when the chanting finally faded into the distance and the smell dissipated in the air, the morning settled down to a finale played by an ensemble of *muodong* owners swooshing their red barrels with brushes made of bamboo sticks like the jazz players swooshing their drums.

"Don't belittle these *muodongs,"* said the director in a dead serious voice. "Messeur Muodong de Shanghai is one of the richest Chinese in Shanghai. He owns all the business on Simoloo, which means the 4th Street, also known as Foochow Road, also known as the Red Light District. He has a monopoly on the city's night-soil, which he sells to the farmers who put it on the vegetables and melons we eat everyday."

"Yuk!" the refugees gave out a cry of shock in unison.

"The spirit of *ashes to ashes and dust to dust,"* the director continued, "is carried out by these people down to their daily lives. They believe that humans are an integral part of nature. By the way, we should all thank Messeur Muodong de Shanghai. He not only cleans up our messes but also makes a generous donation to our center. For example, the *muodongs* you sit on every morning are part of his donation. That is another good example of the spirit of *ashes to ashes and dust to dust.* Bless the gentleman's heart!"

The city was constantly filled with sounds and smells of China. After the wakeup call by *le matin de Shanghai,* the morning of Shanghai was replaced by different sounds and different smells. The hawkers announced their services by chanting, from selling notions, mending bowls and dishes, giving haircuts to pulling and mending teeth. The food stands did not need any advertisement. The customers could just follow their noses. In the morning, it was mainly the smells of frying oil. In the evening, the night air was dominated by the rotten odor of fermented bean curd that rose from the same boiling oil pots that lined the sidewalks of the streets. One could not tell which was more tolerable, the smell of "the night of Shanghai" or *"le matin de Shanghai"*.

"How are we going to survive in this awful place?" was in everyone's mind. But from a different perspective, the consolation was that they could feel through the smells and sounds that they were not only alive but indeed the *chosen people of God.* These pathetic local souls must be the *discarded people of God.*

The refugees soon found out that the European faces they met earlier were not British. They were Jews.

As soon as the refugees started to arrive in Shanghai in shiploads, the local Jewish community gathered up to help them settle in. Two committees were formed. One was called the *Committee for Assistance to European Jewish Refugees in Shanghai (CFA)* and the other one was called the *American Jewish Joint Distribution Committee (JDC).* They set up camps for the new arrivals in Hongkew, where the dominant residents were Chinese, because the British and the French refused to let the refugees into their Concessions unless they had connections and money. On the contrary, the Chinese in Hongkew opened their arms widely to the refugees.

Hongkew was under the Japanese control. Wasn't Japan an ally of Germany? Was this good or bad?

Did the refugees get out of one ghetto just to step into

another one? Only this time they had to live with the local mass, a bunch of miserable looking dirty creatures, who looked so poor and so uncultivated. And this place looked so slummy and smelled so bad. Nowhere in Europe could one see poverty like this. It exceeded anyone's imagination. Which was better, a clean labor camp with rigid rules or a free gutter with no rules? In one, one lived at the captor's mercy; in the other one, one must survive in a hostile and highly competitive environment.

The Chinese did not seem to mind the deplorable condition they were in. Adding more dirt to their environment was just a natural process of life. They even taught their children the tongue-twister:

> *Che juezi, bo jue-ko,*
> *Jue-ko do-lo bi go-lo;*
> *Fu che juezi, fu bo-ko,*
> *Jue-ko fu do-lo bi go-lo.*

Which meant:

> Eat tangerines, peel tangerines,
> Throw the peels to the wall corners;
> Eat no tangerines, peel no tangerines,
> Throw no peels to the wall corners.

"Not even animals can survive in this environment except rats and cockroaches," Rabi commented in disgust. "There are two kinds of wilderness. But why is the animal's wilderness so beautiful and so clean and the human's wilderness so ugly and so filthy? Is that the consequence of being civilized?"

"Calicut is worse," said the Gypsy boy.

"Eh! I don't believe it. Nothing can be worse. Didn't they tell me that there are eighteen levels in the Chinese hell? This one must be the eighteenth level. No wonder the Chinese think nothing of death."

But to the tailor's wife, seeing free Jews stepping forward to take care of their fellow Jews made her feel proud of being a Jew. Unlike the rest of the refugees who kept complaining and whining, Mrs. Rabi was quite satisfied.

"This is heaven on earth," she told her daughter. "The only place that could be better than this is a country of our own. Is this asking too much? Well, we can't ask God to do everything for us. We must find a way to do it ourselves. God only helps those who help themselves. Perhaps this is the place to start."

CHAPTER FIVE

First things first, the very first thing Mrs. Rabi did after hanging up a curtain in the dormitory to mark the territory of her family was to enroll the children in school. By this time, she had wholeheartedly accepted the Gypsy boy as her own. There were several Jewish schools in Shanghai. But those in the Concessions were out of bounds for the refugees. So she enrolled them in the Shanghai Jewish Youth Association School right at the center of Hongkew with the other refugee children from Central Europe. The school was set up by a Sephardic Jew from Baghdad, Sir Horace Kadoorie, and run by an Ashkenazi Jew from St. Petersburg, Miss Lucie Hartwich. What pleased Mrs. Rabi the most was that, as far as she knew, for the first time in modern Jewish history anywhere, Hebrew, Scripture and the history of the Jewish people were openly included in the regular curriculum.

To Lenduai, the first day of school was interesting. Everything was new. Just sitting in a classroom itself was a new experience. He was amazed to see music and kickball brought into the classroom and the school grounds from the streets. But to his disappointment, the rest of the week was repetition and frustration. He could not follow any of it even with the help of his former "shipmate". He honestly tried his best. The second week was boring. Nothing made sense to him. He stopped trying. Came the third week, he was having headaches and blurred vision. He tried to play truant. After getting caught and thrown back into the dungeon a couple of times, he disappeared totally from the school as well as from the refugee dormitory and his adoptive family.

The British might be good buccaneers who traded in guns and excellent bureaucrats in managing their booty. But when it came to the more civilized *free trade*, they had to take a second seat to the Jews. In Shanghai, the commercial-financial world, such as real estate or the import export business, were all in the hands of the Sephardic Jews from the British colonies in the Middle East. Such names as Hardoon, Sasoon and Kadoorie ranked among the richest not only in Shanghai but also in all of China, including the British colony of Hong Kong. The latecomers, the Ashkenazi Jews from Russia, also did well, but on a smaller scale such as in restaurants, groceries, bakeries, printing houses, etc. The central European Jews were the last ones to arrive. They were mostly professionals: lawyers, doctors, engineers, accountants, printers, musicians, etc. These Jews were highly literate in comparison to the other ethnic groups, including the local Chinese and the colonialists. The newspapers were the best evidence. While the Chinese had not more than three or four Chinese newspapers in greater Shanghai and the British had just two English newspapers in their own Concession, the Jewish community had over fifty newspapers and magazines published in ten different languages including Chinese.

The British had tried repeatedly to suppress the Jews with all kinds of harassments but to no avail. One of the most notorious stories that was going around was on the screwing of the real estate tycoon Hardoon.

"Jews are not loyal to the Empire. They are loyal only to money," the Viceroy of the British Concession once challenged his friend Hardoon, an Iraqi Jew.

"I can't speak for the others. But I am as loyal to the Union Jack as anyone in this Concession including your honorable,"

Hardoon retorted, with an equally challenging laugh.

"Prove it!"

"How do you want me to prove it? Do like Sir Raleigh did, laying down my jacket for the Queen to walk over a puddle when she comes to inspect the Concession?"

"So that little Jew is trying to be a smart-aleck?" thought the Viceroy to himself. Suddenly his eyes lit up. "All right, I'll let him have it."

"Yes, something like that," said the Viceroy.

"When is Her Majesty coming to the Concession?"

"I don't know."

"Very well, I will be waiting for Her Majesty in my best suit."

"But we must be prepared well in advance."

"How?"

"How about paving the Doomoloo with rosewood instead of your jacket, Aaron?"

Doomoloo was the Broadway, the Champs-Elysées and the Trafalgar Square in the heart of this tiny British colony and were treaded on by millions of feet from all over the world. Rosewood, on the other hand, was exclusively for making elegant furniture to be sat on by the rich and the nobilities. How could the two be put together? Besides, rosewood trees were not native to China. They grew in the tropics, in Thailand and Burma.

Nevertheless Hardoon complied without uttering one word of defiance. But when his premium shipment arrived, the Viceroy said to him,

"By the way, Aaron, I forgot to tell you. I want the blocks to stand on their ends."

Hardoon not only complied to the absurd demand by ordering more shipment, but he also went to supervise the project himself from time to time.

Anti-Semitism was a foreign idea. A Westerner is a Westerner, Christian or Jew. There had never been any indigenous anti-Semitic activity in Chinese history, although there had been Jews living in China for hundreds of years, if not thousands as claimed by the Jews themselves. The Hardoon story immediately became a national media sensation. No one dared to call it a scandal to the face of the British. Hardoon was, thereby, dubbed *the Merchant of Shanghai* after *Merchant of Venice*. Every visitor to Shanghai wanted to take a walk on this "anti-Semitic street that was paved in rosewood". As a consequence, the price of the land along Doomoloo soared sky high. What the British Viceroy was not aware of was that Hardoon owned most of these properties along Doomoloo under different names and different companies. What he did not own, he bought before he started to pave the street.

Rabi was not aware of the intricate relationship that was going on among these local peoples. Besides the Jews and the British, Shanghai's international community was made up of many other nationalities, colonialists as well as subjects from other colonies. There were the French, the Germans, the Americans, the Canadians, the Scandinavians, the Dutch, Russians, Portuguese, Indians, Filipinos, the Chosens (Koreans), the Annanese (Indo-Chinese), the Jews... and, of course, the Japanese. Although the Chinese were still the majority, they were living under the domination and mercy of all of the above, politically and economically. Every one had an edge on the Chinese coolies. If one considered the foreigners fish in a tank, then the Chinese were the water in the tank, in which the fish ate and defecated. If the newcomers wanted to survive in this tank, they must also swim in this water regardless of whether it was muddy or clear.

But Rabi found that he did not have to swim in this water. Being a tailor from a fashionable European metropolis, he saw no problem in making a living among the colonialists and the foreign contingent in this fashion capital of the Orient. He was neither a fish nor the water. He was a fisherman.

One day one of the major benefactors of the refugee camp

showed up at the camp. Rabi went to put on his best suit, the stylish Shetland mohair suit that he had worn to see the Chinese consul in Vienna before coming to the Orient. His attire immediately caught the attention of the visiting dignitary.

"Nice suit," the man commented. "What kind of style is that? I have never seen it here in Shanghai."

"It is the latest style in Vienna, sir," Rabi said. "I made it myself."

"Are you a tailor?"

"Yes, sir."

"Do you think you can make one for me?"

That was how Rabi established his business. From then on, his name was passed on from one customer to another in the high society of Shanghai. What was good about his profession was that he did not need to invest a single penny as *start-up capital.* He had brought with him his scissors, measuring tape, chalk line and even the pins. That was all he needed. The best thing was that there was no one to compete with him in this place. Although there were plenty of good tailors in Shanghai, none of them had kept up with the recent trends and styles in the European society as he had. He was immediately issued a pass to all the Concessions.

The pass led Rabi into a totally different world. Once he crossed the Garden Bridge (over the Soochow River) and got his feet on Doomoloo, the place even smelled different, no *matin-de-Shanghai* or stinking fermented bean curd. The scenes of wooden shacks were replaced by the scenes of tall buildings. As he ventured further into the Concession, rags on the streets disappeared. Suits and furs appeared. Tall buildings that lined the Bund were replaced by mansions of white marble and European houses of red bricks. Unlike in Europe though, where building styles varied only from region to region, architectural designs from all parts of Europe and the British isles could be seen here in the Concessions. Rabi felt that he was back in the civilized world. He realized that he owed it to the colonialists and his fellow Jews. If they had not come before him, he could have landed in an isolated desert of culture. Without the guidance of these wise predecessors, the refugees could have drifted astray to worship gods made in silver or animals made in gold.

Many of Rabi's customers lived in these big mansions on shaded boulevards. He felt especially proud to be able to play a role in this civilization, namely to bring the fashion of the city up to that of the modern world.

With almost an instant and very comfortable income, Rabi moved his family into the upstairs of a home in Teelanchow. Just a few doors down there was a European coffee shop called Little Vienna Café. It was beyond the loud city noise and the decadent smell of Hongkew although there was still the smell of *matin-de-Shanghai* in the morning and the equally repelling odor of the fermented bean curd in the evening. But strangely speaking, those smells were more bearable in Teelanchow than at the refugee camp. There was a tram stop next to the building where he lived. With the sound of the tram together with the smell of coffee brewing coming out of Little Vienna Café, the Rabis felt as if they were back in Vienna. All in all, life became more tolerable.

The tram stop was so close that Rabi had ample time to catch the tram from his flat after hearing the clanking bell of the approaching tram. Once on the train, it took him less than twenty minutes to get to the Bund, the International Settlement and the heart of business in Shanghai, or a few blocks further to Avenue Joffre in the French Concession. The flat was also close to their daughter's school on Chow Poong Road, just six short blocks for her to walk.

The place was the best one Rabi could find in the so-called *Shanghai Ghetto.* It was owned by an enterprising Chinese who, like many Chinese in Hongkew, grabbed at the opportunity created by the arrival of the new refugees and cashed in on renting his property out. He moved his own family to the small servant's quarter downstairs and rented the rest of the house out, the upstairs to the Rabis and the smaller downstairs to a Polish family. It was not big but roomy enough for the tailor to spread out his work. Although the place was far from matching what they had in Vienna, his wife did not mind. Now for the first time in her life, the tailor's wife could hire domestic helps just like the rich gentiles back home. For a minuscule fraction of her husband's income, she hired an *ahma* (nanny), a *dahyishangnin* (laundry-woman) and a *dahsifu* (cook). The only drawback of the place was that there were no flush toilets, no hot water and the kitchen had to be shared by three families. But with her domestic help, it did not impose too much inconvenience to her family. The *muodongs* were emptied every morning by the laundry-woman; grocery shopping and cooking were done by dahsifu; for hot water, there was a hot water vendor at the other end of the street. For a few coppers, one can have a thermal bottle filled.

Mrs. Rabi's house staff was from different places within two hundred miles of each other along the Lower Yangtze River. Yet they all spoke different dialects.

Ahma was from Chongming, an island at the estuary of the river. Her dialect was rough to the ears. She lived in with the Rabis and shared a room with their daughter whom she took care of. When the girl was at school, she cleaned the house from floor to ceiling everyday.

Dahsifu was a roly-poly person with red cheeks and a jolly personality. He laughed a lot. He was a typical metropolitan Shanghainese, who did not only speak Shanghai and Mandarin but also spoke some pidgin English which he had picked up when he cooked for an English family. Dahsifu came early in the morning after visiting the fresh food market. After cooking breakfast and lunch, he would make another trip to the market to shop for fresh vegetables and meats for dinner. It was usually dark when he went home after serving dinner and cleaning up the kitchen.

The laundry-woman, Wang-sao, took care of the rest of the house chores such as laundry, ironing, mending, emptying the garbage and taking the *muodongs* out to the street and swooshing them with a bamboo brush after they were emptied. Wang-sao was exactly the opposite of Ahma and Dahsifu. She was tiny and thin and had bound feet. She was a person of very few words. She spoke only when spoken to. Even then, she spoke with such a low voice that one could hardly hear her. She never smiled or laughed. As a matter of fact, she couldn't even stand hearing people laugh. Whenever Dahsifu laughed, she would cover up her ears or walk out of the place.

When Wang-sao first came to interview for the job, she was told, "You come in the morning and go home at night."

"I can sleep on kitchen floor. I bring own bed-roll," she said.

"No, you sleep at home," Mrs. Rabi made it very clear. "You come in the morning. I'll pay for your tram fares."

"I don't have home."

"Don't you have relatives or friends in the city with whom you could stay?"

"No. I am refugee from Nanking."

The word *refugee* touched on Mrs. Rabi's empathy. But refugee from what? Weren't both Nanking and Shanghai part of China? Weren't both places under the Japanese control now? It did not make much sense to her for someone to run away from one Japanese control into another Japanese control. But then on second thought, weren't the Rabis doing the same thing, running away from the control of one tyrant into the control of another tyrant? Didn't both Germany and Japan belong to the same league, the Axis? The Chinese in Hongkew had accepted the Jews without asking any questions. Why should she question Wang-sao?

As all domestic helps in China, Mrs. Rabi's house staff worked 365 days a year without a single day off. She thought that was too harsh. Everyone needed a break from work. But when she gave them a day off on the first Sunday, she immediately received complaints from her friends.

"You are setting a bad example, Sara," her friends told her. "Don't spoil these coolies. The words, *Vacation* or *Holiday*, do not exist in the Chinese dictionary. Let us respect their culture. This dump is already miserable enough. Without the servants how are we going to survive?"

Regardless of how much Mrs. Rabi hated the idea, she eventually gave in. The result was she ended up with a lot of free time to herself. The first thing she did was to decorate her apartment.

"Where can I get some curtain and drapery material?" the tailor's wife asked the owner of the Little Vienna Café.

"You won't find any in Hongkew," said the proprietor of the café, a Viennese. "The Chinese don't use curtains. Haven't you noticed that they paste their windows with newspapers in winter?"

"I have noticed it. I was just about to ask you. Why do they do that?"

"Just look what they have on their bodies. Do you think they can afford any material to cover their windows?"

"Where shall I go then?"

"There are many fabric stores on Doomoloo."

"I'll ask my husband to get me some next time he goes into the Concessions."

"A Jew can go anywhere in China. But to enter a Foreign Concession in this city, he needs a pass."

"He has a pass."

"How did he get one?"

"One of his customers got it for him."

"He's very lucky. Are you new here?"

"We came on the last refugee ship."

"We are having a neighborhood meeting tonight. Would you care to join us? You can meet some new friends."

"Where is it going to be held?"

102

"At Ohel Moishe Synagogue?"

"Where is that?"

"Not far from here on Changyang Road."

That was how Mrs. Rabi met Mr. Topas.

"Welcome to Shanghai, the paradise of adventurers," said Boris Topas to Sara Rabi when they met that evening. Thank God, there was Yiddish. Otherwise, how could a Russian communicate with an Austrian? "How do you find your accommodations here?"

"I told my daughter that the only thing that could be better than this is to have a country of our own," said the tailor's wife.

"Did you say a country of your own?"

"Oh, I mean figuratively."

"Why figuratively?"

"Is it possible? We are Jews, Mr. Topas!"

"We used to have a homeland. A great one too."

"That was a long time ago."

"Length of time is just a concept in the mind. Look, no human time could be considered long when compared to the age of Creation."

"Why are you telling me all this?"

"We can have a country of our own again," the Russian gentleman's voice suddenly became excited. He sounded so sure of himself that it stopped Mrs. Rabi from raising another question. Then she heard the Russian continue, "You want to join us?"

"Join what?"

"Kadimah."

"What is that?"

"A Zionist organization that I founded a short time ago."

"When will it meet?"

Mrs. Rabi found her paradise in Shanghai. Whether the Jews could really have a country of their own or not was not that important to her. To be able to participate in the efforts to bring it to reality brought satisfaction and a tremendous excitement to her new life in this strange place. Back home even dreaming about it was unthinkable. Suddenly the smell and the noise in the streets did not bother her any more. In fact, for her *Le Matin de Shanghai* even symbolized freedom.

The next thing on Mrs. Rabi's agenda was piano lessons for her daughter. With her husband's *lucrative* income they could certainly afford them. The problem was not that there was a lack of good piano teachers in Shanghai. The problem was that besides the Jewish refugees there were no other Westerners living in Hongkew. So she settled on having Miss. Hartwich, the headmistress at the Shanghai Jewish Youth Association School, give her daughter lessons. The advantage of taking lessons from Miss. Hartwich was that there was a piano at the school. Her daughter could practice on it after class as long as she wished.

CHAPTER SIX

At the sound of the school bell, the younger children rushed out of the school gate looking for their nannies. The older students were equally anxious to get out to go to their extracurricular activities. But the tailor's daughter always stayed behind. This was the only time the piano was available for her to practice as long as she wished. But on this day, the school choir needed it for practice. So she left early.

She did not quite know how to spend her extra time before going home. All the students were gone. There was no one in the abandoned schoolyard except herself. Suddenly she was jolted by a voice,

"Moishe!"

She had not heard that name for more than four years. She turned around and looked. There was no one but this man standing at a distance from the gate. She looked at him. That face was rather cute but she could not relate it to anyone she knew. How did he know that name? Coincidence? She looked around. There was no one else but the two of them. Ever since the family landed in Shanghai, she had gone back to her birth name. No one knew the name Moishe except... Then their eyes met.

"Lenduai?" she whispered in hesitation and nostalgia.

"So it IS you, Moishe!" said the man excitedly. "I was not sure."

"Lenduai! Where have you been all this time?" Moishe asked in disbelief. There was nothing for her to relate this man to that childhood playmate of hers. He had hair on his face. He did not have that high-pitched voice any more. He was wearing a pair of long trousers with creases and a shirt, not in shorts and naked above the waist. He stood there like a man, not restless like a boy any more. His hands were resting on the handlebar of a bicycle. A bicycle! That would cost a fortune! How could he afford to own such a luxury? Did he...? Then she recognized those two big brown eyes. That brought back all the memories of the refugee ship and the lifeboat. Her mood changed from surprise to joy, then from joy to anger and then from anger to accusation.

"Why did you run away without letting me know?" she asked. Tears suddenly welled up in her eyes.

"Because I did not know where I was going."

"All these years?"

"Yes, all these years."

"Why didn't you contact me?"

"Because I did not know what I was going to do."

"Why do you come back now?"

"It's a secret."

"What's the secret?"

"It's a secret. I can't tell you."

"A secret!" Moishe wiped out her tears and burst out in rage. "I shared my secrets with you and you don't want to share yours with me? Didn't we have our blood clot together?"

"Since I have promised you not even to tell your secret to yourself, how could I tell my secret to you?"

The man stared at the schoolgirl before him. He could not believe it was the same girl, he meant boy, with whom he had climbed trees and mooring lines. Then he saw a smile appear on her rosy cheeks.

"Now tell me. What is the secret?" Moishe asked. "I promise I won't tell anybody, not even myself."

"Lately I suddenly had an urge to see you."

"Is that all?"

"Isn't that enough?"

"Now that you have seen me, are there more secrets?"

"You want to go *ashore?*"

"*No Jews allowed.* Remember?"

The two old friends broke out into a hearty laugh.

"You want to go or not?" the young man asked again in a more serious voice.

"Where?"

"The Concessions."

"No Jews allowed."

"Says who?"

"Papa said they have big red-turbaned Indian guards at the border to stop anyone without a pass."

"How does he know?"

"He has a pass. His customers all live in the Concessions."

"But there is no border for Gypsies. Remember?"

"Shall I go like this?" Moishe patted her school uniform.

"You don't look like a Gypsy."

"Then I'll go change. Come home with me."

"I'll wait here."

"Don't you want to see Mama and Papa?"

"Another day."

"Mama is probably as anxious to see you as I am."

"Go! I'll wait here. Hurry up."

It did not take long for Moishe to return in a blouse and a colorful full skirt. She touched the two big rings hanging on her earlobes with her hands and asked, "Remember these?"

"What did you say to Mama?" Lenduai asked.

"She was not home. But I told Ahma that I was going to a birthday party."

"Who's Ahma?"

"The woman who takes care of me and cleans the house."

"Will she tell Mama?"

"It depends."

"On what?"

"Whether she thinks I will get a scolding from Mama or not."

"Why does she protect you like that?"

"She's my friend."

"*Yotahning?*"

"No, she's Chinese. She's from the countryside."

"What does she do besides being your friend?"

"She takes care of me."

"You have a maid all to yourself?"

"There is also Wang-sao. She brushes my hair."

"A maid to take care of you and a maid to brush your hair? What have you turned into during the time I did not see you? A Princess?"

"Actually it's not Wang-sao's duty to brush my hair. Her job is to wash clothes for the family. But she likes my hair so much that she wants to brush it for me every night. She said my hair reminds her of her baby's hair."

"Where is her baby?"

"Dead."

"What does she look like?"

"Small with bound feet."

"Bound feet? How does she walk?"

"Like people wearing high heels."

"Does your ahma have bound feet too?"

"No, Ahma is a peasant. She used to work in the field. Wang-sao is a city woman. She used to not work at all."

"Is she also your friend?"

"Sort of. But she does not talk much. I have never seen her laugh either. She can't stand to hear people laugh. When I laugh, she covers her ears with her hands and buries her head between her legs. Sometimes she cries."

"Why would she do that?"

"I don't know. It reminded her of her baby perhaps."

"Well, Your Highness, who else do you have in the house?"

"The cook."

"A cook! You mean Mama doesn't cook any more?"

"Not any more."

"I can't believe it," Lenduai shook his head and said. Then he looked around and ran into the schoolyard. A moment later, he came back out with a big sunflower in his hand.

"What's that for?" Moishe asked.

Lenduai put the flower behind Moishe's ear and said, "To match that freshly brushed hair of yours. Now you look like a Gypsy."

"You mean a Roma," she laughed uninhibitedly like a boy. Suddenly Lenduai saw his lifeboat shipmate standing in front of him.

Lenduai pushed his bicycle away from the wall. Patting the top-tube he said, "Come, climb onto this *hawser.*"

"Hawser? I don't see any *mouse-stop,*" Moishe suddenly felt like she was the kid again, who had climbed onto the ship's mooring hawser to sneak ashore.

Lenduai rubbed his hands over the bicycle's handle bar and said, "This one will stop any mouse, including you."

Moishe bent her knees and slipped her small body skillfully into the space formed by Lenduai's arms and the handlebar. She tipped up her toes and lifted her hips onto the top-tube.

In front of his eyes, Lenduai saw a Gypsy girl sitting sidesaddle on a donkey. He mounted the "donkey". With a push, the two old friends rolled off on their venture to the Concessions.

The couple weaved through the foot traffic that was shared by man-pulled rickshaws and flat carts as well as buses and trucks. Moishe found herself winding in narrow streets that she could never even imagine existed on earth. The streets were paved with mud and trash. They were so narrow that no vehicle with an axle could travel on them. The buildings along the streets looked like beaten up matchboxes. Some were patched with rusty cut-up tin cans, some pasted with newspaper, but none of them were painted. The only things that looked clean were the laundry lines that were strung among the rooftops. Moishe suddenly felt like a stranger on Mars. She could not see a single European face. She wondered, if the Europeans thought a Jewish ghetto was dirty, what would they think about this? A garbage dump in the ghetto? Was this where their family cook returned to every night?

Lenduai maneuvered skillfully through the *dump*. He was even able to avoid the potholes and the splash of grey water thrown into the streets by the residents. Moishe was so shocked by the scene around her that she was speechless throughout the wild ride. Finally, they were out of the impoverished environment and came upon an open field. Green patties lined the road on both sides.

"What is that green vegetation?" she asked.

"Rice sprouts."

"That's what Ahma told me her home was like."

"Where is she from?"

"Chongming, an island in the estuary of the Yangtze. Are we still in Hongkew?"

"I am not quite sure."

"Were those streets we just rode through still in Hongkew?"

"I guess so," Lenduai said.

"Why did we have to go through such a long route to get to the Concessions? Papa just rides the tram car."

"Remember the red-turbaned Indian guards your Papa told you about?"

"Yes, where are they?"

"Taking this long route we don't run into any of them."

"Is Calicut like these streets?"

"Similar except that there were a lot of beggars in Calicut."

"Does that mean the people here are better off?"

"Or you may say the people here are so poor that no one

could afford to give anything to the beggars."

"But I have seen beggars in Teelanchow."

"Yes, because there are Jews."

"What does it have to do with Jews?"

"They are much better off than the Chinese. So they can afford to give."

"Why are they better off than the Chinese?"

"Because they are Jews. They have rich Jews to help them."

"Are there no rich Chinese?"

"Yes, there are lots of rich Chinese."

"Why don't they help their poor fellow Chinese?"

"There are too many poor Chinese. Besides, they are not Jews."

With no traffic to dodge, Lenduai took notice for the first time of the young lady who was sitting in front of him on the top-tube and balancing between his two arms. Was this the same sweaty and smelly half-naked playmate of his on that refugee ship? How he hated her hair brushing against his face at night in that crowded space of the lifeboat! He had tried to turn around and sleep head to toe. But her feet smelled even worse. Now the feeling of this girl's hair brushing on his chin was totally different. He bent down his head to let it brush on his face.

Moishe could hear Lenduai panting next to her ear as they climbed up a slope. She could feel his warm breath blowing on her face.

"You want me to peddle for a while?" she asked.

"How are you going to peddle in a skirt?"

"I can pull it up."

"And show your panties to everybody?"

"What's wrong with that? I put my bare bottom in your face. Remember?"

"Whew!"

The two riders broke into a hysterical laugh. Lenduai lost his balance. They fell and crashed.

Moishe Fantasy

Lenduai got up and saw a young lady he couldn't recognize lying on the ground. Her skirt was hooked onto the fallen bicycle's handle bar, just like her shorts on the lifeboat's floorboard before, exposing a pair of bare legs that could more than qualify for joining the Ziegfeld girls on stage. He could not take his eyes off them. He had never seen a girl so beautiful in the entire city. Was this the same timid Jewish "boy" whom he had guided grip by grip to climb up the tree to see the bird's nest? Have those bald chicks grown full feathers yet? This one certainly has.

"Don't just stand there, Lenduai!" Lenduai was brought back to earth by the girl's voice. He saw an arm stretched out to him. "Help me get up! My skirt is tangled in the mouse-trap."

The "boy" he knew did not ask for his help when *he* was on that tree. *He* was more independent. Is that the difference between a boy and a girl? He gave her his hand and pulled her up.

Lenduai was right. They were in the French Concession without encountering any guards, Indians in red-turbans or Indochinese in straw hats. Everything in the Concession looked so European, the houses, their roofs, the stores, the streetcars, the people in the streets, even the sycamore trees that lined these streets. These Gypsies were so amazing. In less than an hour on a bike, Lenduai could take her from the ghetto through the dump back to the Europe she had once known and forgotten.

They stopped in front of a red house. It had a red wall, a red roof and a red door. It even had a matching name, Red House. Lenduai parked his bicycle and led Moishe into the red house.

Inside Red House there was a fancy hall with lots of people. It was the first time Moishe had ever been inside a restaurant. Back home Papa had never taken the family to any restaurant. The place was dimly lit. All the tables were covered with white tablecloths and decorated with flowers and candles, just like Mama's dining table on the high holidays. The waiters were also in white to match the tablecloth. A waiter came and showed them to a table, pulling out a chair for her. She looked at the waiter and did not know what to do or what to say. Then she heard Lenduai saying,

"Sit down."

As she was sitting down, the man in the white jacket pushed in the chair, just like in the movies!

Moishe let Lenduai order the food for her. Lenduai had always known what to do. On the refugee ship, she had let him make all the decisions. When the waiter came back with the first course, he only served Moishe.

"Why are you not eating, Lenduai?" she asked.

"I don't eat that stuff."

"What are they?"

"Escargots."

"What are Es...?"

"Snails."

"Yuk!"

"They taste good."

"But..."

"You eat ox tail, don't you? You know what is closest to the tail on an ox?"

"Then why don't you also have some?"

Lenduai did not offer an answer. He just stood up and walked out of the dining hall. Moishe was at a total loss. Why did Lenduai suddenly behave so strangely? Did she say something wrong? Why did he abandon her, without saying anything or getting mad? He had never behaved that way before. How was she going to get home? The waiter kept serving her more fancy food. She looked around. There were women in fancy dresses and men in suits? How was she going to pay for this? Why did Lenduai bring her here and leave her to sit all by herself? Just then she saw three men in black tuxedos walk into the dining room, one carrying a double bass, one a violin and one an accordion.

Moishe Fantasy

The one holding the violin was Lenduai!

The trio walked quietly to a corner of the dining room and started to tune their instruments. Before Moishe could grasp the situation, the random plucking of strings and tapping of keys drifted into a melody without any announcement or beating of hand. The violin was in the lead. Moishe was so flabbergasted that she left all the food in front of her untouched. She had never known that Lenduai could play the violin. Was that the boy who climbed trees, sneaked ashore on a mooring line and stole the quinine pills for her? She could not imagine.

The trio played one piece after another. Some of them were familiar to Moishe but most of them were not. They were all beautiful though. The music finally stopped. While the musicians were taking a break, Lenduai came over to the table. Moishe did not know what to say. She just stared at the young man standing in front of her. In the black tuxedo he looked like a movie star. He even had his hair waxed and combed! Lenduai did not say anything. Nor did he sit down with Moishe. Instead, he put the violin under his chin and started to swing his body with the bow as music poured out of the tiny resonant box. The tune was very familiar. She was sure that she had heard it before. Suddenly she remembered. It was the Gypsy love song that the King played on the violin Papa had given him when they first arrived at the camp. When Lenduai came to the end of the song, he did not stop. Going into the second refrain, he played with just one finger like the King did to challenge Papa to play. At that time Moishe could not understand why it had brought tears to Mama's eyes. Now her own eyes were red and watery. Then Lenduai played another one.

"What was the last one you played?" Moishe asked. "It is very beautiful."

"Moishe Fantasy."

"Don't joke. I am serious."

"I am serious too. It was composed by Paganini. Have you heard of Paganini?"

"Yes, but why did you pick this one to play?"

"I like it, particularly the name Moishe. I always thought of you when I played it. I fancied that it was written for you."

Moishe's face flushed.

"I see that my group is back from their break," Lenduai said after taking a look at the accordion and the base. "I must go back to them."

On their way back to Hongkew late that evening, Moishe tried to match in her mind the young man in creased trousers to the musician in the black tuxedo. Do I know either one of them?

"Is that what you do for a living, Lenduai?" she asked.

"Yes," he said.

"Every day?"

"Every night," he corrected.

"How did you learn to play the violin?"

"I am a Gypsy."

"I know, but you still must have studied under somebody."

"We Gypsies don't study. We just pick it up."

"Then from whom did you pick it up?"

"The King and others in the tribe."

"How come I never saw you play during our journey to Venice?"

"I did not have a fiddle. Besides, I had you to play with. What else could I ask for?"

"Do you like what you are doing now?"

"Yes, very much. What can be better than playing to make a living? I am free to do anything I want. I play whatever comes into my head, just like being with you in the woods or on the ship. No one tells me what to play."

"I want to have a life like that."

"Like what?"

"Like what you have. Doing what you like."

"Doesn't everybody do that?"

"Not Papa. I don't think he enjoys working with scissors. His real love is the violin."

"Then why doesn't he play?"

"He doesn't have enough fingers on his left hand."

"Don't give me that! Didn't you see me play with one finger? Didn't you see the King play with one finger?"

"You are different."

"How so?"

"You are Gypsies."

"Well, if he really misses playing the fiddle that much, he could restring his fiddle and play with his right hand"

"No one plays the violin with it resting on the right shoulder."

"Why not? It certainly could not be the violin's fault. A violin without strings is symmetric."

"That would be against nature. Most people are right-handed."

"Then think about those who are left-handed. Isn't a left-shouldered violin against their nature?"

"Traditionally..."

"Forget about tradition. Music has no bounds."

"It won't work anyway."

"Then ask your papa to learn to play with two fingers."

"But no orchestra would take him."

"He can come play with us. We can certainly use a second violin. The restaurant goers don't give a damn whether he plays with one finger or four fingers, on his left shoulder or his right shoulder as long as he can play. They come for the food and the company they are with. Or he could start his own group. They have more restaurants in Shanghai than musicians."

It was already past midnight when they reached Moishe's apartment in Teelanchow.

"Come in with me," Moishe said to her long lost friend.

"It's too late."

"I am sure Mama and Papa are still up."

"This late?"

"Yes."

116

"Always this late?"

"No. They are waiting for me."

"Then go. I'll wait until I see you are in safely."

"Come, at least to say hello to them."

"Papa will scold me."

"I'll be with you. He will scold me too and Mama will probably cry."

"You are their daughter."

"I don't want to face them alone."

"Won't your Ahma be there to protect you?"

"She can't protect my feelings. I want you to be with me when Papa scolds me. Just like that time when we returned to the ship from our *shore-leave* in Singapore, remember?"

"You have to learn to accept the consequences of your own decisions, Moishe. Isn't this what Papa has been telling us? Free will? The price is that for every action you take, there is a consequence. I'll come see you again."

"When?"

"When I come."

"Come soon."

"I'll try."

"Then..."

"What?"

"Oh, never mind."

CHAPTER SEVEN

Winter in Shanghai was not as severe as in Europe. It rarely snowed. When puddles and lakes froze, the ice was never thick enough to be walked on. However, the humidity in the air made the cold pierce right into your bones and made you feel as if it were coming out of your body. The Chinese were used to having no heat just like they were used to the smell of *Le Matin de Shanghai.* The Concessions were another world. The foreign contingent had always had the luxury of heat. Even the sycamore trees in the Concessions had the luxury of being wrapped in straw ropes. That left the refugees in Hongkew in the cold. Those who had extra money could have one room for the family heated for a few hours during the evening. One room was what many families had anyway. For most people, the only luxury they could afford was to fill their thermos bottles and kettles from the hot-water vendors for a few coppers while looking forward to summer.

"Hey, Yotahning! You are one copper short," the old man who tended the hot water tank shouted to Moishe in a contentious voice. The man almost always found one or two coppers short whenever Moishe went to have the bottle filled. He never complained when Ahma or Wang-sao went to have the bottle filled. He was a typical Chinese, always trying to take advantage of the vulnerable and cheat the kids and the foreigners. But what could Moishe do? The man complained only after he had pocketed the coppers. There was no way to recount.

Moishe threw the copper on the ground. If he wanted it he had to pick it up. As she turned around in disgust, she bumped into an old woman. She knocked the thermal bottle in the old woman's hand to the ground. It broke into a hundred pieces of shiny mirrors.

"Yotahning! What are you trying to do?" the woman shouted. "You pay!"

Moishe did not know what to do. Her arm was seized by the woman's hand. Her ears were deafened by her shrieking voice, "You pay! You pay!" Moishe realized that a thermal bottle was a very expensive item. Ahma told her that on her farm she could not even afford to own one. What she had in her pocket wasn't even enough to buy the bamboo holder. If she asked her mother for the money, she would definitely get a scolding. She could not ask Ahma either. It would take several of her monthly salaries. Just as she did not know what to do, she heard the hoarse voice of the man who had just cheated her of one copper,

"Let the kid go, old woman! I'll pay for it."

Suddenly Moishe felt so bad about throwing the copper onto the ground. While she was looking for words to say, she heard the familiar contentious voice, "Go home, Yotahning!"

Moishe thought she had made a new friend. But the next time she went to fill her bottle, the nasty old man found her short of a copper again.

When summer finally arrived, the contentious voice of the old man vanished from Moishe's mind together with the thermal bottle. People forgot the miserable winter and started to complain about the heat. Summer in Shanghai was more unbearable than winter. Unlike the cold, the heat treated everyone equally, the poor Chinese and the Jewish refugees in Hongkew as well as the rich and the high-ranking colonialists in the Concessions. The humidity trapped the heat inside people. It was worse than the dry heat on the Red Sea. There was no escape, not even a breeze like that stirred up by the headway of the refugee ship. The more one sweated the harder it was for one's body heat to dissipate. People would pray for typhoons. Only a typhoon could bring wind and rain to relieve them from their misery. A few broken windows, some blown-away roofs, a few over-turned cars and the backed-up sewer in the streets were worth having as collateral damage.

When the weather became intolerable, winter or summer, Rabi always thought of home.

"When is this goddamn war going to end so that we can go home?" he would complain to his wife.

"Where do you call home?" she asked.

"Vienna, of course."

"People back there were so anxious to get rid of us before the war. You think they will welcome us back after the war? If they do, I'll call it a just war then. To me, a home is a place where we are welcome. An ideal home is a place where we can rule ourselves and run our own government."

"Where is that?"

"For home, I know we are welcome here. As for a place we can call our own, I don't know. But at least this place allows us to think about it."

"But these pagans are not our kind. Living with them for a short while is all right. We can't live among them for the rest of our lives!"

"Look, there are so many of us here in Hongkew that it almost looks like a Jewish town."

"You mean a ghetto."

"Why are you always so negative, Papa? If we consider this place our home, then we can rebuild it to our taste. No one says it has to be a ghetto. Look at what the British and the French did in the Concessions."

"You think the Concessions were created by the British and the French peoples? No, they were created by their governments. Where is our government? We are refugees from everywhere: Germany, Austria, Hungary, Poland... all over

Europe. You think we could work together instead of fighting each other?"

This discussion between the couple kept being repeated as long as the Shanghai climate did not improve.

While her parents were complaining, Moishe found her own hiding place to get out of this horrible Shanghai summer heat. The place was just a few blocks from where she lived. It had a roof with a high ceiling and no walls. It was open on all sides such that any motion of air from any direction would breeze through it. She kept it to herself as a secret. To have too many people know about it would definitely ruin it. But she did not have to worry. The smell of the place would keep most people away.

The boys at school had already changed into short pants. The girls had taken off their long-johns underneath their skirts. Moishe could not wait to hurry to her hideaway on the very first day of her school summer break.

The auction was over before dawn. The fishing boats had gone back to sea. All the auctioned goods were already wheeled away to various fresh food markets throughout the city. The place had been hosed down and scrubbed, though it still smelled fishy. How could it be called a fish market without the smell of fish? She would get used to it just as she had gotten used to the smell of *le matin-de-Shanghai* that permeated all of Hongkew in the morning. Like everything else in China, every detail of life was labeled by its smell. A little while later, the unpleasant fishy smell was overwhelmed by the smells from the steaming food stands. Noodles, wontons, dumplings and chicken feet were served to the freshly enriched fishermen and the worn-out fishmongers. It turned a fish market into an eatery market.

As Moishe walked into the fish market, all heads turned towards her, making her aware of her intrusion. She found a bitt (used for tying the mooring lines of the fishing boats) on the dock and sat down on it. Then she dropped a fishing line into the water and picked up her book to read, pretending that she did not notice the stares that were focused on her. She figured that they would fade away just like that fishy smell.

At noon, even under the high ceiling roof and the open space on the sides, the fish market could be intolerably hot. By then the fishermen would have all gone back to sea. The fishmongers had all lain down on their straw mats on the cement floor to catch up with the sleep they had lost during their early morning work.

Moishe barely settled down on the bitt on the very first day when some women vendors walked over to find out about her. Over the noodles and steamed buns they offered, they found out everything about her from her age to where she had come from. Moishe talked and laughed with these women like old friends. On the second day only a few heads turned when Moishe arrived to occupy her bitt on the waterfront. On the third day, no head turned except some nodding to acknowledge her presence. Before long, Moishe had become a fixture of the fish market like a statue in a plaza fountain in a European city. When Ahma wanted to look for Moishe, she knew exactly where to go. She could always count on finding her little girl sitting on the same bitt with a fishing line in one hand and a book in the other hand, looking like the statue of the fishermen's goddess *Tianhou ningniang,* the Heavenly Queen Holy Mother, standing at the other end of the fish market.

Every afternoon, a group of rowdy boys between eight and ten would come to the dock. They would shed their clothes and dive into the Whampoo.

"How is the water?" Moishe asked as the boys climbed back up to the dock for another dive. "Is it warm like the air?"

"Warm?" the youngest one of the bunch responded while the bigger ones just ignored her and dived right back into the river. "Are you kidding? Look at my birdie. It has shrunk to the size of my pinkie."

That was exactly what Moishe wished for, to cool herself down so that everything on her could shrink down to the size of her pinkie. The muddy water became more tempting everyday. Finally one day, with the encouragement of the unbearable heat at high noon and the cheerful voices of the kids, Moishe gathered enough courage and jumped in. When she got back up on the dock, she was surrounded by a bunch of naked kids staring at her.

"Look at her!" one of them exclaimed in an astounding voice. "She went in with her clothes on!"

"What's wrong with that?" Moishe retorted.

"Did your birdie shrink?" a sympathetic voice came from the little one who had complained to Moishe earlier that the water was cold.

"I don't have one," Moishe's answer shocked the kid into silence. The rest of the kids kept staring at her with their mouths open. "Why do you think I jumped in with my clothes on?"

All the kids broke out laughing. They all jumped back into the river. Moishe followed.

Ahma had a fit when Moishe returned home that day.

"Look at you!" she scolded her in anger. "You are soaked like a drenched chicken! What happened?"

"I went swimming."

"So unladylike! Look, Miss, you are not a flat-chest tomboy anymore!"

"What does that have to do with flat chest or not?"

"You shameless girl! Where did you go swimming?"

"In the Whampoo."

"Ah-ya, that river is a sewer! I mean sewer. The city dumps its sewage into that river. Didn't you see trash floating on it?"

"It's a flowing river. It is constantly being flushed out to the sea," Moishe argued. "Besides, it is being replenished twice a day with clean fresh sea water."

"The sea is so far away."

"It is so big and the tide is so strong."

"What do you know about tides?"

"I am a fisherman. Fishermen pay attention to tides."

"Go away! How many fish have you caught today, my dear fisherman?"

"Just give me time. I will become the best fisherman in Hongkew."

"What's the matter with you? There are so many trades you can pick and you have to pick that of a fisherman. A fisherman's life is the lowest. Fishermen are vulgar people; they are illiterate; they are poor; they smell and they have no morals. No decent girl will marry a fisherman."

"I am not a boy."

"There are no women fishermen either."

Moishe did not pay any attention to Ahma. She kept on going to the fish market and kept on jumping into the Whampoo River with the other kids. However, she did not have much luck in her proclaimed profession - fishing. Once in a while she would catch one. But the catch was never over two inches long. She would forgo her Whampoo-dip that day and run home to have the cook fix her catch. That would be the centerpiece on the dinner table and the talk of the evening.

One day when Moishe came to her usual pedestal, she noticed that it was occupied. A rope was tied on it. At the other end of the rope there was a boat. It was large, not a sampans that was being rowed with oars. It occupied about half of the fish market dock, blocking off what she and her swimming friends used for diving. The boat had two tall masts topped with small red squares and tell-tale pennants, standing majestically high above the roof of the fish market like two church spires. Her deck was enclosed by two knee-high gunwales. Instead of joining at the two ends, they curved up, like a rooster's tail at the stern and, at the bow, stuck up like a pair of rabbit ears. Right below the rabbit ears there were two big round eyeballs, the size of two large watermelons, gawking just above the waterline. This was definitely not a sampan.

"Is this a dragon boat?" she asked.

That brought a round of laughter from the naked kids around her. "Do you see a dragonhead? The eyes on a dragon boat are high up on the dragonhead, not below the deck."

"What is it then?"

"That is a junk!"

"Shouldn't a junk have sails?"

"What do you think those masts are for?"

"What kind of junk is this?"

"A fishing junk."

A fishing junk? Where else can you find a better place to fish than on a fishing junk? Without thinking twice, Moishe gathered up her fishing gear, which consisted of just a line and a hook, and climbed over the gunwale on board the junk. She walked across the deck to the opposite gunwale that was exposed widely to the flowing Whampoo. The river flowed faster away from the bank. As soon as she dropped her fishing line over the side, she was startled by a voice.

"You won't catch anything there."

She lifted up her head. There was a young man about her own age sitting high up on a thwart on the fantail with one leg dangling over the side and one leg crouching on the thwart like a hound dog. His hands were holding a bowl and a pair of chopsticks. His face was wearing a smirk.

"Is this your boat?" Moishe asked.

"No, I just work here."

"Is this a fishing junk?"

"That is exactly what you have your feet planted on," the boy spoke in a dialect quite similar to the Shanghai dialect spoken by Moishe except that the words sounded like being forced out by a lot of air and saliva. It was loud. Moishe could somehow figure out every word the man said.

"Are you a fisherman?"

"Yes."

"Where are you from?"

"Shinguomen."

"Where is that?"

"Chusan, outside of Ningpo," said the fisherman. Then after taking a suspicious look at Moishe, he asked, "Are you English?"

"No, I am a *Yotahning*."

"Is the *Yotahning* language the same as Chinese?"

"No."

"How come I can understand you?"

"I am speaking Chinese."

"Thank heavens you are not English!"

"What's wrong with being English?"

"Those foreign devils are so arrogant. They think the whole world should speak that tongue-twisting language of theirs."

"Have you talked to them?"

"Are you kidding? They don't talk to Chinese. When they do, they can only yell *'buhao buhao'*. When we cannot understand what they want, they ram their gunboats into us."

Moishe had no doubt about what the boy said about the English. It was interesting to notice that the boy called the English "foreign devils" while assuming that her language was the same as his language. Did he think *Yotahning* were not foreigners? Now, why couldn't her father learn to speak Chinese? Then he wouldn't have been considered a foreign devil and he wouldn't be feeling so miserable about his life in Shanghai. The trouble with her parents was that they clung too close to their old culture. They socialized too much with their own kind. Every time they got together, they reinforced each other in their misery by telling each other how bad this place was and how cultureless the Chinese were and how much they looked forward to returning to their civilized Europe. She could not understand why they would continue to dream about going to America while they were repeatedly refused visas by that government.

"You come everyday?" the young fisherman asked, this time without the smirk on his face.

"Yes."

"Fishing?"

"Yes, but I don't catch much."

"No fish in Whampoo."

"Why not?"

"Too narrow. Too shallow. Too muddy. Too dirty. Not fresh enough for carp and not salty enough for yellow croaker."

"Where do you catch your fish then?"

"Out at sea."

"Then why are you not at sea at this time?"

"We are waiting for the tide to turn around and go out."

"Can't you sail against the tide?"

"Yes, but stick out your finger and feel it. Do you feel the air moving?"

"Do fish really go with the tide?" Moishe remembered telling Ahma that tide had everything to do with fishing.

"Yes, but that's not what we are waiting for."

"What are you waiting for?

"An ebb tide and some wind. Why buck against the tide while in a few hours it will go our way?"

"Can I go with you?" Moishe asked.

"Go where?"

"To sea."

"Why do you want to go to sea?"

"To catch fish. Didn't you say there are no fish in the Whampoo?"

"You'll have to talk to the *laoda.*"

"Who is the *Laoda?*"

"The captain."

"Where is he?"

"Over there working on the bow."

Moishe's voice suddenly turned femininely sweet. "Can you ask him for me? Please!" she begged.

The young fisherman hesitated for a while. Then he came down from the fantail and went forward. It was too far away for Moishe to hear what they were saying. She saw the old man turning his head to look at her. After a while the man returned to where Moishe was standing.

"He says it's bad luck to have a woman on board," said the young fisherman.

"Does that mean no?"

"He says you don't look Chinese."

"What does that mean?"

"He says he could not tell whether you are a boy or a girl from the way you dress."

"Tell me, is that good or bad?"

"But he says you can go with us."

"He really said that?" Moishe cried out in disbelief.

"He says just this once."

"What shall I do next?"

The boy cast a look to survey Moishe from head to toe, just as the *laoda* had done a while back from the bow. "Take off those shoes," he said. Then after another look, he said, "Those thin clothes of yours won't work. You must put on something heavier. It's cold out there."

"Cold in the summer?"

"You must tie up your hair. It blows at sea. You must... Eh, follow me."

Moishe followed the young fisherman into the cabin.

It was dark and stuffy inside. There was no window. The ceiling was so low that she had to keep her head stooped all the time while she was in the cabin.

When she came back on deck, there was no *Yotahning* and no woman. There were just two teenaged fishermen.

"What's your name?" the shorter one asked the taller one.

"Ah Bong. What's yours?"

"Moishe."

"Ah Moi?"

"Yes, call me Ah Moi. I like that."

CHAPTER EIGHT

Sailing on the Whampoo brought Moishe back to her first impression of the Orient. She remembered standing on the deck of that rusty refugee ship. Just like now, she was a boy, many years younger. Just like now, she had been fascinated by everything that she saw. The sky was lit up by the city lights in the distance like dawn. The river was filled with strange looking boats that she had never seen before. She remembered holding her breath as she watched those daring junks with big gawking eyes and patched sails cutting daringly across the bow of the refugee ship.

Moishe could not believe that she was actually on one of them now! Only this time, all she could see in front of her were two huge patched sails like the wings of a dragon in a fairy tale. Through the crack between the sails, the busy river traffic flashed by like scenes in a peep show. She felt as if she were inside a carpet factory peeping out through the hanging carpets.

Suddenly, the crack was blacked out. At the next moment, a huge monster popped out of the crack and was coming at the junk. She braced herself against the nearby railing and cleats and held her breath. She felt the junk roll, her weight shift and the deck slip away from under her feet. She heard the sails flutter and the bamboo battens rattle. Then she heard the canvas pop. A gust of wind came from nowhere and blew her hair across her face.

She swept her hair back and looked through the crack again. The monster was not there any more. All she could see was a little bit of the river and a short section of the shoreline. She turned her head back. There she was! A huge iron structure towering over the stern, trying to catch up with the junk. She pushed up a heap of white foam swallowing up the wake of the junk.

Before Moishe regained her breath, there came another steel wall... another high rising bow... another switching of the tilting deck... another heap of foam... Then another one. Each time, the junk either turned away with the ease of a swimmer who flipped around at the end of a swimming pool or dashed across the white angry foam like a jumping dolphin. One after another, the big sea monsters kept coming, plowing through the Whampoo and not yielding to anything in their way like a buffalo plowing through a rice field not yielding to the cranes, frogs or insects in front of it. The daredevil junk kept making somersaults and dashing away from these sea monsters. Her deck kept switching from one inclination to another while Moishe's sweating hands held on tightly to the railing and her feet struggled desperately to keep on deck. Would she tip over?

"When will the deck be leveled?" she asked, as she couldn't hide her fear any longer.

"When we start fishing," Ah Bong said.

"When will that be?"

"If this wind prevails," said the young fisherman after tilting his head to the clouds in the sky. "Probably by tomorrow morning."

"You mean we are not going home tonight?"

Moishe did not go home that night. In the late afternoon, Ahma went to the fish market to look for her. At first she could not believe it when the naked kids told her that Moishe had gone out to sea on a junk. When she finally realized the truth, she almost fainted.

"Was she kidnapped?" was her first reaction. "What junk?"

When she was told that it was a fishing junk, she immediately swore to herself, "Those low-down, dirty, no-good fishermen! How many times have I told that silly girl to stay away from those immoral beings? They must have drugged her! Oh, my Heaven, she will be gang-raped!"

Where did the junk go? Would the junk come back? When? What if she never came back? What if the junk got caught by the Japanese? What if the junk ran into a storm? What if she got washed overboard? What if they sold her to a whorehouse? What if... As one horror after another ran through her mind, raping almost seemed to be a blessing. Oh, that brat! How was she going to break this horrible news to the Rabis?

Moishe did not come back the next day, not the following day, not the day after that, not...

Neither Ahma nor the Rabis knew what to do except to lose sleep and their appetites. They certainly could not report it to the police. The Japanese ran the police. That would be like asking a wolf to look for a lost sheep. On the other hand, even if the police were willing to look into this, how could they trace a fishing junk to sea? What was the name of the junk? Do junks have names? A junk at sea was like a seagull in the ocean. There were so many of them. No one could even tell which one or how many failed to return to shore. To the beachcombers, there were always so many of them out there and nothing could wipe them out. They were an integral part of the everlasting seascape.

Once the junk got out of the Whampoo and into the Yangtze, she stopped changing tack so frequently. Consequently the deck did not switch its inclination so often. Now Moishe could try to feel out the situation. She noticed that the junk did not look as neat inside as she looked on the outside.

The deck was divided into two parts lengthwise by the cabin, a flat fore deck and a slightly raised poop deck. Lining along the centerline on the fore deck there were two masts and a row of hatches in between. Under the hatches were the holds used for storing the catch. Next to the hatches there were two piles of sampans stacked on top of each other. The rest of the space was filled with ropes, baskets of fishing lines and poles with flags. The poop deck was a small space barely large enough for a couple of people to stand on it and for the helmsman to walk from one bulwark to another when he pushed on a five-foot long tiller to change the heading of the junk.

The cabin was divided into two compartments, a small galley open to the poop deck and the crew's sleeping quarters forward of the galley. In the galley there was a wood-burning stove on one side and a sleeping bunk on the other side. In the inside quarters there were two platforms, each one large enough to accommodate at least six sleepers.

"Go lie down for a while in there," said the *laoda* to the girl pointing at the bunk in the galley. "We are going to be under sail for quite a while."

"But there is only one bunk," Moishe observed.

"Take it," said the *laoda*. "That's mine."

"Aren't you going to sleep?"

"I won't get to sleep until we get to the fishing ground."

"Where are you going to sleep then?"

"I'll sleep on one of those platforms in the crew's quarters."

"I can sleep there."

"You? You can't sleep there!"

"Why not?"

"They are all men."

The junk zigzagged all night in the muddy water. Every time she changed tack, Moishe woke up to switch her posture such that her back was always positioned leeward in the bunk. Just as she was getting used to it, the rolling stopped. Moishe came up on deck. The deck was level and the sails were furled. All hands were gathered there. Dawn was barely breaking over the horizon. After a quick breakfast of hot rice gruel with some salted fish, the sampans were lowered into the water.

"Are you ready to go fishing?" Laoda asked Moishe in high spirit.

"Yes!" the girl responded excitedly.

"Then get into that sampan with Ah Bong."

"Ah Bong?"

"Isn't he your friend? Get your lunch before you go."

"Lunch?"

"You are going to stay out there for a whole day."

Moishe watched the crew put on the bottoms of their rice bowls some salt fish that was leftover from breakfast and then packed them tightly with rice. She skipped the salted fish and just packed the rice. With the rice bowl in one hand, she jumped into the sampan. The impact of her weight almost capsized the tiny boat.

"Careful!" shouted Ah Bong. "Move to the center!"

The sampan reminded her of the beggar boats at the entrance to the Whampoo. The only difference was there was no top. The sampan had no deck either, just a couple of thwarts. Moishe's bare feet not only felt the roughness of the bottom but she could also feel the ocean hitting the sampan on the other side of its thin planking.

"Don't stand there!" ordered Ah Bong, "Go sit down on the sheet at the bow."

Moishe was surprised to hear Ah Bong speaking in the authoritative voice of a *laoda*. Where was that soft-spoken Shinguomen fisherman? But on second thought, why not? There were just the two of them. If Ah Bong did not act like a *laoda*, who was going to handle the sampan?

Moishe watched Ah Bong fitting a scull to a rounded bolt on the stern. Then he picked up a rope that was attached to the bottom of the sampan and hooked it on the tip of the handle of the scull.

"I can row," Moishe volunteered.

"Row?" Ah Bong laughed. "Look around. The sea is so

big. You won't get anywhere by rowing. Besides, this is not an oar. You don't row, you scull."

But don't the gondolas in Venice do the same thing? Moishe thought to herself. The scull looks almost like the single oar that is used on a gondola. The difference is that the scull is mounted on the stern of the sampan and the single oar is mounted on the side of the gondola. Boats are so strange! Each one is different from all the others.

A junk is different from a ship, a sampan is different from a junk, a gondola is different from a rowboat and a rowboat is different from a sampan. Moishe felt like a toddler learning to walk all over again. So far nothing she did or said was right. So she kept quiet.

Moishe watched Ah Bong take out a long bundle from under the thwarts. He unrolled it. It turned out to be a pole attached to a piece of ragged cloth. Ah Bong stuck the pole into a hole in the middle of the forward thwart. Then he climbed back to the stern with a line in his hand. The line was attached to the corner of the ragged cloth, which was fastened to a stick attached to the pole. With one hand on the handle of the scull, one foot on the aft thwart, he pulled in the line. The sampan suddenly came alive. It leaped up like a horse responding to a jerk on a rein. It stopped rocking and headed straight away from the junk just as swiftly as the junk did in turning away from the steamships in the heavy Whampoo traffic.

The sampan sailed until the junk shrunk to look like a seagull on the horizon. Ah Bong loosened the sheet in his hand and wrapped it around the mast together with the sail. The sampan became limp and resumed rolling in waves and even to just a tiny movement of her occupants.

"Do you know how to scull?" the boy asked. Seeing no response from his sampan mate, he demonstrated it to her as he explained, "See, there is nothing to it. With this end tied down, you simply push and pull on the handle while applying a slight twist as it goes. The tricky part is when the sampan is lifted up by a wave, the scull will get out of the water. You stop sculling until it is back in the water."

Moishe tried it. She quickly got the feel of it. Ah Bong tied a floating flagpole to the beginning of the fish line and threw it into the water. Then the two youngsters went to work. With Moishe sculling and Ah Bong baiting the hooks, they let a long line out of a wooden tub. The line slid over the side and sank into the deep blue water, taking the hooks and the bait with it. It did not take long to have all of the line played out of the tub.

"Wow! How many days do I have to sit at the fish market to have so many hooks set in the water?"

"Now you can stop sculling," said Ah Bong as he tied another floating flagpole to the end of the line.

"Then what?"

"We'll let the hooks work for us."

"What are we going to do?"

"Nothing. We sit and wait, just like you did at the fish market. Look how busy those sea gulls are diving? I bet we are going to catch some fish today."

Moishe could still vividly remember sailing on the refugee ship through the Mediterranean Sea, the Red Sea, the Indian Ocean and the South China Sea. But it was always the ship sailing on the sea. She could only watch the sea from a high deck. She could never touch the sea. Only occasionally the sea would climb up to touch her. Now she was "on the sea" just like a ship. To touch the sea, all she had to do was to reach her hand over the gunwale. She could watch the waves roll and break at eye level and let them spray on her face. She fancied that she was a seagull.

"Ah Bong, will the seagulls bite on our hooks?" Moishe asked.

"No."

"Why not?"

"They are set too deep in the water."

"What if there is one seagull who can dive very deep?"

"Then it will get hooked."

"What shall we do with it?"

"Unhook it."

"Will it live?"

"Sure, they are tough. All creatures in the sea are tough. If you unhook a fish, it will also live."

"How do you know?"

"I've caught fish that had rusty hooks in their mouths."

Moishe went back to her daydreaming. This time she dreamed that she was a fish and was hooked. She wouldn't like that. She'd rather be a fisherman. Being out there on the sampan, she sort of missed the junk. The bunk she slept in the night before was quite comfortable. She wouldn't mind to have a bunk like that at home. That was a luxurious wish. Even on board the junk, only the laoda had a bunk.

"Ah Bong!"

"What?"

"Why did Laoda give me his bunk to sleep in?"

"I don't know."

"Why did he say I could not sleep on one of the platforms?"

"I don't know."

"Is he married?"

"Yes."

"Does he have any children?"

"He had a daughter."

"How old is she?"

"She should be about your age if she were alive."

"What happened to her?"

"One day the Japanese soldiers went to his village and killed her."

"Why didn't Laoda stop them?"

"He was at sea."

"Why did they kill her?"

"Because she clawed them."

"Why did she claw them?"

"They gang-raped her. But they were not satisfied. So they turned to rape her mother. She got up and tried to stop them."

"Why didn't her mother fight back?"

"She was tied up."

"Did the Japanese kill her mother too?"

"No."

"Why not?"

"Because she did not hurt them and they had their satisfaction."

"Why couldn't she hurt them?"

"I've already told you. She was tied up."

Moishe did not keep quiet for very long before she asked again.

"Ah Bong, was that why Laoda did not want me to sleep on the platform?"

"What do you mean?"

"I mean the crew might..."

"No, as long as Laoda is on the junk, nothing will happen to you. Besides, we may be illiterate, but we are not animals like the Japanese."

"Then why did he yield his bunk to me?"

"He just wanted you to have a good night's sleep, I guess. Being first time at sea is tough enough."

Moishe did not say anything any more.

The morning was chilly and the water around her was blue. The summer heat in Shanghai and the muddy water of the Whampoo had completely disappeared. She was so relaxed that she suddenly felt the call of nature.

"Where can I go to the bathroom?" she asked.

"Bathroom? There is no bathroom here. Can't you see with your own eyes?"

"I mean I want to use the toilet."

"What toilet?"

"I want to go!"

"Then go."

"Where?"

"Anywhere."

"How?"

"Just like you do on the junk."

"How do you go on the junk? I have not done it before."

"Do it anyway and anywhere you want, as long as you don't leave anything inboard."

"How?"

"Sit on the gunwale."

"Gunwale?"

"The side," Ah Bong patted on the gunwale and said.

"What about you?"

"It's you who wants to go. I don't want to go."

"You know what I mean."

"Don't expect me to give you a hand!"

"I don't mean that! Can you turn your head?"

"Oh, that! No problem. But don't sit on that side. Go sit downwind or it is going to be blown back onto you. Hurry up, it's time to pick up."

Picking up was more exciting than setting. Moishe could not believe what they were pulling out of the water. Instead of the fish line, a string of silver ribbons came up over the gunwale. They glittered under the sun. They even outshone the reflection of the sun on the water and the whitecaps. They were fish! Before she got to the tail of one, the head of another one came up.

"They look as if they are biting on the tails of the ones before them!" Moishe said excitedly. "What do you call these silver ribbons?"

"Silver Ribbons."

"Don't joke. I am asking a serious question."

"What else would you call them?"

"You mean I have just given a name to a fish?"

"If you want to think of it that way."

"Hey, I have just made an original contribution to ichthyology!"

"Ich...gy? What is that?"

"Science."

"What is science?"

"Study."

"Then stop studying. Pull. Be careful when you unhook them. They have sharp teeth. And don't tear their mouths. Don't let them bite you and don't let the hooks hook on you."

Seeing that his sampan-mate was doing all right, Ah Bong let her do the unhooking. He picked up a square wooden bucket and started to scoop water into the sampan.

"What are you doing, Ah Bong? You want to sink the boat?"

"To keep the fish from suffocating in the air."

"Suffocating in air?"

"Fish breathe water, not air like us humans. We want to keep them alive until we return to the junk."

After they had picked up the entire line, they made three more settings. On the third setting, Moishe had fully managed the process. She did not get bitten even once. Not a single word of instruction or warning was heard from her *laoda* either.

As they were sailing back to the junk, Moishe felt as if she were drunk. She could not tell whether it was from being exposed too much to the sun or from the sight of the colorful clouds over the western horizon or from the boatload of wiggling silver ribbons around her bare feet. Whatever, it was the most exciting day of her life.

Moishe and Ah Bong were the last ones in. All the other sampans had gotten back to the junk an hour before them.

"Screw you!" Moishe heard Laoda yelling to the fishermen standing on deck watching Ah Bong and her pulling alongside the junk. "You guys insisted that women would bring bad luck. Look at what she's brought! Shame on you!"

Only Ah Bong and Moishe had a decent catch that day.

When Moishe planted her feet back on the deck of the junk, she felt that she had always belonged there. She felt secure like she was standing on solid land.

"*Yotahning* doesn't count," some of the crew still clung to their superstition. "She's not an ordinary woman."

"Save your breath," said Laoda as he watched Moishe's and Ah Bong's sampan being hoisted up on deck. "Go lash down everything. Let's go find an easier fishing spot for these so-called 'old hands'."

Moishe felt so good about her achievement that the simple dinner of steamed rice and boiled Silver Ribbon tasted better than any meal she had ever had in her life. Even the inclined deck did not bother her any more.

After dinner, the cook handed a hot towel to Laoda. Moishe watched with great interest as Laoda wiped the towel around his face several times in a circular motion. Then he wrapped his index finger in it and stuck it into his mouth. He rubbed his teeth just as he did his face. When he finished, he cleared his throat and handed the towel to Moishe.

"Clean yourself," he said in the tone of a caring father.

Moishe did not know what to do with the towel in her hand. She handed it to Ah Bong. Then she heard Laoda say,

"That's for you, not for those thieves."

Moishe did not know whether she should wipe her face and rub her teeth or give it back to Laoda. She knew it was a gesture of favoritism. She turned around and lifted the towel to her face. She did not wipe her face. She wiped her hands and then ran it over her messy hair.

"Don't be shy," said Laoda with a friendly smile. "The junk is only so big. There is no place for you to hide from others."

All the deckhands turned in after dinner except Laoda, who stood the tiller watch all by himself. Moishe fell asleep as soon as she hit the sack in Laoda's bunk.

The next thing Moishe knew: she was being awakened to

get out on deck. It was still pitch dark.

"Guys, go catch them Silver Ribbons at their early feeding!" Laoda said to the crew after their breakfast of hot rice gruel and salted fish. "Let's hope that you do better than the *Yotahning xiao-niang-bi* today."

Moishe was half asleep while Ah Bong stepped the mast and sailed the sampan into the dark abyss. Morning at sea was quite chilly. Even wrapping her arms around herself, Moishe still could not stop her teeth from chattering. Suddenly Ah Bong's voice woke her up.

"You want to bait the hooks today?"

"Me?" Moishe asked in disbelief.

"Yes, you."

"Are we there already?" She looked around. It was still pitch dark. But the sampan had stopped.

It was such a compliment! But baiting was not so simple. She had to move fast to keep up with Ah Bong's sculling. Moishe wished that Ahma were here to see her. No one in the entire Hongkew could do what she was doing.

"What does *xiao-niang-bi* mean?" Moishe asked when she and Ah Bong finally sat down to let the hooks do their work. It had been bothering her since they sailed away from the junk.

"Where did you hear that?"

"Didn't you hear Laoda calling me *Yotahning xiao-niang-bi?*"

"Oh, that. It means *little-girl.*"

"What does *bi* mean?"

"Just the way we Ningponese talk."

"There must be a meaning."

"You don't want to know."

"I do."

"You do?"

"Yes."

"That's what you women pee with."

Moishe was more hurt than shocked to hear that. "What do

you think the *laoda* has against me?" she asked.

"Ha, ha, ha, ha!" Ah Bong could not control himself in laughing. "That is an endearing term."

"Endearing or cursing?"

"When it is combined with *little-girl,* it becomes endearing. This is the way we Ningponese talk. You call your daughter with that. Didn't you hear him calling us thieves? Did you see me stealing anything? What is there to steal on a junk?"

Moishe baited for all the settings that day. Give her a few more days, she thought to herself, perhaps the *laoda* would give her a sampan to skipper, if what Ah Bong said to her about the endearing word was true.

Ah Bong and Moishe had another good day of catch. After they pulled in the last Silver Ribbon, Ah Bong went to sit down on the sheet at the bow and said to Moishe,

"Set sail for the junk, Ah Moi!"

"Me?"

"Why not?"

Moishe unfurled the sail and climbed back to the stern with the sheet in her hand. She fit the scull onto the pivot and hooked its end to the anchor rope. As soon as Moishe pulled in the sheet, the sampan surprised her by leaping up like a wild horse and went into a gallop over the waves. For a moment Moishe did not know whether she should hold on to the sheet or to the scull. Then she heard Ah bong's voice.

"Pull in the sheet more! Never mind the scull."

Moishe did as told. Miraculously, the sampan tamed down into a steady heading.

"Now pull the sheet a little bit tighter..." said her coach. "You see how she goes into the wind? Now try slacking it up... See her heading falling off? Hold it right there... See how steady she is holding her heading? You see, you can steer just by handling the sheet without using the scull as a rudder."

"Why do we need a rudder then?"

"The wind is never steady. Any change in its direction or

strength can change the heading of the boat. So you need a rudder to compensate."

"Wow!" Moishe was so thrilled at being able to control the sampan. "How do you know so much, Ah Bong?"

"Science."

"That's not the way the word 'Science' is being used."

"Didn't you say science means study?"

"Study of what?"

"Wind and sailing. Now push on the scull..."

Moishe followed Ah Bong's instructions, taking in and letting out the sheet and pushing and pulling on the scull. The sampan responded to Moishe's commands, making turns and tacks as in an equestrian performance. Moishe broke out screaming and laughing like a little girl on horseback.

"Raise the sail higher, sailor!" she called out to her crew. "Raise it to the top! I want to go faster."

"Now that you've got the feel of it," Ah Bong said. "Let's head back to the junk."

On the following morning when Ah Bong got into his sampan, he saw that the mast had already been stepped in and Moishe was already at the scull with a limping sheet in her hand.

"Give me a heading, *Laoda,*" asked Moishe in high spirit.

While the sampan was bouncing on the waves and heading toward a dawn-breaking horizon, Ah Bong went aft and squeezed by Moishe to sit on the stern sheet. He threw something overboard.

"What did you just throw out?" Moishe asked.

"A troll line."

"What is a troll line?"

"A fishing line."

"What for?"

"To catch fish. What else do you think?"

"Aren't you going to wait until we get to the fishing

ground?"

"A troll line catches different fish."

"How different?"

Before Moishe got her answer, the troll line stiffened.

"We've got a strike!" yelled Ah Bong as he quickly pulled in the line, giving instructions to his sampan mate at the same time, "Let go of the sheet in your hand! All of it!"

The sail swung out, spilling out the wind instantaneously. The sampan came to a standstill. A sheet of ragged cloth fluttered on the rocking mast with a dangling rope. The troll line took off to the side of the sampan. Ah Bong ran forward while pulling in the line as fast as he could. The line became taut again and started to veer from one side to the other.

"Look!" cried Moishe excitedly when she saw a dashing shadow coming up from the deep blue water. Then suddenly before her wide-open eyes, a flashing sword shot out of the water. The next moment, it was flipping and jumping on the bottom of the boat.

Unlike any sea creature Moishe had seen at the fish market, this one had a raised forehead like a bent knee and a golden green body like a gold-gilded Buddha draped in a green transparent chiffon.

"What is that?" asked the bewildered girl.

"A fish. What else?"

"What kind of fish?"

"A dolphin."

"You mean a porpoise?"

"No! A porpoise is not a fish. Porpoises are fishermen's friends. We would never hurt a porpoise."

"Why do you call a dolphin, I mean porpoise, a friend?"

"If a fisherman fell overboard in a group of porpoises, they would come hold him up."

"Really? Have you ever seen that?"

"I have never fallen overboard."

"I mean seeing them help others."

"I have never seen anybody falling overboard."

"You mean a dolphin wouldn't do that?"

"A dolphin is just a fish."

Fish or friend, its vigorous struggle for life was too vibrant not to win the heart of this compassionate girl.

"Let's put it back into the water," she suggested.

"Are you crazy?"

"Quick!" pleaded Moishe. "It's suffocating. It's going to die."

"What is not going to die? One day you are going to die too."

"But I don't want to kill it. For that matter, I don't want to be killed by someone either."

"Then why do you want to come fishing with us?"

"To catch silver ribbon."

"What's the difference, dolphin or silver ribbon?"

"One is for eating and one is not."

"What are you talking about?"

"Look how scared it is."

"A fish does not know what it is to be scared."

"Why is it jumping then?"

"It's a reflex."

Suddenly the fish stopped jumping. Moishe could not believe her eyes. The shine on the fish quickly faded. It became tarnished, like metal turning rusty. Just then a streak of reflection on the surface of the ocean blinded Moishe's eyes. A deep red sun broke out on the horizon.

"What happened to it?" she asked in bewilderment.

"It is dead," Ah Bong said in a matter-of-fact tone as he picked up the fish. He brought it to his mouth and bit on its tail, on one side then on the other side. Then he dug his fingernails into the new wounds on the fish. Spreading out his elbows, he tore at the fish. The tarnished green skin peeled off like the skin of a banana exposing a snow-white flesh.

Ah Bong tore off two pieces of fillet from the bones. He

handed one to Moishe and said,

"Eat it while it is still fresh."

Moishe did not know how to react to the situation. She saw a Stone Age savage in front of her. She had never seen a life extinguished like this, not to mention being eaten.

"It's not cooked," was all she could say as she watched Ah Bong eating it like a wild animal.

"Try it. It's so much tastier than anything cooked."

"How cruel!"

"Cruel?"

"It was alive just a while ago."

"Do you think cooking it would make it less cruel?"

"At least one wouldn't be thinking of it being alive."

"You think that would make you more civilized?"

"It's not fair to the fish."

"Fair? What does that mean?"

"Good deeds get awarded; bad deeds get punished."

"How do you think it got caught? It stole my fly and ate it. You call that fair?"

"Your fly was not alive."

"The fish didn't know that."

"But I know."

"What you think does not count. As long as the fish thinks it is alive, it is alive. Do you call the fish cruel? There is nothing fair in the world. There is only fate. Why do you think we caught the silver ribbons yesterday and none other did? Why do you think the rain falls on us and not on others?"

Moishe did not want to appear to be a sissy to her sampan mate. She bit on the piece of white fillet in her hand. She must admit that this piece of raw fish, even untreated and unseasoned, tasted better than anything she had known, lox or pickled herring. It made the boiled Silver Ribbon tasteless at dinner.

The crew turned in after dinner as usual, leaving the *laoda* on the poop deck all by himself. Moishe's bunk was open to the poop deck. Lying there she could see Laoda's legs pacing the deck. Tilting up her head she could see the night sky. There were more stars in the sky at sea than all the city lights in Shanghai. They were also brighter than the city lights. But they did not light up the sky like the city lights did to the city. She could not close her eyes. After a while, she broke the silence,

"Laoda, why aren't you in bed?"

"I am on watch," the old man said.

"Watching what?"

"Watching the junk."

"What for?"

"So that nothing happens to her."

"What can happen to her? It's water all around us."

"Who knows? Something may come up."

"Like what?"

"Oh... maybe some steamship runs onto us."

"Can't they see us?"

"Maybe, maybe not. But never depend on someone else to watch out for you. You must watch out for yourself."

"Why do only you stand watch every night?"

"The crew has to go into the sampans in the morning. Besides, I am the *laoda*. If anything happens, I am responsible not just for the junk but for all fourteen lives, now with you on board fifteen lives."

"Why doesn't Ah Ting stand watch? I didn't see him going into any sampan."

"He's our purser."

"What's a purser on a junk for?"

"He keeps track of our sales at the auction."

"Can't you do it?"

"Yes, but I can only keep numbers in my head. I can't enter them in a book like he does."

"Why not?"

"I can't read or write," said the old man.

"Can't someone else on board do it?"

"Are you kidding? None of the crew even knows how to recognize his own name."

"Doesn't Ah Bong know?"

"If he did, he wouldn't be a fisherman. He would be working somewhere on shore. This life is not even fit for a half decent person."

"Why doesn't Ah Ting work on shore?"

"He represents the owner on board."

"Owner of what?"

"This junk, our catch, ... everything. You watch. When Ah Ting goes ashore, he puts on shoes. At the auction he always puts on a pair of glasses to look intelligent and respectable."

Moishe couldn't imagine that someone like Ah Bong who knew so much about sailing, fishing and how to tell the weather could not recognize his own name in writing. If he could learn to use the word "Science", why couldn't he learn his name and how to enter numbers in a book?

Ah Bong let his sampan-mate steer the sampan and bait the hooks again on the following day. She did both very well. But her beginner's luck had run out. The two morning settings did not yield much. They picked up the line and made a run. They did not go far when the wind died down and the sea became as calm as a lake.

"It's just as good here as anywhere to set our line," said Ah Bong. "We are playing a game of hide and seek with the Silver Ribbon anyway."

Without a breeze, the sun at noon was baking the unshielded fishermen as mercilessly as it did the residents in Shanghai.

"At least at the fish market we had a roof over our heads," grunted Moishe.

"Here we have a sea."

"What can the sea do? It is under us. The sun is above us."

"Then get under it."

"How?"

Without saying another word, Ah Bong stood up. To Moishe's shocking, he took off all his clothes right in front of her like the kids at the fish market and jumped off the sampan. Moishe's eyes followed Ah Bong until he disappeared into the deep blue water where they had pulled up the golden green dolphin.

It felt like many, many minutes had passed. There was no sign of Ah Bong anywhere. Moishe started to worry. Did he know how to swim? Had he drowned? Could he be swallowed by a shark, just like the fly on the troll line by the dolphin and the dolphin by Ah Bong and herself? Perhaps a porpoise would carry him up. But she did not see any porpoise around them.

"Ah Moi!" she heard a voice calling her. It came from the other side of the sampan. She turned around. There was a head bobbing in the water at a distance and a hand waving. Moishe gave out a sigh of relief. The head disappeared again.

After another long while, the sampan suddenly tilted to one side as if it was going to capsize. Moishe quickly threw her body to the other side to balance it as a natural reaction she had acquired during the past few days. Before she realized what was happening, a bronze statue, dripping with water, was standing in front of her. It resembled one of those naked gods in the city fountains back in Europe. The water and the sunshine made the masculine muscles stand out under a tight bronze colored skin. Only then did she realize that there were no naked statues in Shanghai. Back home you could see them everywhere, female as well as male, in fountains, in city squares, on buildings and in galleries and museums. The statues here were all heavily clothed. They looked unnatural.

"Is the water cold?" she asked just to make conversation. In the meantime, her eyes instinctively moved down from Ah Bong's chest to his abdomen. She suddenly felt a burning sensation in her cheeks. She lowered her eyes. There was no place to hide. She turned around. There was just the clear blue ocean around her. She jumped into it.

She held her breath and buried herself deep into the water. She opened her mouth and tasted the ocean. It tasted salty. She swallowed some. It was bitter. But thank God it did not have that muddy taste of the Whampoo. After thoroughly cooling off, she came up to the surface and swam back to the sampan. From where she was, the freeboard of the sampan appeared as high above her head as the railing of the junk when she was sitting in the sampan before being hoisted up. She looked up. There were two naked legs straddling high above her head.

"Give me your hand," she heard a familiar voice.

She stretched up her hand. She felt a jerk. She thought her arm was coming apart from her shoulder. In a split of second, she found herself inside the sampan pinning to something as solid as the mainmast of the junk. She could feel a strong vise locked on her small back. Her feet were dangling on thin air. She could feel bulging muscles burning every inch of her body from her thigh all the way to her chest. It felt good after emerging from that cold ocean. While she let her body thaw, she felt an unshaved face rubbing against hers. Her arms reached back and unlocked the muscular vise. She pushed herself away. She was surprised that her captor did not resist her push.

There standing at a loss before her, was the bronze statue that she had adored earlier. His eyes were staring at her. But they were not on her face or her eyes. She followed the stare. She was shocked by the sight of her own body. Under the tightly clinging dripping wet clothes, she looked as if she were naked.

"Stop staring at me like that, Ah Bong!" Moishe said. The young fisherman did not respond. He was scared stiff, like a young tiger cornering a doe on its first solo hunt, like Adam, waiting for Eve to take the first bite on the apple. Moishe did not know what to do either. Her voice turned to begging. "You are making me nervous."

Was she begging to her temptation or was she begging to her conscience? Curiosity plus the instinct to surrender to the call of nature was burning her mind and her body. The only hesitation in throwing herself into the arms of this young stallion at arms reach was the traditional sense of decency pounded into her by her parents and the thought of Lenduai. She didn't know what she would have done if it were Lenduai instead of Ah Bong standing in front of her. She turned her back and proceeded to strip herself slowly. In total nakedness and with the wet clothes dripping in her hands, she hesitated for another moment. Then she wrung the clothes dry and wiped herself before putting them back on. When she turned around, the bronze statue still remained in the same position. His eyes kept on burning her body.

"Put on your clothes," Moishe was surprised to hear her own voice talking authoritatively like Ahma ordering her after a bath. "It's time to pick up."

Ah Bong put on his pants obediently. But he left his body bare above the waist. "Why don't you do the pick-up?" His voice sounded as if he had just gotten out of a trance. "I'll scull."

Moishe went to the bow and started pulling in the lines and coiling them into the wooden tubs. Every time she unhooked a silver ribbon and turned around to throw it into the pool of their day's catch at the bottom of the sampan, her eyes would meet the burning stares of Ah Bong. They were fixed on her twisted torso that showed all its prominences under the tightly wrapping wet clothes. "That voyeur!" thought Moishe amusingly. "So that's why he asked me to do the picking up."

Life at sea was raw, from relieving oneself on the gunwale to eating raw fish, from taking a dip in the sea to being stared at by her sampan mate. "Is this how this simple man expresses his feeling toward a girl?" Moishe asked herself. "Is this the way he courts a girl, flexing his muscles and fanning his gorgeous feathers like a peacock suitor? Couldn't he just say to me *I love you?"* In a way, she kind of felt good about this. Look, in China, life was raw and unprocessed. From morning till night, one was constantly being reminded of its essence by its smells and sounds in the streets and by the uninhibited yelling and laughing of its participants. Now life had just revealed to her its most intimate essence through sight and touch.

The fishermen had seen their last day of nice weather. On the following day, the sky became overcast and the sea churned up. That made the sampan jumpy as it headed out to its fishing spot. By noon, the sea was heaving up like many little mountains. Half of the time the horizon was buried under these water mountains. White caps were breaking out and the sampan started to shift in water. Moishe suddenly shouted to her sampan mate,

"Look over the horizon! What is that?"

"Where?"

"Over there," Moishe pointed to where their junk was supposed to be.

"I don't see anything."

Just then another streak of smoke rose above the waves.

"Let's pick up the line and go back," Ah Bong said to her.

"Now?" asked Moishe. "We have plenty of time for two more sets."

"No more."

"Not even one?"

"Laoda wants us back now."

"How do you know?"

"Didn't you see that rocket?"

"Was that Laoda?"

"Yes."

"Why does he want us back?"

"The Peach Blossom Storm should be around this time of the month. Look at that sky. It is going to get worse."

Moishe Fantasy

By the time Ah Bong and Moishe had retrieved the entire line, the sea had become very ugly. It was so rough that Ah Bong could only raise half of the sail. Rollers were continuing to climb into the sampan and lifting the scull out of the pivot.

"I wish we had a real rudder," Ah Bong murmured to himself as he cut off the painter from the bow to tie down the scull so that it would not jump out of the pivot again. "That stingy Ah Ting! How much would it cost to buy a few boards and a few fixtures?"

Even though Moishe was bailing nonstop, the water level in the bilge kept rising. Ah Bong had to lend a hand from time to time. After struggling for three hours to cover the distance that had taken them only half an hour in going out, they finally made it back to the junk. Half of their catch had been washed away in the sloshing bilge water.

The other sampans returned one by one. As each one came broadside to the junk, which was rolling more severely than the approaching sampan, the men on the junk would keep the sampan away with long poles until the men in the sampan were safely on board. During all this time, Laoda did not utter a single word. He sat on the fantail all by himself looking worried. By nightfall, all the sampans were stacked on deck and lashed down except one. Laoda lit up a storm lamp and raised it to the top of the mainmast. In the meantime, he ordered a rocket fired off every hour.

As the night advanced, the world around them turned upside down. One could only hear the howling of the storm through the ropes on the masts and the rolling and breaking of the seas in the night that was as dark as in the navel of the earth. From time to time, the breakers would climb up to the poop deck and pour into the cabin. There was not a single dry body. All one could see was a lone oil lamp swinging and drawing circles on the masthead high above the deck. In order to reduce the destructive attack by the billowing seas, Laoda raised four bamboo battens of sail to keep the junk as close-haul as possible and yet trying to hold her position such that the last sampan could find its way back to the junk.

By dawn, the missing sampan still had not returned. With the aid of daylight, Laoda decided to abandon the position he had held and to start searching for his two lost junk mates. For the whole day, the junk zigzagged all over the area that Laoda thought could have been covered by the sampan in sailing and in drifting. While all the other fishing junks in the Chusan Archipelagoes had gone in to seek shelter, the junk Moishe was on continued to comb the sea through the storm. After a couple of days, the sea finally calmed down. There was still no sign of the lost junk mates. On the fourth morning, Laoda ordered all the sampans put into the water.

"We'll stay here and fish for a few more days," Laoda said to the crew. "Look out for any remnant of the wreckage. Take some rockets with you. Give me a signal if you pick up anything."

Fishing was suddenly not fun to Moishe any more. What was the point of getting more fish? Would that make up for the two junk mates' lives?

"Why are we still fishing?" she broke the silence after they set all the hooks and lines into the water. The question had been bothering her for the whole morning.

"You see those seagulls over there?" Ah Bong asked.

"Yes."

"Did you see them before the storm?"

"We see seagulls everyday. But I don't know whether or not these are the same ones that we saw before the storm."

"Do you know if any seagull is missing from that storm?"

"How can I tell? They all look the same. Besides, there are so many of them."

"You think anybody at the fish market would notice that we are missing two crewmen? Do you think they would miss us at all if we never showed up again?"

"I don't know."

Moishe Fantasy

"What do you think the sea gulls are doing over there?"
"Fishing, I guess."
Ah Bong acted as if he did not hear what Moishe had said.
"I think it's time to pull in the lines," he said as he went astern
and fit the scull into the pivot. "I'll scull. We can still make two
more sets before the sun goes down."

Ahma went to the fish market every morning before the pre-
dawn auction to check on the fishing junks that came in during
the night. She asked every fisherman if he had seen any
Yotahning girl or if they had heard of any fishing junk that was
lost at sea. After the auction was over and the final bid shipped
away, she went to sit on the bitt that Moishe used to occupy,
hoping that some miracle would bring her little girl back or
would turn the clock back to the time before Moishe
disappeared so that she could stop her from going. She
promised Buddha she wouldn't scold the girl. She would sit
there all day blowing her nose and rubbing her eyes until the
place became totally dark. At first, people would come to
comfort her and offer her food and drink. As time went on, she
had also become a fixture of the fish market like Moishe. No
one even noticed her presence. At the end of each day, Ahma
would go to the temple to burn incense to Guanyin Buddha
before returning home to face a tearful Mrs. Rabi.

Finally after ten days in the East China Sea, the junk
returned to the fish market with a full load of Silver Ribbon.
When Moishe came ashore, Ahma could not recognize her little
girl. Her skin had changed into a deep bronze color; her hair
had turned into a bundle of entangled straw and her body
smelled fishy. With those rags hanging on her, she looked
exactly like one of those low-down dirty fishermen from
Shinguomen. She even walked like them, wobbling on her bare
feet like a duck. Where was her pretty *Yotahning* Miss?

Laoda gave Moishe a bagful of Silver Ribbon to take

home. "You can come fishing with us any time you want," he said to Moishe. Then he added, "But I don't advise you to do so. You have seen all there is in fishing. It's not a life for you. We have no choice because our ancestors were fishermen. We don't know anything else. We can't read or write. We will go to our graves without ever seeing a pair of shoes or being able to recognize our names in writing. Look, I don't even want my own *xiao-niang-bi* to marry a fisherman. And you, a *Yotahning xiao-niang-bi,* will have a bright future waiting for you ashore in the City. Stay there."

Summer was over. The Shanghai Jewish Youth Association School was back in session. Moishe promised her parents that she would never do any such silly thing again. In particular, she promised them she would never even go near the sea any more. When the next summer came, Moishe kept her promise. She did not return to the fish market. After all, there were no fish in the Whampoo. As for catching fish, she did not need to go to sea. Ah Bong always brought his entire share of fish to Moishe whenever his junk came into port. He had no relatives or any acquaintances on shore to give. On that day, the Rabis and all their friends and neighbors would feast on fresh fish. When the silver ribbon season was over, they would have yellow croaker. When the yellow croaker season was over, they would have snapper delivered to their door.

CHAPTER NINE

Lenduai kept his promise. He showed up at the school auditorium one day while Moishe was practicing on the piano.

"Hey, you never told me that you could play the piano. I see you play very well!"

"I have been taking piano lessons from Miss Hartwich. But just the other day she told me that she could not help me any more."

"What were you playing?"

"The part in this trio she wanted us to do for a school program."

"Are you still taking lessons from her?"

"Yes."

"Didn't you just say...?"

"Yes, but there is no other piano teacher in Hongkew."

"Let me ask around."

"Will you really? When do you think you can let me know?"

"Not now." Then he changed the topic. "I came because I have two concert tickets for tonight at the Lyceum Theater. Come to think of it, you have just lucked out. Tonight you will meet the best piano teacher in town."

"Then what are we waiting for?"

Lenduai went to get his bicycle and met Moishe at the school gate. Moishe did not wait for Lenduai to get off his bike. She bent her knees and slipped right into her usual place between Lenduai's arms and the handlebar. She skillfully moved her hips onto the top-tube. The two rode off.

Lenduai took Moishe to Kavkaz, a Russian restaurant on Avenue Joffre. As the war dragged on, food in China had become more and more scarce. Supplying the Japanese army was the first priority. Many foodstuffs for the civilians were put on ration: rice, flour, cooking oil, sugar and meat. Only vegetables were the exception. In such an austere situation, the Russian restaurants had become the most favorable places for people to go. They knew how to make vegetables into delicious borscht.

Almost everyone in the restaurant was going to the concert after dinner. It was a performance produced by the local ballet company, the Ballet Russe. During the intermission Lenduai ran into a friend of his.

"Hey, Jue. Didn't you tell me that your piano teacher is the conductor for the ballet?" said Lenduai to his friend.

"Don't you believe me?"

"But I did not see any orchestra."

"It's in the pit. Have you ever been to a ballet or an opera before?"

"No. Why do they hide in the pit?"

"People come to see the ballet, not the orchestra."

"How can we meet him then?"

"Meet whom?"

"The conductor, your piano teacher."

"Why do you want to meet him?"

"Moishe wants to find a piano teacher." Lenduai turned around to introduce Moishe. "This is Moishe. This is Jue."

Lenduai had tried to call Moishe by her true name. But he found it not only sounding awkward but lacking in all her personalities. It might sound all right to her parents and her friends at school, but certainly not to Lenduai. Besides, calling her Moishe made her closer to him and his inner circle of friends. To the Chinese, a foreign name was a foreign name. There was no differentiation in ethnicity or sex.

Jue had not noticed Moishe until then. But from that moment on, the young Chinese boy could not take his eyes off the girl before him. He finally found words to break up the awkward situation, "You play the piano, I assume."

"Yes."

"Who is your teacher?"

"Miss Lucie Hartwich."

"Never heard of her."

"She's the head mistress at our school."

"Which school do you attend?"

"Shanghai Jewish Youth Association School."

"For *Yotahning?*"

"Yes. I have been taking lessons from her for four years. Recently she told me that she could not teach me any longer. She said I am too advanced for her. She suggested that I find another teacher."

"Where do you live?"

"Hongkew."

"Oh... I don't think the Maestro will go to Hongkew."

"I can go to his place," Moishe suggested.

"Paci never sees students at his place."

"What? A pianist without a piano?"

"I don't mean that. I don't know whether he has a piano or not. But I have studied under him for four years already. I have never been to his place even once. If one has a full orchestra to play, why would one need a piano?"

"Oh..."

"I tell you what. Let us do this. Why don't you come to my place when I have my next lesson? He can listen to you play. If he accepts you, we can ask him to schedule our lessons back to back at my place. That will solve your problem and save him time and wear in travel."

"You don't mind?" Moishe did not know how to respond to such a generous offer.

"Of course I don't mind. Lenduai, why don't you bring her

160

to my place next Tuesday?"

"Where do you live?" Lenduai asked.

"Don't you know?"

"How could I? Like to your piano teacher, you have never invited me to your place."

Lenduai and Moishe came to Ziegawei, the exclusive residential district in the French Concession. They checked and rechecked the number on the post. There was no mistake. It was exactly what was written on the piece of paper in Lenduai's hand. But the place did not look like a residence. They were speechless when they peeped through the wrought iron gate. Behind the gate there was a garden as large as one of those small public parks along Avenue Joffre. It was shady. There were lots of flowers and trees. At one end there were two tennis courts. At the other end there was a mansion that looked like a miniature Schonbrunn.

While they were peeping through the ironwork with awe, a man came out of the gatehouse.

"Hey, what are you two doing?" he scoffed in an authoritative voice. "Go away! This is not a public place."

"Is this the Shen residence?" Lenduai asked.

"This is the Shen residence," the gateman's tone sounded as if he belonged to this family. "Why do you ask?"

"Is there a Jue...?"

"You mean our young Master?" the arrogance suddenly disappeared in the gateman's voice.

"He gave me this address."

"Is the young Master expecting you?" a big smile came on the gateman's face. His voice turned humble and polite.

"I think so." Lenduai said.

The gate opened. As Lenduai pushed his bicycle through the gate, the gateman said to him, "I'll take it, Mister. I'll keep it here for you."

Moishe Fantasy

The inside of the house was like a museum. There were all kinds of porcelain and crystal. The walls were decorated with flowery wallpapers and scrolls of paintings. There were many rooms including a separate piano room where there were two baby grand pianos!

Jue introduced Moishe to his teacher, Maestro Mario Paci. The maestro immediately put Moishe at one of the pianos.

"Let me hear you play something," he said.

"What shall I play?" Moishe asked timidly.

"Anything."

Moishe sat down at a baby grand. Her heart started to pound, partly because of her fingers touching a grand and partly by the presence of the maestro. She played her part in the Piano Trio that she had been practicing for the forthcoming school concert. She had it all memorized. At first, she was hesitant. The keys on the grand were stiffer than the old upright at school which she was used to. A few minutes later, she got the hang of it. But then she heard the maestro's voice,

"Terrible! Terrible! Where did you pick up all those bad habits, Miss?"

"I don't know." What she meant was "*I don't know what bad habits you are talking about.*"

"But I see that you've got a feeling for the music. I'll have one of my advanced students straighten you out."

"You mean you accept me as your student?"

"That depends on whether or not you can get rid of your bad habits. Habits are hard to be gotten rid of. But you are still young. We'll see."

Moishe did not dare to ask the maestro how much he would charge for a lesson. After the maestro had left, Jue told her how much he was paying for a lesson.

"I'm afraid I won't be able to afford it," she said in great disappointment. "My father is a tailor."

"Imagine where our musical world have been if Rachmaninoff had said the same thing at your age."

162

"What do you mean?"

"You heard what the maestro just said. You've got a feeling for music. Not too many people have it. Music is all about feeling. Technique is only an instrument to express those feelings. I am sure you will get rid of your old habits in no time. My parents will be more than glad to pay for your lessons. They always feel proud to be able to contribute to launching a new talent to the world."

"I cannot accept it."

"What about if I ask them for a loan. You can pay it back when you start to charge admissions for your concerts."

Moishe started on her lessons the following week. The young teacher whom the Maestro sent to give Moishe lessons took her teaching assignment very seriously. After two hours she was still working on Moishe's fingers. Lenduai could not wait. He had to go to work at Red House. "Jue, can you bring Moishe home when she finishes her lesson?" Lenduai said to his friend.

When the lesson finally ended, Jue's mother said to the teacher and Moishe, "It's rather late. Would you two care to join us for dinner, just our usual plain meal?"

The young teacher accepted the invitation without the usual polite decline that was required of a well-mannered guest, partly out of the long hours at Moishe's first lesson and partly out of the smell of the food. Moishe did not know what to do. She looked at Jue, who was supposed to take her home. He did not seem to be in a hurry to move. Instead, he sat himself down at the table. Then pointing to the chair next to him, Jue said to Moishe, "Why don't you sit here?"

Moishe was glad that she stayed. The dinner was totally different from anything she knew, in looks, in smell, in taste and in table manners, European as well as Chinese. At home, the servants never let her see them eat. On the streets and on the junk, people piled whatever they had on their rice bowls and squatted wherever they could find space, very often one at the bow and one at the stern. They had chopsticks, two thin bamboo sticks. But they used them only for shoving food from their rice bowls into their mouths. She liked to watch them eat. They sucked, slurped, gulped, chewed and making all kinds of sounds, just to get the food down their throats without using their hands.

The table setting at the Shens was simple and elegant. At each place there were a small saucer for the rice bowl, a smaller saucer for the soup spoon and a tiny intricately carved rack for the chopsticks. The soup spoon was shaped like a slipper rather than a spoon. The chopsticks were jade on the upper part and silver on the lower part.

The food was served on large plates that were placed in the middle of the table with no serving spoons. There was no knife on the table either. The food was all pre-cut into small pieces so that one could not tell beef from pork or chicken from bean curd.

Moishe wondered where the family got all that food? Later she found out that there was a black market where one could get almost everything, provided one could pay the price. She was curious about what Jue's father did for a living. She wondered if the Japanese knew about the way this family lived and ate.

Moishe was glad that her mother had taught her the *"universal table manner",* do as others do. She noticed that they did not pile their food in the rice bowls as the fishermen and the street people did. But once picked up, the rice bowl and the chopsticks never left the hands of the diner. The chopsticks did all the work. They picked up food from the community plates; they put the food into the mouths without touching as a mother bird feeding her chicks; they shoved the rice from the bowls into the mouths; they even picked bones from the mouths and placed them in a saucer where the rice bowl was sitting before it was picked up. Moishe could not tell what she was eating. Nevertheless, everything tasted and smelled good.

"This food is different from the fermented bean curds they sell on our streets in Hongkew!" Moishe said, just to make conversation.

"That is the most favorite delicacy for Shanghainese, rich or poor," Jue's mother said. "Have you tried it?"

"No," Moishe regretted what she had said as soon as those words got out of her mouth. But it was too late.

"Then you must try it," said Jue's mother.

Moishe did not know how to respond. But this much she knew. Refusing is considered bad manners in Chinese etiquette; one never admits one is hungry before dinner and never says one is full after dinner. So before she knew it, the stinking smell hit her nose. A small dish was brought out, just for her. In it there was a cube of some brownish, greenish, grayish looking thing. All conversation ceased. All chopsticks froze. All eyes were trained on the centerpiece - Moishe. She realized that she had to do it. What the heck, after eating live dolphin, she could eat anything. She shut her eyes.

All those around the table held their breath as Moishe put the chopsticks into her mouth. Then her eyes opened wide.

"It doesn't taste like it smells," she was surprised. "I even swallowed it!"

"You like it?"

"Uh... Yes," she lied out of politeness. "But nothing could taste better than raw dolphin."

"Dolphin? Raw?" Moishe could see that she had gained respect around the table.

After dinner that evening, Jue took Moishe home in the family car, a chauffeured big black Packard.

CHAPTER TEN

It soon became a routine. On the day Moishe had her piano lesson, Lenduai would pick her up on his bicycle and Jue would be responsible to take her home after dinner in his chauffeured family Packard. But Jue did not always stick to the routine. Sometimes they would sit in the living room after dinner and talk until very late; sometimes they would play duets all evening in the piano room; sometimes Jue would take her to see a movie after dinner; sometimes they would go out to dinner and then to a concert afterwards; sometimes they just went to explore the city on foot. They would walk all the way from the shaded residential Zegawei to the fashionable Avenue Mercier just to get some pastries at the Russian pastry shop, DD's. Pretty soon all of the latter took over as their routine. Ahma could never tell when her little girl would come home from her "piano lesson". But as long as she knew that Moishe was with Jue, Ahma did not worry. She liked that boy, more than she liked Lenduai and certainly much more than that fisherman, whom Ahma could tolerate only because he brought the family fresh fish. As for Moishe's mother, Ahma always covered up for Moishe. Both of Moishe's parents were busy in their endeavors and not home most of the time anyway. So Ahma was the one with whom Moishe spent most, if not all, of her time when she was home. She was more of a daughter to Ahma than to her own mother.

One day Jue said to Moishe, "My parents and I are going to visit some relatives in Hangchow. Would you like to come along?"

"What about your parents?"

"They asked me to invite you."

"Where is Hangchow?"

"In another province, on another river, and they speak another dialect and it has another culture that is totally different from that of Shanghai. It is not far from here."

"You mean they are not Chinese?"

"They are Chinese. But Chinese come in different types."

Ahma gave Moishe her full support. "Go ahead," she assured Moishe. "I'll take care of your parents."

Secretly, Ahma had been praying for something like that to happen. She had great expectations of this trip. A proposal perhaps? Moishe was such a sweet girl and Jue was from such a good cultural and rich family. Above all, he was Chinese.

Hangchow turned out not to be on any river. The city spread itself along a lake. The lake was as big as a bay. It reminded Moishe a little bit of the Chusan Archipelagos with the exception of its mirror-like water and its beautiful bridges, pavilions and pagodas. Its *Longjing* tea grown locally was renowned as the Cognac of China. Its scenery had no comparison in the Western world. The closest comparison was perhaps the Peterhof enlarged many, many times with much, much more water. It made Moishe long for the sea again.

While Jue's parents were socializing with their relatives over *Longjing* tea, Jue and Moishe sneaked out to the lake.

"Too bad we got here so late," Jue said. "The boatmen have all gone home. Otherwise it's a perfect night to show you the lake. The lake looks totally different with a full moon like this."

"There are so many boats here," Moishe said. "We can borrow one of them."

"Are you joking? They are privately owned. That's

immoral."

"How can it be immoral if no one gets hurt and no one notices it?"

"Stealing is immoral."

"If nothing is lost, how can it be called stealing?"

"What would the owner think about someone using, even though not taking, his property without asking?"

"The boatman won't find anything missing or worn out when he comes back in the morning. He won't even notice his mooring line being touched. If it still bothers you, you can leave a big tip."

"But without the boatman how are we going to get the boat out?"

"How about hiring a boatwoman?"

"Where can we find one at this time of night?"

"Right here."

"You?"

"Just watch."

Jue could not believe that this nice *Yotahning* girl could handle a boat as if she were born on the water. "Where did you learn that?" he asked with great admiration.

"When I was fishing."

"Where did you fish?"

"At sea, of course. Are you thinking the Whampoo River? There are no fish in the Whampoo." She even talked like an old salt.

"Where at sea?"

"Around the Chusan Archipelagos. In the East China Sea."

"When did you do that?" Jue asked in disbelief.

"Last summer."

"All by yourself?"

"Of course not. There were other fishermen on the junk."

"Did you say junk?"

"Yes, a boat run under sails."

"With junk fishermen?

"I'll introduce you to a junk fisherman one of these days. But at sea we use a scull. This one is like a gondola in Venice except..."

"You've been to Venice?"

"There is only one oar on the gondola. Here we have two. Everything else is the same: rowing standing and facing forward."

"Well, you might have been to Venice and the Chusan Archipelagos all right," Jue changed the topic. "I bet you have never seen three moons shining at the same time."

"Have you?"

"Yes."

"Show me!"

"All right. See those three short pagoda-like stone vases in the water over there? Row over there."

Having the entire lake and the moon to themselves, Jue and Moishe roamed all night until the moon was about to spill over the brim of the lake. During all this time, they were taking turns reciting poems to each other. Neither of them understood what the other was reciting, Moishe in German and Jue in classic Chinese. But they all sounded poetic.

"It's just like what Su Dongpo was doing in the Song Dynasty," Jue said.

"Who's Su?"

"A poet. The difference is: we are reading poems while enjoying the lake; Su Dongpo was composing poems while designing the lake. So no one around him understood what he was saying."

"A poet designing a lake?"

"Yes, West Lake was designed by Su Dongpo."

"How long ago?"

"The Song Dynasty was between the 10th and the 13th centuries. But I have no idea when Su Dongpo came in."

When Moishe tied the sampan back to the post where she had borrowed it, dawn was breaking. A mist rose from the water and covered the lake where she and Jue had spent the night.

"At sea it's time to set the sampans in the water," she said.

"What did you say?" her friend asked.

"Never mind."

"My parents are giving a Christmas party," said Jue one day to his friends. "You want to come?"

"Christmas?" Moishe asked. "Isn't that a Christian holiday?"

"What does it matter?"

"What does that have to do with us? Lenduai is a Gypsy, I am a *Yotahning* and you are a Buddhist."

"I am not a Buddhist," corrected Jue. "My parents are."

"What are you?"

"Nothing. The new generation in China does not go for any of these superstitions," the young Chinese intellectual said.

"You mean religion," corrected Moishe.

"All right. Religion, superstition. What's the difference?"

"Then it sounds even weirder. An atheist, a Gypsy and a Jew are being invited to a party given by two Buddhists to celebrate a holiday of the Christians."

"There is no religious discrimination in China. All religions were imported anyway."

"It has nothing to do with discrimination," Moishe said. "If one believes that there is only one God, then what does it mean to observe the celebration of the birth of another so-called God which is assumed not to have existed in the first place?"

"When people say there is only one God," Jue explained, "they do not mean there is only one God. What they want to say is there is only one God for them."

"Then why does he celebrate the birthday of another god, someone else's god?" Moishe argued.

"Look, I have just one mother. Can I give a party to celebrate the birthday of your mother?"

"But it is different in religion. When one says there is only one God, one means there are no other gods, not even for other people."

"That's even better. If the other gods are non-existent, celebrating something that does not exist does not constitute a right or a wrong."

"Then why do it?"

"Because all the foreigners here celebrate it: the English, the French, the Russians, the Americans and the Portuguese."

"What does it have to do with the Chinese?"

"My parents want to keep up with the Jones. Why do you count years in the Christian Era? Do you have to accept Christianity to do that?"

"Back to my first question," said Moishe. "Why Christmas? Why not Chanukah?"

"What is Chanukah?"

"It's a holiday the Jews celebrate at about the same time as Christmas."

"You mean at Winter Solstice?"

"Yes. Why not celebrate Winter Solstice for that matter?"

"We Chinese do. But that is no fun. It's just a family dinner."

"Then why not the Chinese New Year?"

"That we also do. But we do different things. We kowtow to our ancestors, we feed the Kitchen God with a traditional banquet, we give kids red envelopes, we burn firecrackers, etc. etc."

"That sounds like fun. I'd like to be invited to a Chinese New Year's party."

"Are you willing to kowtow to my ancestors?"

"They are real, aren't they?"

"But dead."

"Why not? They were real people at one time."

"Then you are invited," said Jue. "But you have to wait for another month. I am talking about now. Do you want to come to my parents' Christmas party or not?"

"Why not?" Lenduai said.

"If you go, I'll go," Moishe finally consented. "What day is Christmas Day?"

"In Shanghai, we celebrate Christmas on Christmas eve, not on Christmas Day," Jue said.

On Christmas Eve, Lenduai went to Hongkew to pick up Moishe. He was surprised to see a strangely dressed coolie in the apartment. He was barefooted and smelly.

"This is my former sampan-mate, Ah Bong," Moishe introduced him to Lenduai. "He brings us fresh fish whenever his junk comes into port. Oh, Ah Bong, this is my former lifeboat-mate, Ah Len."

"Lifeboat?" the fisherman asked.

"Yes, we spent a long time together in a lifeboat when we were coming over from Europe."

"You had a shipwreck?"

"No. There are many lifeboats on a steamship."

"What for?"

"I guess just like you have sampans on the junk."

Although having lifeboats and having sampans was for different reasons, Moishe knew that would be enough to satisfy the simple-minded fisherman.

"I must go back to the junk now," said Ah Bong.

"Is your junk going back to sea?"

"Not right away."

"When?"

"At ebb tide."

"When will that be?"

"Tomorrow morning."

"Then why don't you come to the party with us tonight?"

"Party?" Ah Bong repeated the word mechanically without knowing what it meant.

"Where people meet."

"For what?"

"To celebrate Christmas."

"Christmas?" There was another strange word for Ah Bong.

"Worshipping a god."

"A Buddha?"

"No, a foreign god."

"Why me?"

"Ah Len and I are going."

"Why?"

"To see how these foreigners worship their god."

"Uh..."

From her past experience with Ah Bong, Moishe knew that it was a yes. She took a step back and looked at the fisherman. Then she said,

"You look all right except that you need a pair of shoes."

"What for?" Ah Bong asked.

"For your feet."

"I won't be able to walk in shoes."

"Never mind. We are going by car."

"Car?"

"I mean bicycle. Ah Len, do you think you can carry another person on your bike?"

"If he doesn't mind standing on the spokes of my rear-wheel axle."

"You see, Ah Bong? You need to wear shoes to stand on those steel spokes. They are hard and narrow. Let me see, I think you will fit into Papa's shoes."

"What is your Papa going to wear?"

"He has more than one pair."

"What for? He's got only one pair of feet."

"So that you can borrow his other pair."

"You mean...?"

The gateman at the Shen residence ran his eyes up and down the fisherman. He had never seen any coolie looking like that: his hair was bleached to the color of a *Yotahning;* his skin

173

was baked to the color of a turbaned Indian guard; his clothes were tanned to the color of fishnets; his trousers were as wide as a woman's skirt; ... But his leather shoes were as shiny as those worn by an English gentleman.

"He is with us," Lenduai said before the gateman could raise any questions.

"He can wait in the gatehouse."

"He is going in with us," Moishe said. "He is a guest of Mr. Jue."

"He is?"

"Why don't you ask Mr. Jue to come out to the gate?"

"Oh, he cannot be bothered. There are too many guests in there."

"So?"

The gateman shook his head. If I can let some man dressed in red robe in, he thought to himself, why not this one dressed in fishnet? He let all three of them in.

The fisherman thought he had come to a public park. Once inside the building, Ah Bong could not believe what was before his eyes. It had more gold than a temple. The floor was as shiny as a lacquered vase. The men were dressed like generals in a capital drama. The women were dressed like the ladies in the cigarette ads. They smelled like flowers.

Moishe could not find any altar, candlestick or incense urn anywhere. The place was decorated more like a ballroom on New Year's Eve than a place to worship god. The music that filled the place did not sound sacred at all. The thick rug in the living room had been removed. Couples were holding each other closely and twisting their bodies awkwardly to the music played by a Filipino band. People who were not on the dance floor were wandering around with glasses in their hands. There was no priest, no cantor and no master of ceremony. What kind of celebration was this? It was more like a cabaret she had once peeped into when she was a kid in Vienna.

Lenduai could not understand why the dancers were

jammed so tightly against each other. How could people watch them? How could they whirl around? How could the boys tease the girls? How could the girls ruffle their skirts? He noticed that none of them was wearing a skirt. They were all tightly wrapped in their Mandarin gowns. Of course, this was China!

Was this a religious celebration or a dancing party? After half an hour, the teen-agers could not take the noise any more. So they left. No one noticed it and no one missed them either.

CHAPTER ELEVEN

The rise of the Third Reich in Germany led to the self-glorifying superiority of the Aryan race. In order to keep this superior race pure and uncorrupted, the *Untermensch* must be purged from the human race. Who were these "sub-humans"? The Jews, the Gypsies, the Blacks, the mentally retarded, the physically defective,...

Since among the *Untermensch* the Jews were the largest in number, the most industrious and the most successful in assimilating into the mainstream, in fact, the most threatening, they became the first target. At first, it was contempt, later it developed into hatred and then followed by exclusion of Jews from all aspects of life: cultural, social, scientific and economic. When the Jews demonstrated great tolerance, agreeing to live a subservient coexistence, the Nazis decided to get rid of them once and for all. They started to expel Jews from the European countries they occupied. Then someone came up with the idea of using them as free labor. The able bodied were rounded up and sent to labor camps. Those who were unfit to work were sent to concentration camps. Why the concentration camps? Weren't the ghettos concentrated enough? Why destroy old ghettos and build new concentration camps?

It was too late when the Jews finally realized that something really bad could happen. But it had already become very difficult to get out of the Third Reich's rule. Getting out of Nazi control was difficult, being accepted by a free country was equally difficult, if not more so. No one, including all the

British Commonwealth Nations and the United States, would accept Jews.

Many foreign individuals rushed to their rescue. Among them were three courageous diplomats, who acted on their own conscience without the approvals of their governments. An audacious Swedish consul, Raoul Wallenberg, issued several thousands Swedish passports to the Jews; a sympathetic Chinese diplomat in Vienna, Heh Fengshan, issued over a thousand visas to the fleeing Jews without asking to see their passports or any certificates; a dissenting Japanese consul in Lithuania, Chinue Sugihara, issued visas to some 1,500 Polish Jews.

But when a shipload of refugees arrived in Yokohama with Sugihara's visas, they were not allowed to disembark. They were immediately shipped to China, which remained the only country that accepted the Jews.

After the last shipload of refugees arrived in Shanghai, no news ever came out of Europe any more. No one could even guess what was taking place "at home".

"Papa, didn't you say that the Germans hate the Jews?" the tailor's daughter asked him one day.

"Yes," answered her father.

"Hans said the Germans don't hate us."

"How is that so?"

"He said there is only this one bad man who hates the Jews. He said the rest of the people in Europe all accept us as their equals."

"Who is Hans?"

"He plays the violin in our trio."

"He must have come from Germany."

"He came from Berlin. He always calls himself a German of Jewish ancestry, not a Jew from Germany."

"That's the trouble."

"What trouble?"

"The German Jews were thoroughly assimilated. Like the

Germans, they think they are better than the rest of us."

"Didn't you also say something like that, Papa?"

"Me? Never."

"Didn't you say that all those who come from Poland are not as educated as we are?"

"That's true though. That's why there are so many Polish Jewish musicians. One does not need to go to school to learn music. But in Germany, the Jews were completely assimilated into the German mainstream. They thought they were Germans. They lived among the Germans. They went to universities just like the Germans. That's why there are so many Jewish intellectuals, scientists and doctors in Germany. They tried to distinguish themselves from the rest of us. Let me tell you..."

The tailor stopped abruptly. He suddenly remembered what the King had said to him by the fire in the Gypsy camp on the night before they parted. *"Ha, you call that home? What kind of home is it? You accepted them. Did they accept you?"*

The German pride was contagious. The Japanese had the same superiority complex as the Germans. But instead of dividing people into a super race and *Untermensch,* sub-humans, they have humans and non-humans. The Chinese were the non-humans. They believed that humans and non-humans could coexist just like the coexistence of man and animal, as long as man could harness the animals to serve them as labor and raise them as food and breed them for pleasure. For animals, one did not need to be concerned with their "treatment" or "condition". No one hated the animals they kept. Some animals were even elevated as pets.

The Japanese did not even bother to build concentration camps or POW camps. The Japanese soldiers were free to ransack, rape, torture or kill the POWs and civilians whenever and wherever for whatever reason. When they captured China's capital city, Nanking, they staged a one-week celebration of their victory by slaughtering the civilians with knives, bayonets and bare hands, but no bombs. What they could not finish off they buried alive in trenches dug by the victims. Raping and head-cutting competitions were being held every day. They took so much pride in these "sports" that they reported all events in their newspapers with vivid photographs. Even a Nazi officer, John Rabe, who represented Germany in Nanking, was shocked beyond belief. In his report to the Nazi Headquarters, he estimated the number of slaughtered to be as high as 600,000 versus 300,000 reported by other sources. Which one was closer to reality? It did not matter. The vast discrepancy between these two estimates indicated how insignificant the Chinese lives were. Would a farmer care whether 300,000 or 600,000 maggots were being annihilated when he cleaned out a cesspool? Would the maggots themselves care? Each one might care about being annihilated. But it certainly did not care how many other maggots were being annihilated at the same time.

On the other hand, the predicament for the Jews was quite different. The Japanese did not consider them sub-humans or non-humans. On the contrary, they found the Jews quite civilized with Western music, arts and science. The Japanese did not have any indigenous culture. In the past, they had adopted the Chinese culture. Ever since they had opened to the West, they adopted Western culture with a frenzy. They wished they could acquire and make contributions to the Western culture as much as the Jews did. Besides, the number of the Jewish population was too insignificant to be threatening. They were just one small group out of a vast number of foreigners in Shanghai. Therefore, the Japanese never came up with any special policy for treating the Jews.

With the help of the local Jewish community in the Concessions, a new Jewish community was created over night in Shanghai. In a matter of months, over 30,000 European Jews came to settle in the Hongkew District. In fact, this number was larger than the combined number of Jewish refugees taken in by the rest of the world. They not only had their own schools, synagogues and hospitals; they had restaurants, theaters, concert halls and domestic servants. They were also free to carry out various political activities from Utopian Socialism to Revisionist Zionism in the open. Many leading Zionist activists such as Mrs. Raymond Elias Toeg, Boris Topas, Judith Ben-Eliezer and Leon Ilutovich started their movements in Hongkew.

There was no barbed wire, no barracks, no guards and no boundary for Hongkew to be qualified as a concentration camp. Some called it a Jewish Ghetto; some called it Shanghai Ghetto. But that would be ungrateful to their Jewish brethren who so generously provided the refugees with temporary housing, public kitchens, schools, hospitals and job training programs. Moreover, what about the Chinese residents of Hongkew who were living there before the arrival of the Jewish refugees and made room for the newcomers and accepted them as more than their equals? Why was it not called a Chinese Ghetto or Hongkew Ghetto? The rest of the city except the concessions would be more qualified than Hongkew to be called Zabei (Outside of Checkpoint) Ghetto, Nanshi (South City) Ghetto, etc. Unless one considered the Chinese people as one of the despicable elements like the rats and cock roaches that constituted the ghetto environment.

"These *Yotahning* are used to the luxurious life style of the Europeans," the Chinese made excuses for their guests while not being aware of their negative sentiment. "They won't be able to survive even for one day in our primitive living conditions."

"But not without a price," pointed out the refugees. "The Concessions are occupied by the European colonialists and the rest by the Japanese aggressors. The Chinese are living at the mercy of these occupiers. When we arrived, the Chinese thought they could take advantage of us. So rents in Hongkew went up. New produce and meat stands appeared in the market. The Chinese housewives found jobs as domestic help in our homes. Rather than say we owe the Chinese something, we

180

believe we have brought prosperity and culture to them. Besides, it is not up to the Chinese to say. This place belongs to the Japanese now."

Shortly after the attacks on Pearl Harbor, the Japanese soldiers marched into the Concessions. All the citizens of the British Commonwealth and the Americans were put into internment camps. The only Western faces that still remained to be seen on the streets of Shanghai were the Germans, the Portuguese, the Russians, the Jews, the French who were loyal to the Vichy government and the stateless. The Jewish refugees in Hongkew continued to be allowed to carry on with their cultural and political activities since they were not in conflict with any Japanese policy. That dealt a slap on the face to the Nazis, an ally of Japan.

In July 1942, the chief representative of the Nazi Gestapo in Japan, Colonel Josef Meisinger, arrived in Shanghai to propose to the Japanese Occupying Authorities a plan for the "final solution" to the Shanghai Jewish Refugee problem. But to the Japanese, the Jewish problem was a German problem. Even if it were their problem, genocide would not have been the solution. "If you killed all the inferior races, who is going to work for you?" the Japanese argued. To the Colonel's great disappointment, the Japanese Authorities did not implement the *German Solution* as recommended.

The Japanese dragged their feet for a whole year and when they finally implemented the "solution", it was to enclose Hongkew with barbed wire. One wondered whether the barbed wire was put in place to distinguish the Jewish refugees from the Jewish residents in the Concessions or to hide them from Colonel Meisinger. The Jewish refugees were still allowed to go in and out of Hongkew with passes. A green pass was good for one month and a pink one for one week. To further appease the Nazi colonel, the identification cards for the German Jews were marked with red stripes and those for non-Jewish Germans were marked with green stripes. Otherwise, life in Hongkew went on as usual. The only change that could be felt was the shortage of food supplies. But that was a general phenomenon in all of the war-torn China. It had nothing to do with the "solution". Those who had money could still get anything they wanted from butter to caviar on the black market and could continue to hire domestic help. In fact, the Jews in Hongkew could now brag that their situation was much better than that of the British and Americans in the internment camps. They were free.

The reluctance of the Japanese to subject the Jews in Shanghai to Meisinger's "final solution" was not accidental. It could be traced back to the Russo-Japanese war back in 1904. Japan won that war through the financial support and arms sales by the American Jews. Since then they had been nurturing this relationship. Now that they had launched an ambitious conquest on a much larger scale, they might call upon their "friends" again one day. They certainly did not want to do anything foolish to spoil this relationship.

The Rabis kept their Teelanchow apartment. Since many of Rabi's customers were taken to the internment camps, his income suddenly dwindled to almost nothing. To make ends meet, Mrs. Rabi had to dismiss all her domestic helpers.

"But Mrs, Miss needs someone to look after her," Ahma pointed out to her employer. "She's just a kid, so innocent, so defenseless and so emotional. She acts so impulsively. If she could sneak out to sea on one afternoon as casually as she sneaked into the Concessions on Ah Len's bicycle, who knows what she will do next?"

"I can look after her myself."

"But you are not a Chinese, Mrs."

"What does that have to do with looking after my own daughter?"

"You won't be able to tell the Japanese from the Chinese. But those Japs can spot you right away. You are a *Yotahning*."

"How do the Japanese come into this?"

"They are beasts, worse than any wild animals when they see women, especially since Miss is so young, so pretty and so white."

"But I can't afford to pay you."

"Pay me? Who's talking about pay? You have paid me enough all these years, Mrs. Besides, if I don't work for you, where can I find work? I don't know anyone in this city."

"You can go back to Chongming Island."

"What is there in Chongming? There is no electricity, no paved streets and no street vendors. My husband and my son can more than take care of the small plot we rent from the big landlord. I will just become one more mouth for them to feed."

"At least you will be with your family."

"Family? A husband stubborn like a mule and a son dumb like a piece of wood. Sons are not like daughters. Miss talks to me every night. She tells me everything, even about boys."

"Boys? What did she tell you about boys?"

"That is between Miss and me."

Moishe had been going out a lot with Lenduai and Jue. They were called the Three Musketeers by their friends. But Mrs. Rabi could never get her daughter to tell her anything about them or, for that matter, what had happened on her fishing trip. Come to think of it, Mrs. Rabi thought, her daughter was indeed more attached to Ahma than to herself, both physically and emotionally. Ahma never let Moishe out of her sight except when she was in class or out with the boys of Ahma's approval. At night they slept in the same room. When Moishe cried, she always ran to Ahma. Perhaps, she should not have spent so much time in the Zionist movement, thought Mrs. Rabi, which seemed to be leading to nowhere.

The next morning, Mrs. Rabi was waken up by the chanting of *le matin de Shanghai*. She jumped out of her bed and rushed to the bathroom. But it was too late. The honey-pots were not there. They had already been taken out to the street to join the long line of red barrels. She went downstairs and found Wang-sao washing clothes in the backyard.

"Didn't I tell you to go home?" Mrs. Rabi asked.

"I don't have home to go"

"What about Nanking."

"I have no one in Nanking."

"Aren't you from Nanking?"

"Yes."

"Don't you have any family members there?"

"All killed."

"Who did it?"

"Japanese."

"All of them?"

"All."

"You sure?"

"I saw it. They killed my baby with a bayonet..." then she started to cry. It was the first time any one had ever seen Wang-sao giving away to any emotion. "Then they buried my man alive... chopped my father's head off with a saber... raped my mother then cut her stomach open..."

"And you were there?"

"First they made my family watch while they raped me again and again. Then it was my turn to watch them kill my family one by one. They spared me because I was young and could be raped again."

"Do you have other relatives?"

"All killed."

"The same way?"

"I don't know."

"How did you get away?"

"I don't know. All I remember is hearing them laughing while I was being raped. After seeing what they did to my family, I had no feeling left. Then I lost hearing. I guess I

184

passed out. A foreigner found me later and put me in a camp with many young girls."

"All rape victims?"

"I don't know. They were all very young. Later the foreigner shaved my hair and put me on a train. I ended up here."

"What about the other girls?"

"I don't know."

"Who was this foreigner?"

"I don't know. But I kept the letter."

"You still have it?"

"Yes, I will never part with it. It is my life."

"Can I see it?"

Wang-sao opened her collar and reached her hand into her bosom. She pulled out a wrinkled envelope and handed it to Mrs. Rabi.

"Oy Vey!" Mrs. Rabi yelled out as she unfolded the letter. She almost fainted when she saw the sign of Swastika on the letterhead. Then the rest of the letter became blurred.

"Are you all right, Mrs?" Wang-sao asked worriedly.

"I am all right," answered the tailor's wife. It took her a while to get hold of herself. Suddenly she realized that she had been so engrossed in self-pitying her own suffering that she had lost sight of seeing the suffering of others. It took a Nazi officer to get her out of it. She suddenly felt ashamed. She took a look at the name of the letter writer, John H. D. Rabe. It missed by one letter from her own name.

"But I won't be able to pay you," she said to the laundry woman.

"I don't want pay, Mrs. I just want a place to stay," Wang-sao pleaded.

"You may stay as long as you want. But you are not to do any housework. No laundering."

"But who is going to empty your *muodongs* for you?"

"Taking the cans out on the street and lining them up with

the rest of the *muodongs*? I can certainly do that."

"How are you going to swoosh them afterward? Do you know what to swoosh them with?"

"Why don't you show me?"

"Do you see any *Yotahning* doing it? No? But it's so easy for me to do."

"But I told you I cannot pay you any more. This is a hard time. Mr. Rabi cannot make enough money to support this family."

"Why do you *Yotahning* always talk about money? You have money, you pay. You don't have money, you don't pay. I get paid, I spend. I don't get paid, I don't spend. But the fact is your *muodongs* must be emptied and swooshed and your clothes must be washed. Look at your hands. They are too delicate to do these rough chores. These chores are only for rough hands like mine."

The tailor's wife had never seen Wang-sao talk so much. She could have gone on and talked for the whole day if the cook had not shown up. In his one hand was a basket full of vegetables and in his other hand was a live chicken, being held upside down.

"Dahsifu, I told you not to come back, didn't I?" asked Mrs. Rabi. "Besides, who asked you to buy chicken?"

"I went to the market early this morning," said the cook. "There was this live chicken. Just one. I grabbed it before anyone discovered that there was no meat for sale today. The food supply is getting worse and worse everyday. The Japanese armies must be having a hard time at the front. I mean there are not enough in the farms for them to rob."

"We can't afford to eat chicken."

"That's all right, Mrs. I have money."

"You don't understand. We can't repay you."

"That's all right."

"Not ever."

"I understand."

"Mr. Rabi lost all his customers."

"Then Mister stays home?"

"Yes. No more chicken."

"But I need to learn how to make chicken-a-la-king."

"You don't make chicken-a-la-king with a whole chicken. Chicken-a-la-king is next to the garbage can."

"Garbage can?"

"Trash. Chicken-a-la-king is like your pan-fried chicken intestines, the leftover so to speak. Let me show you what you can do with a whole chicken. But don't come back any more. You hear that?"

"But you *Yotahning* are too delicate to mingle with the rough Chinese crowd in the market. Food is becoming more and more scarce nowadays so that you have to go very early in the morning and fight with all the shoppers. Then you have to bargain with the vendors."

"Just shop for me then." Mrs. Rabi did not know how to refuse a good will gesture. She realized that these Chinese people could interpret it as an insult.

"I am thinking about finding a job as a Western cook in one of those big mansions or hotels after the war. I need to keep practicing at cooking the Western meals you have taught me. Will you teach me more dishes?"

"With food scarce like this, you won't have much to cook with."

"We have a saying in Chinese. A real chef can turn water into a delicious soup."

"I don't know how to thank you people," said the tailor's wife as she wiped the tears from her face. "I will repay you one of these days. I swear."

"Coming to live among us in Hongkew is already giving us a big face," the cook said. "Before you *Yotahning* came, no foreigners would even come near this place."

Moishe Fantasy

The tailor kept going to the Concessions to look for new customers when he was not working on a suit. Because of a lack of material, most of his work was reduced to alternations rather than making new suits. One day he came back from a long day at the Bund and decided to unwind over a cup of coffee. He walked into Little Vienna. He heard a Schubert piece being played on a violin. Since when did they have music in this place, Rabi thought to himself? He sat down and listened to it over his coffee. The player was so bad that he was not only murdering Schubert but also piercing the tailor's eardrums. He could not even finish his coffee. He paid and stood up.

The music suddenly stopped. Just as he reached the door, his shoulder was pulled back with a jerk. Before he realized what was happening, a hand flew over and landed on his face. It almost knocked his head off his neck. In front of his dazed eyes was this man dressed in a poorly tailored Western suit with a violin and a bow in his other hand.

"Don't you *rike* my *praying?*" he shouted in a shrieking voice in English that matched the scratchy sound of his violin. The heavy accent, particularly the way he pronounced the letter "l", was distinctively Japanese. He was rubbing his right hand on his trousers, trying to ease the pain from the slapping.

"Yes, I like your playing," stuttered the tailor in apprehension. The Japanese reminded him of the Gestapo back home. The Germans were music lovers. But their taste was much more sophisticated than this Japanese. The tailor forced a smile on his face and went on, "You play very well. But, you see, my wife is waiting for me. I must go home."

"Don't you *rie* to me!" shouted the Japanese.

"No, I mean it. You play very well," said the tailor, thinking that he had seen this person somewhere before. "Especially... the way you did the staccato."

"Did you say staccato?" the tone of anger in the Japanese's voice suddenly changed to that of curiosity and vanity. "You *pray* the violin?"

188

"No, sir," the tailor answered as respectfully as possible while stretching out his left hand to show his missing fingers.

"You know music," said the Japanese. "You *rike* music?"

"Yes, sir." It suddenly dawned on him that this guy was the one who issued him his pass to go out of Hongkew during the day. Thank God the man did not recognize him. He was put in charge of the Jews in Hongkew after the Japanese had taken over all the Concessions. His name was Goya. But he called himself "the King of the Jews". Since none of his fellow Japanese could appreciate his talent in Western music, he liked to show off to the Jews, who were musically oriented. Rabi heard that "the King of the Jews" would pop up in public places from time to time and force people to listen to him playing his violin.

"You know Mendelssohn?"

"Yes, he's one of my favorites."

"Then *risten* to this!"

The short man jumped onto a tabletop. He quickly surveyed his compulsory audience. There were about half a dozen people including the owner. He put the violin under his chin and started to play.

Rabi sat down and ordered another cup of coffee. He could feel his face still burning and probably swelling from the slap. But come to think of it, this was nothing in comparison with how the Chinese were being treated. They got beaten everyday. Once he saw a rickshaw coolie literally beaten to death simply because he had asked his Japanese rider to pay for his ride. Rabi tried to keep his eyes on the violinist. The Western suit on him was brand new. Its style was of the last century. It was so poorly made that it could only be found on farmers in Europe. He tried to listen to him play. It was off tune half of the time. The bow was sliding all over the place like a drunkard on an abandoned street, making scratchy sounds. "He would do better playing the piano where he could only hit the wrong notes and never play off key," the tailor thought to himself. "People who do not have an ear for music should not be allowed to touch the violin. It is a sin to murder music with a violin!"

CHAPTER TWELVE

Rabi had a Pink Pass to go out of Hongkew. It was good for only one week. Before it expired, Rabi went back to have it renewed.

"Didn't I meet you somewhere before?" the diminutive Japanese in a badly cut business suit asked.

"Yes, sir, Mr. Goya," said the tailor. "At Little Vienna."

"Oh, yes. I remember now. You *rike* my violin *praying* very much."

"Um, um," Rabi made some sound that could be interpreted as an agreement or just an acknowledgement.

"I see that you have always had a pass to go into the Concessions since you arrived in Shanghai. What do you need a pass for?"

"My customers all live in the Concessions."

"What is the nature of your business?"

"Making clothes."

"So you are a tailor. What kind of clothes do you make?"

"Men's suits."

"Business suits?"

"Yes, sir."

"Then make one for me."

"Sure. Let me measure you," Rabi reached into his pocket and took out a tape measure.

"Not here, you dumb ass!" The Japanese shouted angrily. The tailor was confused by the sudden change of tone from the voice. "You think this is a marketplace? I have the respect of all the Jews in Hongkew. I must maintain my dignity."

"Where do you wish to have the measurement made, sir?"

"At your place. Don't you have a shop?"

"No, I work at home."

"Then let's go to your home," said *the King of the Jews.*

The first thing the Japanese noticed as he walked into Rabi's place was Beethoven's picture on the wall. "Are you the Fiddler on the Poop Deck?" he turned around toward Rabi and asked.

"What do you mean, sir?"

"Some of your fellow Jews who came on your voyage of Exodus told me that they had seen a man *praying* a 'fiddle' on board," said the King of the Jews, trying to show off his knowledge of Jewish history. "I take it a fiddle is a violin. No?"

"That must be someone else," Rabi stretched out his left hand to show the missing fingers to the Japanese.

"Yes, they told me that the fiddler had just two fingers on the finger board. But they said he *prayed* rather well. I am curious to see how one can *pray* with just two fingers."

"I don't play."

"Don't *rie* to me. Go get your fiddle out and *pray!*"

Rabi thought that if he refused he would get slapped again and might even be beaten to death like the rickshaw man. He got his violin out and hesitantly tried out the Mendelssohn piece that he had been forced to listen to at Little Vienna. With just two fingers he could not get all the notes. Truly or faking, he missed a lot of notes and slurred over many.

"No, no, no, no!" the Japanese jumped up hysterically after listening for less than a minute. "You are murdering the Jew."

"Sir?"

"Mendelssohn. Wasn't he a Jew?"

"I told you that I couldn't play, sir."

"Why do you keep a violin then?"

"I like to fool around with it."

"Let me show you how to *pray* Mendelssohn properly," the

Japanese snatched the fiddle from Rabi's hand and put it under his chin. Oh, no, thought Rabi, am I going to sit through the whole ordeal again? To the Japanese, he had gotten a captured audience. Not an ordinary audience. A violinist who loved and knew music but did not play as well as he did. Unlike the rest of them whom he had to slap and kick to make them listen to him playing, this one should appreciate his artistic talent. He totally forgot that he had slapped Rabi in Little Vienna for walking out on him.

Thank God, "the King of the Jews" did not finish the piece. Only a short while after he had started, Goya stopped playing abruptly. He took the fiddle off his chin. He turned it around, peeped through the sound holes and patted it like someone selecting a watermelon.

"This violin sounds better than mine," tapping its back with his knuckle, the Japanese said. "I'll take it. It's too good to be wasted on a crippled hand like yours. Sometimes I just can't figure out about you Jews. Now, make the measurement. I am a busy man. I don't have a whole day to waste on you."

CHAPTER THIRTEEN

As the war dragged on, living conditions in Hongkew deteriorated more and more. The occupying Japanese had become more ruthless. Victims of beating and raping by the soldiers were not just limited to the Chinese any more. Many Jews had become their targets. Food supplies had dwindled to vegetables only. Even so, fresh vegetables were hard to get. When the refugees first arrived in Shanghai, the wealthier ones went to live in the Concessions. Now they were all ordered to move to Hongkew. Hongkew suddenly became more crowded. Many schools were closed.

On the brighter side, that gave Moishe's trio more time to practice as the date of their performance at the Lyceum drew near. They would be the youngest chamber music group to perform at the Lyceum, the most prestigious music hall in the entire Orient.

One day when Lenduai showed up to pick up Moishe for her piano lesson, he did not hear music.

"I came early today so that I could listen to you play," Lenduai said to Moishe as he walked into the school auditorium. "I did not realize that you guys have already finished practicing."

"Hans did not show up," Moishe said while the rest of them, including Miss. Hartwich, remained quiet.

"Who's Hans?"

"Our Violinist."

"What happened?"

"For some time he has been talking about going to Chungking, China's war capital, to join the Kuomintang in fighting the Japanese."

"But he promised not to do it before we have our concert," the 'cellist interjected.

"What can a *Yotahning* do among the Chinese?" Lenduai asked.

"He says that sooner or later the American marines will land on the Chinese shore."

"So, what can he do?"

"He says when the Americans land, the Chinese underground will respond with an attack from behind the enemy. He says to coordinate this operation, they will need interpreters."

"How does he plan to get to Chungking? The Japanese occupy all the land between here and Chungking."

"That's his problem, not mine," said Moishe. "My problem is how are we going give a concert without the violin? He is playing in the trio as well as the sonata."

"What can we do?" the 'cellist asked. "When they closed our school, remember, even Miss. Hartwich could do nothing. She's the headmistress! We are just students."

"But Paci promised me that he would come to our concert. Lenduai, why don't you fill in for Hans?"

"Me? No way."

"Hans left his scores here. Can you at least try?"

"I can't read music."

Lenduai's answer sent a shockwave through everyone. Suddenly the place became quiet. All eyes turned to the Gypsy boy. Everyone knew that he played at Red House. And he could not read music?

"I came to take you to your piano lesson, Moishe," Lenduai said.

After he brought Moishe to Jue's house, Lenduai immediately went to work at Red House. It was not Moishe's day. She made so many mistakes during her piano lesson that after a while her teacher refused to go on.

"What has happened to you?" her teacher asked in anger. "Go home and practice! Don't come to take new lessons if you do not practice your old lessons. I will never be able to hand you over to the Maestro if you don't practice. I don't want to waste my time on you."

She gathered up her things and left.

"Is there something bothering you?" Jue asked.

"I just lost the violinist in my chamber group."

"Oh, forget about the concert," Jue tried to comfort the girl. "There is always another time."

"But when will I have another chance to play in the Lyceum Theater?"

"You will. Another time. Let's go to a movie."

"Not today."

"Then you can practice your piano here."

"I want to go home."

"I'll take you."

"I think I'll go with Lenduai."

"We can go out to dinner," Jue's voice was almost begging. He had noticed that whenever that girl was down in spirit, there were only two people she would run to, her Ahma or Lenduai. With Ahma, Moishe could hide her head in her bosom and cry; with Lenduai she could pour her heart out. But why couldn't she share her grief with Jue? A strong feeling of jealousy suddenly surged through Jue.

Being jealous of Lenduai? But Lenduai was his best friend. Perhaps jealousy was a form of love. He suddenly realized that he was madly in love with this girl. He had never noticed it, or rather admitted, before. Should he express it to her explicitly? Did love need to be expressed in words? In poems perhaps. But he could only recite poems, not write them. If he put it into words, would it ruin the feeling? Wasn't love mutual? Had Lenduai sensed his feelings toward Moishe? Wasn't Moishe

Lenduai's girl? Could friendship and love coexist among friends?

"Next time, Jue," Moishe said.

"But Lenduai has to work."

"I'll just go sit there and listen to him play."

"It's going to take a whole evening."

"I know. I need to have my mind completely occupied. Besides, I haven't heard Lenduai play for quite some time. I sort of miss that Gypsy air."

"We can play a duet."

"Not today."

"I can try to play the Gypsy way."

"That's very sweet of you, Jue. Perhaps next time."

"At least let me take you there."

Although Moishe was sitting away from all the customers by herself in a corner at Red House, Lenduai walked up to her several times during the evening and played the tunes that the Gypsy King and the tailor used to play by the camp fire. It brought the long forgotten memories of the Gypsy camp to Moishe. At the end of each of Lenduai's performances, Moishe could almost hear the laughter of the two men at the Gypsy camp and see them passing a bottle to each other by the camp fire. But even that could not cheer her up.

On her ride home on Lenduai's bicycle, Moishe sat quietly on the top-tube listening to Lenduai's heavy breathing from peddling. Not a single word was exchanged between them. They hadn't done this for quite a long while. Ever since Moishe started taking piano lessons at Jue's place, it was always Jue who brought her home in the black family Packard or on his Harley-Davison after a dinner or a movie.

Hongkew was under curfew. But they had their own secret passage to sneak through. Just before they got to Teelanchow, Moishe abruptly turned her head around, crashing her nose into

Lenduai's. She broke the quiescence. Her voice sounded almost cheerful.

"Lenduai, I have an idea."

"What?"

"I can ask Papa to read it and then hum it to you."

"Read what?"

"The violin part in the pieces we are playing."

"I don't know about that."

"You shouldn't have any difficulty memorizing it."

"It's not that."

"Think how exciting it will be for you and me to play music together. We have done so many things together, but never music."

"An illiterate Gypsy playing Beethoven?"

"Yes, it's going to be an adventure!"

"I'm just a street violinist."

"Think how the King would be proud of you."

"I don't think so."

"For us, it will be like climbing down the ship on the hawser again."

"Hm..."

"And roaming on the streets of Singapore."

"Uh..."

"And having ice cream."

"That's the best ice cream I have ever tasted. Nothing in Shanghai can match that."

"What do you say?"

"Here we are," Lenduai stopped in front of the building at Teelanchow. "Your Ahma must be worried to death about your where-abouts."

"Come in with me."

"You want me to get chewed up by your Ahma?"

"Let's go ask Papa."

"He must be in bed already."

"I'll drag him out."

"Wouldn't he be mad?"

"We'll see."

Surprisingly, Rabi did not get mad. At first, he was totally confused about what his daughter was talking about. He was surprised to see Lenduai. For that alone it was worthwhile to be awakened in the middle of the night. When Moishe repeated in detail her scheme, his spirit suddenly soared like that of a young Mozart hearing a new theme in his head.

"You play the violin, Lenduai?" he asked in disbelief.

"Yes, sir."

"Since when?"

"When I started to work at Red House."

"I mean when did you learn?"

"I never learned. I just picked it up."

"When?"

"At the camp."

"On our journey?"

"As far back as I can remember. As long as I have been with the King."

"You mean you picked it up from the King? Let me hear you play a little bit."

"I don't have my fiddle with me, sir. It's at Red House, where I work."

"Go get it. I hope you play as well as the King. Do you have the score?"

"Moishe has it," said Lenduai.

"I haven't heard that name for quite a while," the tailor said in surprise. "She does have a name, you know."

"I know. But to me she will always be Moishe."

"Call her whatever you want," said the tailor. The boy was not a boy any more, he noticed. Then turning to his daughter he said, "Let me see the score."

"It's at school, Papa."

"Go get it then," said the tailor excitedly.

"Papa, you know what time it is now?"

"What time?"

"It's almost one o'clock in the morning."

"Oh, oh... then go, Lenduai. Come back tomorrow morning, I mean later this morning. I'll make a virtuoso out of you... that is provided you are good. But you'll have to give me a bit of time to familiarize myself with the score. I haven't read a music score for ages." Then the tailor turned to his daughter and said, "By the way, what are you playing?"

"They are all Beethoven."

"Beethoven, you silly girl! There are so many. Which ones?"

"The 'Grand Duke' Piano Trio, the 'Spring' Sonata for Lenduai and me and I am going to play the 'Moonlight' Sonata."

"Wow! Do you know what you are getting yourself into?"

"Miss. Hartwich picked them for us."

"But for Lenduai... I mean... he's a Gypsy, perhaps 'Moishe Fantasy' is better than 'Spring'."

"Is it by Beethoven?"

"No, it's by Paganini."

"Then isn't it for the violin?"

"Yes, it is played on one string though, the G string."

"But the concert is not supposed to be for the violin, Papa! Besides, it's not Beethoven."

"Okay, okay, the 'Grand Duke' or the 'Spring', no big deal for me. I've played them both. But I don't know if Lenduai... Well, let me not say anything until I hear him play. Go get the scores. While Lenduai is getting his fiddle, I can study it a little bit."

Lenduai was not paying any attention to what was going on between the father and the daughter. His thoughts were somewhere else. He had been to the Rabi apartment several times before. He had met Ahma. But he had never seen the tailor or Mrs. Rabi since he ran away. They were too busy with their own endeavors, Rabi in making expensive suits and Mrs.

Rabi in the Zionist movement. He remembered that he had been
used to seeing them everyday on the ship. In fact, he could
never get out of their sight during those days regardless of how
hard he had tried. Then he thought of the pirates.

"Mr. Rabi," the Gypsy boy said timidly. "Do you still have
my pistol?"

"By God! I have forgotten all about it. Of course, it must
be somewhere among my things."

"May I have it back?"

That startled the tailor. "What do you want it for?" he
asked.

"To show it to my friend."

"That's dangerous under the occupation of these savages,
you know."

"Isn't it also dangerous for you to keep it, Mr. Rabi? I
don't want you to get into any trouble because of me. May I
have it back?"

"I'll have to look for it. I'll give it to you next time you
come. But I don't want you to think that I am giving it to you
just because I want to pass the buck to you. You should get rid
of it. I'm serious."

The lesson started a few hours later on the same morning. As
the tailor read the music, he imagined that he was playing the
violin himself. He would hum or sing aloud. That boy was so
good that he not only picked it up right away but could also feel
the music with his ears better than most people reading from the
composer's score. When the boy misinterpreted an expression,
Rabi could not show it to him on the violin. He surely missed
his fingers. He just sang it over again by exaggerating the
expression. Amazingly the boy would always pick it up, if not
on his second trial then on a third trial. He never had to tell his
student the fingering either. He would let Lenduai figure out his
own fingering. Since he was not playing in an orchestra, he

could do whatever suited him the best.

Rabi felt more like a conductor than a tutor in these sessions. He enjoyed every minute of it. It sure beat making suits. Why hadn't he thought of teaching violin for a living? Back home, such idea would never occur to him. There were too many master teachers. He wouldn't be able to compete with them. Besides, he was so ashamed of what he was doing that he would never let people know that he had been a professional violinist once before. He would prefer people think of him as a simple tradesman rather than to remind him that he was a washed-out musician.

But here in Shanghai, the situation is different. The Chinese are just beginning to acquire Western culture. They certainly need some music instructors who are qualified not just to teach technique on the instrument but also to convey to the students the feelings and expressions of Western music. What was going through Beethoven's mind when he wrote the piece for the royalty? What was the mentality of the royalty? When did Beethoven need to apply the drums to wake them up? Did literature, fine arts and religion influence his composition? What were they like in Beethoven's time? All that required a rich cultural background, which an instructor living in a totally different culture would have great difficulty comprehending.

But where would he get his students? Perhaps he could start with Lenduai. The boy played at Red House every night. That was good publicity. People who went there frequently to have Western food would be most likely to have their children take Western music lessons of some sort. They would definitely notice Lenduai's improvement and be curious to ask him if he had been taking lessons. The tailor's name would get around by word of mouth just like his tailoring business. Yes, Lenduai was a perfect student to start with. These Gypsies were born with music in their blood.

Since Rabi did not have too many customers, he went to every practice session of his daughter's trio. He was pleased with his student's performance. But one day, as the violin came to a passage needing to lead in forte, Rabi jumped up and yelled,

"Terrible! Terrible! It sounds murderous!"

Lenduai put down his violin without saying anything. Moishe immediately protested to her father,

"What are you talking about, Papa?"

"The violin sounded terrible."

"I couldn't hear it. I thought that was our best practice session. Don't you guys agree?"

Disregarding his daughter, the tailor turned to his student and said, "Can you go find a better violin, Lenduai? That fiddle of yours sounds so awful."

"Where can I find another violin, Mr. Rabi?"

"Borrow one, rent one, steal one... Do anything. Don't tell me there is not another violin in the entire city."

"Very few Chinese that I know play the violin. When I play with them, they either play piano or an *erhu.*"

"Er-?"

"*Erhu,* a two-string Chinese instrument played on the knee."

"Why don't you let him use yours, Papa?" Moishe suddenly came up with the idea.

"I don't have it any more," the tailor's voice suddenly turned sad.

"What?" Moishe was shocked to hear what she had just heard. Papa treasured that Stradivarius of his more than anything. Sometimes Moishe even felt jealous of that old fiddle. If he were asked to part with one of them, she did not know which her father would prefer, his Stradivarius or his daughter. Then it dawned on her. Could he have sold it? He had not been going to the Concessions lately. He had been coming to the practice sessions everyday. Yet Mama still kept all her servants. Where did she get money to pay them?

"When did you sell it, Papa?" in a tone of reprimand,

Moishe asked.

"I would never sell it, you know that. Not even over my dead body."

"Then what happened to it?"

"That Jap took it."

"What Jap?"

" 'The King of the Jews'."

"When?"

"When he came to our place for measurement for a new suit."

Lenduai did not give much thought to the Stradivarius. He was quite happy to get his pistol back from Rabi. If he had not asked for it, *the King of the Jews* would eventually find out about it and take it like he did with the Stradivarius.

Moishe was dressed in a full skirt and a colorful blouse, quite fitting for a party. On her ears were two large ring earrings that Lenduai had given her when the refugee ship was in Calicut. Lenduai was in his black suit that he wore to work at Red House. With his violin box in one hand and a small handbag slung over his shoulder, Lenduai walked up to the front door of the French villa with Moishe's hand hanging in his free arm. There were two guards standing at the entrance.

"Konbanwa," greeted Lenduai in Japanese with a deep bow. It startled the guards into clicking their heels. The couple did not go in. Instead, they followed the wall of the compound and walked straight to the back door of the villa where the kitchen was located. All the service people, including musicians, were supposed to go through this back door.

"Why did we have to walk by the front door?" Moishe asked.

"So that the guards will recognize us later."

The night was hot and humid. The back door was wide open to the street to give ventilation to the kitchen. It exposed a full view of the busy operation inside the kitchen.

"It's just the right timing," said Lenduai in a hushed voice after taking a quick glance into the kitchen. "They are going to be at the dinner table for quite a while yet. Let's go."

The couple hastened their pace. They continued to follow the wall and turned the corner into an alley. The alley was lit brightly by a lone street lamp. On each side of the alley, there was a tall wall topped with broken glass all along the ridge. Inside the wall on their right was the backside of the French villa. They could see its balcony on the second floor overlooking the wall. The window to the balcony was wide open, probably for ventilation.

Lenduai and Moishe found a tree and quickly got under it to get out of the lighted alley. Lenduai put down his violin case. He took out a slingshot from his pocket. He raised it up to his eye level, pulled the rubber band back as far as it would go and took aim. Then he let go. The rubber band snapped back. A faint pop was heard and the light went out. The balcony and the window disappeared into the dark. Everything else in the alley was reduced to a ghostly shadow by the faint light that came from the far end of the alley. Lenduai put the slingshot back into his pocket and opened his bag. He took out a grapple that looked just like the one used by the pirates in the Malacca Strait. It was attached to a piece of rope.

"Where did you get this?" Moishe asked in surprise.

"I made it by tying up four of those short tree-forks that the Chinese use to carry the *muodongs* on their shoulder poles."

"What are they for?"

"You watch."

Lenduai swung the grapple in his hand a few times like a pendulum. Then on the last swing he let go his hand. The grapple flew into the dark. A couple of seconds later they heard a clunk. Lenduai pulled in the slack on the rope. When the rope became taut and firm in his hand, a big smile appeared on his face. He tied the end of the rope to the tree trunk and slung the violin box onto his back.

"You sure you can climb?" he asked his teammate.

"I did climb down the ship, didn't I?"

"This rope is not as thick as the hawser on the ship. It is hard to hold on to."

"I know."

"Good thing is you now have that extra padding on your bosom and hips."

"Watch your mouth!"

"Isn't it true though?"

"Mind your own business!"

Lenduai sensed that his humor was not appreciated. He tried to cover up his embarrassment by suggesting, "Let me bundle up your skirt."

"I can do it myself."

"Then tie it up with this." Lenduai pulled the belt off his pants. He handed it to Moishe and then continued, "We go one at a time. This rope cannot support two bodies. I go first. When I get to the balcony I'll shake the rope. Then you come. Watch out for that mouse-stop."

"What mouse-stop?"

"The broken glass sticking out on the wall. They are supposed to stop burglars. They are very sharp."

The faint light that came from the street lamp down the alley showed a smile on Moishe's face. Lenduai was relieved. He knew that he was forgiven.

A few minutes later, the two "burglars" were both standing on the balcony.

The two shadows moved as quietly as two roof cats. Lenduai unhooked the grapple and threw it back into the alley.

"There goes our retreat!" Lenduai said.

"What do you mean?" his accomplice asked.

"That leaves only one way out."

"That is...?"

Moishe did not get an answer. Lenduai had already

climbed into the window. Moishe could only follow.

The Gypsy had the nose of a hunting dog and the eyes of an owl. It did not take him long to find what they had come for. He took the box to the window where there was a faint light from the alley. He opened it. There it was. He could recognize the cheap fiddlehead that the tailor had glued onto it that night back in the tailor's apartment in Vienna. Then he opened the violin box he had brought along with him. He quickly switched the contents of the two boxes. After putting the Stradivarius box back to where he had found it, he whispered to his partner, "Let's go!"

Moishe let down her skirt and returned the belt back to its owner. As Lenduai was putting the belt back onto his pants, his eyes caught a glimpse of a bare leg.

"Oh my God," he said. "You have torn your skirt on the mouse-stop!"

"Where?"

"Give me your hand." He guided Moishe's hand to her back. "You feel it?"

Without saying another word, Lenduai opened his violin box and took out a safety pin. He got down on his knees behind Moishe. As he was pinning up the tear, his finger touched on something wet on the inside of the girl's leg. He wiped his finger on her bare skin.

"Stop that, Lenduai!"

Lenduai licked his finger and said, "Mouse blood!"

"This is not the time to joke."

"Who's joking? Taste it for yourself," Lenduai grabbed Moishe's face with both hands and drew it toward his own face. "Stick out your tongue."

Without thinking, Moishe complied mechanically. She felt something soft and wet touching the tip of her tongue. It tasted salty. Before she could react to it, she felt a strong arm wrapping around her waist and she was pulled into Lenduai's embrace. They froze. And so did time.

207

A moment later, Lenduai's hand suddenly moved away from the slender waist. He straightened his back and pulled on the edge of his coat to take away the freshly made creases.

"We had better leave," Lenduai said. "Listen, Moishe. This is going to be the toughest part, going down the stairs and walking out of the front door to the gate without being caught. Put your hand in my arm and stick close to me. Smile as you walk. Bow gracefully when we are encountered by anyone."

Carrying his violin box in one hand and his partner's hand in his other arm, Lenduai walked out the front door without encountering anyone and headed straight to the front gate. As he came to the guards, he stopped and fished out a slip of paper from his coat pocket. He handed it to the one who looked like the leader of the two.

"Konbanwa!" he bowed as he greeted them with a smile.

The guards immediately recognized the young couple who had greeted them earlier. They snapped their heels together but did not salute. The young couple bowed again and then slowly walked out of the gate.

Once out on the street, Lenduai held on to Moishe's hand and quickened his steps. They turned around a corner. As they passed the kitchen door, they could see that the preparation was still in full swing. The waiters were still rushing into the kitchen with empty dishes and walking out with plates of food. Lenduai and Moishe hurried into the alley where they had been before climbing into the villa.

"Why are we coming back here?" Moishe asked.

"To retrieve my grapple."

"What did you hand to the guard back there?"

"Just something he could not read."

"What?"

"Something I scribbled in German."

"You have learned to write?"

"No."

"How did you know Papa's violin was in that room?"

"I have come to the alley several times before to listen to the *schmuck* practicing in that room."

"Where did you pick up that awful word?"

"Look, I've been with your people long enough."

"How did you know the *schmuck* was Goya?"

"Gosh, listen to how you talk! Don't you know that practically everybody in Hongkew has been forced to listen to the *schmuck* play? You have to be tone deaf not to recognize that awful playing."

Lenduai was pleased to see a smile on the girl's face.

"Do you think he will force his guests to listen to him play after dinner?" she asked.

"You think he will let a captured audience go free?"

"What will happen when he sees your violin in his box?"

"I am thinking about the same thing."

"Will he round up all the Jews in Hongkew like a Nazi would do?"

"He could only blame the French. Look, he did not lose his violin in Hongkew. This is a French Concession. No Jewish refugees are allowed to come here, especially at this hour. I sure wish that I could be there to watch the bastard's face though."

CHAPTER FOURTEEN

Everybody who could get a pass to go out of Hongkew came to the concert including Mr. and Mrs. Rabi. Even Ahma came. It was the pride of Hongkew. But she admitted to Moishe later that she had fallen asleep several times during the performance. "I just don't have an ear for that '*ziliuziliu*' sound you kids made," she said. "Why didn't you play something nice, like something from the Capital Opera, like 'Number Four Son Visiting His Mother'?"

When it came to the end, Ahma applauded the loudest. Moishe was so embarrassed to hear Ahma yelling at the top of her voice, "Hao!" as if she were attending a Chinese Capital Opera.

It was a success. Even before the concert, it was written up in the paper as the youngest trio who had ever performed in Lyceum Theater. Goya was there too. He had to come when so many Jews in Hongkew went to him to apply for passes to come to the concert.

Lenduai had spotted "the King of the Jews" in the audience during the first movement. It was hard not to notice him. The minuscule Japanese was nodding his head, waving his arms and shaking his body with every beat. He moved so emotionally that he even fell off his seat once. Lenduai realized that it would mean big trouble if the Japanese ever recognize the Stradivarius.

Lenduai grabbed Moishe's hand as soon as the applause thinned down and dragged her to the back stage.

"What's the hurry?" Moishe asked.

"Let's get out of here," said Lenduai as he dragged Moishe to the back stage door.

"We are not leaving, are we?"

"Didn't you see the Jap?"

"So?"

"We can't have him see the fiddle."

Goya was so impressed by the performance, particularly the violinist, that he got up right after the applause tapered down and walked to the back stage. On his way he ran into Miss. Hartwich. The Headmistress was flabbergasted to see Goya come to the concert. She stopped him and struggled with her limited vocabulary in Japanese to thank him for coming to the concert and especially for issuing the passes for the Jews in Hongkew to attend the event. She could not believe her ears when she heard from the very mouth of this abusive occupier, in English,

"Being the King of the Jews, this is my pride as well."

Perhaps from now on he would look at the Jews differently and not treat them so harshly?

Outside of the theater, Lenduai and Moishe found themselves alone in the dark alley. Lenduai was still holding Moishe's hand tightly.

"I meant to tell you this a long time ago," he said in hesitation.

"What?" asked Moishe. She noticed the familiar expression on Lenduai's face whenever he had done something not kosher. Did he steal something again? Moishe could not care less. She was too excited over their flawless performance. She wondered what Papa would say. What would Paci say? What would the critics say in the morning papers the next day?

She could not wait to return to the back stage.

"This is your day," Lenduai said.

"Is that what you want to tell me? They are probably waiting for us. I want to hear what Paci has to say."

"I thought I should wait until after the concert."

"Let's go back. We can talk about it later."

"I know I should not spoil your day. From now on, your door is wide open if you want to make it here in Shanghai."

"I can't wait to read about what the critics will say tomorrow."

"Perhaps Paci can recommend that you play a concert with the Shanghai Municipal Orchestra. Wouldn't it be something? You know, Shanghai is not a bad place. But for me, I have been here too long. It's time to move on."

"Lenduai..." Moishe could not complete her sentence. Her mouth was sealed by two sensuous lips. She knew those lips from the balcony of *the King of the Jews.* She opened her mouth and surrendered to Lenduai's expression of love.

Lenduai knew very well that he could stay. Just like with the King's family, the Rabis would take him back as a member of their family. As for the Stradivarius, he could easily think of some way to hide it from Goya. But he could feel the Gypsy blood running restlessly in his veins. He had to do something. He knew that, just like with the King's family, once parted with Moishe, their lives would never come together again. He realized that this was the last time he would see and touch this girl.

Lenduai broke the embrace abruptly and picked up the black box. "I must go," he said.

"Where are you going?" Moishe asked.

"I don't know. Canton, Hong Kong, Singapore... or even Chungking. It doesn't matter as long as it is a different place. China is as big as all of Europe, you know."

"Take me with you."

Lenduai looked at the girl. She was in tears. Yes, he had

thought of that too. But that would break too many hearts.

"You are not a Gypsy," he said.

"I can learn to become one."

Was that what such a nice girl deserved? Lenduai shook his head and said, "You are a city girl. You have your traditions and culture. Your future is here. You wouldn't be happy with the Gypsy life. Maybe for excitement for a while. But when you get into the drudgery, you would regret it. Didn't you notice how boring the King's wife look in the Gypsy camp? Besides, it would be too cruel to rob your Papa of both his loves."

"What are you talking about?"

"I mean his daughter and his Stradivarius."

"Then give the fiddle back to the fiddler. Take me."

"Give the Stradivarius back to your Papa? Are you kidding? Did you see how *the King of the Jews* watched me? You know what he would do to your Papa if he ever found out about it?"

"You mean you would rather have me go face *the King of the Jews?* I see, you prefer the Stradivarius over me."

"The Jap won't bother you. Go back to your parents and your Ahma. Jue will take care of you. Jue is a good man."

Lenduai paused. In all these years in Shanghai, he had made just one real friend, Jue. Their admiration was mutual. Jue first noticed Lenduai in Red House. He was fascinated by the Gypsy music. Then when Lenduai heard Jue play the piano, another dimension was added to his musical world. It was the first time the Gypsy had ever heard someone playing the piano. From then on, the friendship between the two young musicians grew rapidly under the nourishment of music.

"He loves you," with great difficulty, Lenduai finally got these words out of his mouth. He could feel each word stabbing his heart. It was already too late. It had been bothering Lenduai ever since he noticed that Jue was going out of his way to please Moishe and to spend time with her alone. At first, he trusted that friendship. Then it turned into pain. Had the roles been switched; would he still have had the same feelings if he were Jue? How about Moishe? Was she ever jealous of the friendship between Lenduai and Jue? In that sense, Lenduai was glad to see Moishe being jealous of his attachment to the Stradivarius. He wouldn't have known how to deal with the former situation.

"Jue can take care of you better than I can," Lenduai found it difficult to say these words. But he knew that this was true.

"I can take care of myself!" Moishe reacted to Lenduai's patronage. "I don't need anyone to take care of me."

Moishe's response brought a smile to Lenduai's face. "That a boy!" he said. "You are still the Moishe I knew back in the woods and in the lifeboat. Keep up the spirit."

The Gypsy raised up the violin box like a winner raising a trophy and said, "Thank your Papa for me."

Then he disappeared into the crowd that was pouring out of the theater.

Goya could not find the violinist back stage.

"He's gone," he was told. "You can probably find him in Red House."

The Japanese was disappointed. He had been thinking of playing a duet with him or a trio with him and the girl. When he met the Rabis in the lobby later, he said to the tailor,

"I didn't know you have such a talented daughter. I want her to accompany me. This is a nice theater. I have decided to give a recital here so that you Jews do not need to stand in the street to hear me play."

"I don't know how to play accompaniment, sir," Moishe said.

"*Baka!* Just do as I say!"

"But I have never done it before, sir."

"Then start working on it right away. I will meet you at four in your school auditorium tomorrow." Then turning to the tailor he said, "Rabi, you can make me another suit for me to wear at the concert."

"I don't trust that Japanese, Mrs," Ahma told Mrs. Rabi on their way back to Hongkew. "Don't let Miss go with him."

"It's not up to us," said the tailor's wife. "He is the King of the Jews. Don't you know? Whatever he wants he gets. Didn't you see how he ordered Mr. Rabi to make another suit for him? Didn't you see how he took Mr. Rabi's violin?"

"That's just a fiddle, a fancy *erhu*. But Miss is your daughter!"

"What do you want me to do?"

"I'll go with her when she goes to practice with the Jap."

"The Japanese would never allow that."

"I won't let him see me."

"That's hard to do."

"I know, I know. I can disguise myself. Don't worry, Mrs. I know how to handle these Japs."

From that day on, Ahma never let Moishe out of her sight. Thanks to Japanese martial law, the schools were closed, the Jews were not allowed to go out of Hongkew and there was a curfew at night. Moishe could only visit her friends in Hongkew during the day and Hongkew was just so big. When Moishe visited her friends, Ahma would also go along. She knew all the domestic help at Moishe's friends' households. Only when Moishe went to her piano lesson in the Concession, Ahma couldn't accompany her. But Jue was a nice boy. She could trust her Moishe to him. He would always bring her back home before midnight, not like that Gypsy boy who always stayed out with Moishe past midnight. He was polite and, most importantly, his parents were rich. Wouldn't it be nice if that Chinese boy would marry her little Moishe? Ahma tried to be extra nice to Jue every time she saw him.

When Ahma went to the school auditorium with Moishe,

she always kept many steps behind her and walked in the shade or behind the peddlers and food stalls. She did such a good job that, quite often, even Moishe did not realize that she was being followed. The surveillance in the auditorium was a little tricky. Of course she could not go in. But she found a way onto the back stage. She could not see what was happening in there. But she could hear them play. As long as she could hear both instruments playing, she figured it would be all right. What was hard to do was to keep herself from falling asleep in that hypnotizing *"ziliuziliu"* sound.

Then one day, the unthinkable happened. Ahma fell asleep to that *"ziliuziliu"* sound. Suddenly she was awakened by Moishe's shrieking. She got up and rushed to the door to the stage. Through the crack of the door she had left ajar she saw Moishe pinned to the piano. The diminutive Jap kept one hand on her neck and the other hand fumbling on her skirt. Her blouse was already torn open.

Ahma reached into the flap of her peasant jacket. She pulled out a small silvery pistol that was inlaid with pearl and gold on the handle. She cautiously walked through the door and tiptoed to the piano. Moishe's shrieking covered up her footsteps. Goya's animal lust on his helpless prey overpowered his awareness to the environment. Ahma did not want to miss her target. She tried to recall step by step what the Gypsy boy had instructed her to do when he gave her the silver pistol:

"Unlock the safety pin; hold it with both of your hands, right hand on the handle, index finger on the trigger and your left hand on the right hand. Keeping your arms straight and pointing at the target."

With her posture set, she sneaked to a distance as close as she could without raising any alarm. She tried to calm herself by reviewing the Gypsy boy's instruction in her mind:

"Take a deep breath. Then slowly squeeze all your fingers as if you are squeezing water out of a sponge. Don't pull on the trigger. You can pull the gun sideway and miss the target. You must hit your target with one shot. Remember, you don't have the time or the stomach for a second shot."

The Japanese had his back to her and was in line with the gun in her hands. She pointed the gun at that heaving back. She made sure that she was not also pointing at Moishe. She took a deep breath, closed her eyes and squeezed her hand as slowly as she could. The surprising cracking of a firecracker woke her up. She opened her eyes just in time to see the Japanese slumping forward.

There was no one to hear the cracking of the small caliber purse-sized pistol. The school had been closed by the Japanese for many months. Ahma ran forward and pulled Moishe away from the bleeding body of *the King of the Jews*. The poor girl was shivering in delirium. Ahma quickly took off her jacket and wrapped it around the half naked girl. She half carried and half pulled the girl out of the place.

"Was there anyone else in the place?" the tailor asked when he and his wife were told of what had happened at the school.

"No."

"Did anybody hear it?"

"I don't know."

"Did you kill him?"

"I don't know."

"Was he still breathing?"

"I don't know. All I wanted at that time was to get Miss out of there."

"What does it matter whether that beast was dead or alive?" said the tailor's wife. "What matters is that our daughter is alive. What shall we do next?"

"They will come for us."

"I know. We must leave."

"Where can we go?"

"The Concessions."

"We don't have passes except you."

"We can go get them."

"What are you talking about? Only 'the King of the Jews' can issue passes."

"Definitely we can't stay here. Nowhere in Hongkew is safe."

"We can go to Chongming." The tailor and his wife turned their heads simultaneously to the voice. It was Ahma.

"Where is Chongming?"

"An island in the Yangtze River."

"Why Chongming?"

"It's my home."

"Oh, yes, I remember," said Mrs. Rabi. "Are there Japanese soldiers there?"

"Where can you find a place without Japanese soldiers? But they stay on the south shore. Our plot is on the north shore."

"Chongming is only so big. As long as there are Japanese there, they will find us."

"They won't go to our plot."

"Why not?"

"There's nothing on the north shore."

"They can still come search."

"There is no road on the north shore. The Japanese do not like to walk. When they go places they either ride in cars or on horses. The dykes in the rice patties are so narrow that even donkeys cannot walk on them. Besides, the Japanese hate the smell of our fertilizer. We use human shit. Trust me, I have never seen any Japanese soldier around our place, not even once."

"How can we get there?"

"There is a ferry going to Chongming everyday."

"Then we have to go through the town, don't we?"

"Yes."

"It won't work."

"We can hire a junk."

"It would still have to dock in town, wouldn't it?"

"Our farm is next to the shore."

"Where can we find a junk?"

"How about a fishing junk at the fish market?"

"I'll go," Moishe came alive when she heard the words, *"fishing junk"*.

"Are you crazy?" Ahma raised her voice in scolding. "The Japs are after you, not me! Go hide at your friend's place until I come for you. I'll go."

"Are you sure you are going to find one?"

"Mrs, fishing junks are like seagulls. You can always find one. If one day no fishing junk came into port, how would the Japs get their fresh fish? You and I can go without fish, but not the Japanese."

The fish market was abandoned at this hour. It was too late for food stands and too early for the auction. There was not a single soul in the place. But there was a junk!

Ahma walked over to the dock and hollered,

"Anyone there?"

Someone came out of the cabin.

"Ah Bong!" Ahma was stunned to see that boyish face. Her presence also took the young fisherman by surprise. He had never expected to see Ahma at the fish market, especially at this hour. Ever since Moishe stopped coming, Ahma never showed her face. Ah Bong saw her only occasionally when he went to Teelanchow to deliver his share of fresh take-home fish from the catch. He had always sensed her dislike of him. But for one more glance at Moishe, it was worthwhile to see that long face. Surprisingly, Ahma did not have a long face this time.

"When did you come in?" Ahma asked in a voice as if she was glad to see the fisherman.

"Just half an hour ago."

"Why didn't you drop by the house?"

"We have not unloaded yet. I will bring the fish over

tomorrow morning."

"That will be too late..." Ahma suddenly broke into tears. Ah Bong had never seen that iron cold face have any expression except scorn.

"Has anything happened to Ah Moi?" was the first thing that came to the boy's mind.

"You won't find any of us by the time you deliver the fish."

"Why?"

"Someone got killed."

"Is Ah Moi all right?"

"She's all right."

"Who got killed?"

"A Jap."

"Oh..." Ah Bong was finally relieved of his worry.

"We must leave town."

"Why?"

"The Japs will be looking for us all over the city."

"Where can you go?"

"Chongming."

"That is in the middle of the Yangtze River!"

"Can you take us there?"

"Let me go ask Laoda."

Ah Bong went back into the cabin. Ahma heard a loud argument coming out of the opening. She could not catch a single word of it. These Ningpo people! Their dialect sounded so rough that even chitchat sounded like a quarrel. She wished that Moishe were there to interpret for her.

The noise finally quieted down. Ah Bong came out of the cabin and said to Ahma, "Let's go get Ah Moi."

As they were walking back to Teelanchow, Ahma asked out of curiosity, "What happened back there in the cabin?"

"They had a quarrel," Ah Bong said.

"Who?"

"Laoda and Ah Ting."

"Who's Ah Ting?"

"The purser."

"What did they quarrel about?"

"Laoda wanted to take Ah Moi to Chongming. Ah Ting did not want to miss the auction in the morning."

"Isn't Laoda the *laoda?*"

"Laoda is in charge of catching fish. Ah Ting is in charge of selling the fish."

"Couldn't you still sell the fish after you take us to Chongming?"

"Ah Ting says it is such a rare chance that we are in port all by ourselves. We could get a very competitive bid on the price of our catch tomorrow morning. If we go to Chongming, we will miss this once in a lifetime chance. There will be catches brought in by other boats when we come back. The price will drop."

"What did Laoda say?"

"Laoda says he would do anything for Ah Moi. He says for Ah Moi he did not care even if he had to lose the entire catch. Ah Ting says the Japanese will have no fresh fish tomorrow. Laoda says he does not care. He says Ah Moi's life is worth more than his catch, the junk or the entire Japanese army. You know, the old man looks upon Ah Moi as his own daughter."

"Was the purser convinced?"

"No, Ah Ting threatened to report him to the police."

"Let me go talk to your purser," Ahma stopped and said.

"You don't need to. Laoda already took care of it."

"How?"

"He threatened to fire Ah Ting."

"He can still report to the police, can't he?"

"Don't worry. We have tied him up and have thrown him in the fish hold. Laoda also put someone to watch him."

The Rabis and Ahma were scared stiff inside the inclined cabin, worrying that the junk was going to capsize. Moishe was so thrilled that she could take off her shoes and feel the inclined deck under her bare feet once again. She realized how much she had missed the junk, the sampan, the sea and fishing. Without being told, she joined the crew in raising the sails. What had happened in the school auditorium a few hours ago was completely behind her mind.

After the junk was under way, Moishe returned to the poop deck. She could not believe what she was hearing.

"Ah Moi, take the tiller for me for a while," Laoda said to her.

There were so many other old hands. Why didn't Laoda ask any of them? Why didn't he ask Ah Bong? Why did he have to ask her to take the tiller? Moishe had never even touched the tiller before and Laoda knew that. Laoda did not give any instructions before leaving the poop deck. He went straight down into the fish hold.

Moishe had not realized that the tiller was so much thicker and heavier than the scull on the sampan. The junk suddenly became as big and as tall as an ocean-going steamship. She felt that she had the entire river traffic in her hands. But all she could see was through the crack of the two patched sails.

Suddenly a huge black steel hull blocked her view. They were on a collision course. It was so close that Moishe could hear its propeller churning the muddy water. And Laoda was nowhere around to tell her what to do. Moishe remembered that Laoda always waited until the junk's bow almost touched the steel hull before pushing the tiller all the way leeward. But Moishe did not have the audacity to wait so long. She quickly pushed the tiller hard alee and secured it against the bulwark. The junk turned obediently into the wind as Moishe commanded and spilled all the wind out of the sails. The sails, the bamboo battens and the sheets instantly became limp and started to flop on their masts while the bow of the junk continued to swing. A couple of seconds later, the sails suddenly

222

became stiff again. Bagging all the wind they could catch, the sails blew up like two balloons. Moishe quickly untied the tiller and brought it back to dead center. With safe water in front and the junk heading in a steady course, she turned her head back. In surprise she saw Laoda standing behind her.

"A beautiful performance!" Laoda said with a smile on his face. She took a glance at the steamer. She was left far behind the junk. Laoda turned his head to the other person standing next to him and asked, "Ah Ting, can you do what this *Yotahning xiao-niang-bi* just did?"

Moishe felt her head being tapped. She turned around. It was the purser. With an approving smile, he said,

"I am sorry for what I said to Laoda. I just lost my head temporarily when I thought of those Silver Ribbons in the hold. I could only think of what we could have gotten for them at the auction. Now seeing you, honestly I wouldn't trade you for all the Silver Ribbons in the East China Sea."

Did he mean what he had just said or was he just saying it for Laoda to hear?

Laoda let Moishe steer all the way through the busy Whampoo traffic. At each successive tack, the *Yotahning xiao-niang-bi* got a little bit closer to the steel hull.

Before long, the Whampoo ended. A vast brimless water appeared before them. Moishe yelled out to her parents, "This was where our refugee ship anchored for quarantine." Then turning to Laoda, she asked, "Now what direction shall I steer?"

"Keep the same course," said the old man. Another hour later, Laoda said to Ahma,

"We are now at the northern entrance of the Yangtze River. The shore to our south is Chongming. Where is your farm?"

"Across from Yinyang."

"Can you recognize it from out here?"

"Yes, there is a tall bamboo thicket by the riverbank and an old tree with spreading limbs next to it. But I can't see anything in the dark."

Moishe Fantasy

"Then let's drop anchor here and wait for daybreak."

Paul Chow

CHAPTER FIFTEEN

As soon as there was light enough for the shore to show up clearly, the junk weighed anchor and set sail for upstream. Within an hour, Ahma spotted the bamboo. The old tree with spreading limbs was standing right next to it just as she had told Laoda. The junk dropped anchor again. A sampan was lowered into the water and all four passengers, the tailor, his wife, Moishe and Ahma, piled into the sampan. Ah Bong took the scull. He guided the sampan toward the shore until it got stuck onto the shallow muddy bottom. After dropping a stone anchor, he took off his clothes and got into the icy cold water.

Ah Bong piggybacked his passengers to shore one by one. When he returned for the last passenger, he found that she was already standing in the water. She was shivering in her wet clothes that clung tightly to her body. She had the stone anchor in one hand and the painter of the sampan in the other hand. Was he glad that he did not have to make another trip to shore or was he disappointed not to be able to touch Moishe for the last time? Without showing any emotion, Ah Bong climbed back onto the sampan. Standing in the water, Moishe watched the boy putting on his clothes. It brought her back to sea again. The bronze statue in the sampan did not utter a word then. He did not utter a word this time either.

Moishe put the stone anchor back into the sampan. She hesitated for a little while before throwing the painter to Ah Bong and pushing the sampan off the muddy bottom. Then she turned around and waded ashore to join the others. She could

225

feel Ah Bong's stares burning on her back while the water was freezing her lower body.

Ahma's house looked just like any farmhouse on the island, a thatched roof blackened with mold over four mud walls with no plaster and no windows. There was only one opening for its occupants and light to get in. The inside was like a cave. There were a stove, a table, three stools and three stretchers resting on benches, all made of bamboo except the stove.

"You three sleep on these," said Ahma pointing to the bamboo stretchers.

"Where do you sleep?" Mrs. Rabi asked.

"Over there by the stove."

"But there is no bed."

"We will sleep on the ground."

"On the dirt?"

"Oh, no. We will spread out some straw."

"Why don't you keep your beds?" said Mrs. Rabi. "We can sleep on the straw."

"No, you will get sick. The ground is dirty and damp and the air is smoky and stuffy."

"But the place does not get cleaner and the ground does not get dryer for you."

"We are used to it. We come from a colder place. This is heaven for us."

"You are not locals?"

"Yes, what I mean is that our grandparents came from the North."

"Where?"

"Kaifeng. The climate is worse there. The river is muddier. The northwesterly is stronger and colder."

Sara Rabi could not imagine any place worse than this place. But from Ahma's description of that place in the north, she felt lucky that Ahma took them to Chongming, not Kaifeng. Although material-wise this place was worse than Hongkew, it did not have all those smells.

"This is great," Mrs. Rabi said. "We do not have to smell the *muodongs* any more."

"I am sorry, we don't have *muodongs* here," Ahma misinterpreted the comment as an expression of regret for missing the luxury of *muodong*. "You will have to squat."

"Where?"

"In the *outhouse.*"

The tailor's wife looked around. There was no house or outhouse other than the farmhouse they were in. The only other man-made thing she could see was a cesspool with a bamboo platform over one of its ends. The floor had several holes that could accommodate several people squatting at the same time. Ahma's husband put up a bamboo screen around the floor so that their houseguests from the city could have some privacy. But there was no roof. It rained a lot in Chongming. When it rained they had to hold umbrellas while they squatted.

At lunch and dinner that day, Ahma served the Rabis separately.

"Aren't you also going to eat?" Mrs. Rabi asked.

"We'll eat later."

"Why don't we eat together?" Mrs. Rabi suggested. She realized that Ahma was trying to be proper and to maintain the employer-employee protocol between them. In Hongkew the servants eat separately. But they were servants then. Now the Rabis were houseguests of Ahma. The tailor's wife thought they should eat together. Then she realized that everything could become a habit, even injustice.

"You are not used to our food." Ahma insisted. Mrs. Rabi took a look at the food. It consisted of unpolished rice and cabbage. The only other ingredients were green onions and the flaky shells of dried shrimp for flavoring. She noticed later that the food Ahma served themselves was totally different. It consisted of boiled stock corn and potato vines, without any green onion or dried shrimp shells for flavoring.

"We can eat that too," the tailor's wife insisted. But after she tried it, she found out that Ahma was right.

"Spit it out," said Ahma. The tailor's wife thought spitting would be insulting. She swallowed it. But it took her several gulps.

From then on Mrs. Rabi would never argue with Ahma anymore. This was Alma's world. Mrs. Rabi would listen to whatever Ahma said. She followed Ahma like she was her shadow. She volunteered to help, hauling water from the river, bundling straw for cooking fuel and feeding the straw to the stove while Ahma was cooking. She learned how to wash clothes without soap by beating them on rocks by the river. She learned to rub cotton fibers on her lap to twist them into twines. She learned to trot with the wooden buckets bouncing on the yoke on her shoulder. She even learned to scoop up human excrement from the cesspool to put on the vegetable pads.

Peasant life on Ahma's farm was harsh but peaceful. There was not a single soul or house in sight within hollering distance. Above all, there was no sight of any Japanese soldiers. There was no communication of any sort with the outside world.

For the tailor all he could do was to sit in front of the primitive mud house, swatting the flies during the day and mosquitoes at night. If this was called living, he wondered if dying in a German labor camp or being shot by a Japanese firing squad was not better.

The tailor felt that he had been put back into the Stone Age. The only advance these country folks had made from their stone age ancestors was that they raised their food rather than hunting for it and they wove their clothes rather than wearing animal skins. For housing, they merely moved their cave in the mountains down to the field. (As a matter of fact, the mud house was not any more comfortable than the caves.) Verbal communication among these peasants was limited only to life's essentials, which one could do without. Proper names even became unnecessary. A day could pass without hearing a single word exchanged among them. When they did speak, they spoke in their northern dialect, which the Rabis could not understand.

But was he better than these people? With all his rich culture and advanced knowledge, he could not survive a single day without Ahma's family. Nothing in his training could fit in. No one wore a suit. There was not a single peasant or coolie in all of China who did not have patches on his clothes. It was worse in Chongming. No one listened to music. He could not even see any of the primitive Chinese instruments such as the two-stringed *erhu*. One would think being isolated from any society, they could do anything they wanted. No, there was no such thing as free will. The environment dictated everyone's life. The only thing the tailor had was time. He had plenty of time to think. It was a prison without walls and guards. He did not know which was better, a labor camp where there were fellow inmates of the same cultural background with whom he could communicate and share feelings or total isolation where neither capitalism nor colonialism worked.

Sometimes idling could be harder to endure than hard labor.

He finally figured out why these peasants never complained about the isolation. They were one of the elements that made up the isolation like the birds and the insects. They were self-sufficient. Their existence did not depend on the existence of any other human efforts.

However, the world for Moishe was totally different. It was like the wonderland of Alice. On the very next morning after their arrival, Moishe went to work in the field with Ahma's husband and son. She never stayed in the house during the day. Rain or sun, she was out in the field with the men from dawn to dusk. When she returned to the house, she always had a good appetite at dinner and sound sleep at night.

The farm looked exactly like Ahma had described it to her when they were alone in their bedroom at night back in Teelanchow. She was especially excited to finally meet the family water-buffalo Ahma had talked about. She felt as if she had known him for ages.

"What's his name, Li?" she asked.

"Name?" the young peasant was puzzled by the question.

"Yes, his name," patting the grayish black animal as she repeated her question.

"A name for a water-buffalo?" Although he had a name, Li. The whole family had shared it. It was there to be handed down to their descendants. No one had ever used it. When it first came up in this *Yotahning* girl's conversation, he thought she was referring to someone else. Now she was asking a name for a water-buffalo?

"Yes, how do you call him?"

"You just make a sound, IT'll come."

"Any sound?"

"Oh no. In each country people have their own sounds just like different dialects for people. Here in Chongming we say *Da-da-da-da* for the water-buffalo and *Luo-luo-luo-luo* for the pigs. Try it."

"*Luo-luo-luo-luo!*" Moishe raised her voice. The animal paid no attention to her and kept feeding on the weeds by the side of the field. Then Moishe walked a few steps away and then made the sound, "*Da-da-da-da!*"

The animal stopped feeding and raised its head. Then to Moishe's amazement, it followed her.

From then on, *Da-da-da-da* and Moishe became inseparable. When the farmers started their spring plowing, Moishe was put in charge of the water-buffalo, including driving it to plow, feeding it and taking it to soak in the river after work.

One day it rained so hard that one's feet would get sucked into the mud when walking in the field. They all stayed in the house. Moishe helped Ahma grind the soybeans. Afterwards as she watched Ahma squeezing the juice out of them, she asked,

"What are you going to do with the grounds?"

"Serve them for dinner."

"We can't eat all that!"

"Give the rest to the pigs."

"Why not to the water-buffalo?"

"IT can eat all the grass on the tracks by the field and on the riverbank."

"But he likes soybean grounds."

"How do you know?"

"I let him taste some the other day. He went crazy and wanted more. Can I give this to him?"

"No."

"Please, Ahma."

"Okay, just this once. You don't want to spoil IT. Water-buffalo is not a pet. IT is for working."

There were enough grounds to fill two full baskets. Just as Moishe finished filling the baskets, Ahma's boy handed her a shoulder yoke.

"Why, it's new," Moishe noticed. "The bamboo is still green."

"I made it for you," the boy said.

"Why? You already have so many yokes around here."

"They are all too long for you."

"How do you know?"

"I watched you. They all bounced too slow on your shoulder."

"So?"

"You have faster pace. This one is shorter, more suitable to your pace. You will feel more comfortable."

"Take it, Miss," Ahma cut in.

As Moishe was hitching the baskets to the new yoke, Ahma threw an encouraging glance to her son and said, "Go help her feed the animal."

In just a few weeks, Moishe was baked as dark as the Chinese peasants. She learned to trot barefoot with two full buckets of watery night soil on her shoulder. With the new yoke, she was not spilling as much as before. She found out that as long as it did not spill, it did not smell too bad.

"It's market day today," the older farmer said to his two young field hands on one of the days when they did not go to the field. "Let's go to the market."

The market took place once every ten days in a village at about two hours' walk from Ahma's farm on the winding narrow tracks that divided the rice fields into so many small plots. Moishe had never seen any place like that. On this day, the only street in the village was busier than any street in Hongkew or the Concessions. It was crowded with farmers from the vicinity. Some of them came from as far away as half a day's walk. Both sides of the street were lined with baskets that displayed all kinds of farm products from colorful seeds for planting to suckling pigs for raising. A pot mender was working right next to someone sitting on a stool to have a tooth "mended". While Moishe was nudging from one basket to another and listening to the farmers bargaining, she suddenly heard someone yelling,

"Hey, you!"

She turned around and saw a Japanese soldier at the end of the street pointing at her. She turned her head. The soldier yelled louder and started to walk toward her. She hastened her steps towards the other end of the street.

"Stop!" the Japanese soldier yelled. Moishe pulled a scarf over her head to cover her blond hair and blended into the marketers. As she squeezed through the crowd, she could hear the Japanese yelling in a mixture of broken Chinese and Japanese, *"Baka Yaroo!* Where did she go? Where did that *gaijin* come from? I'll get her one way or another!"

Moishe got out of the village and ran back to the farm as fast as she could with Ahma's husband and son trailing behind.

Life on Ahma's lost farm by the Yangtze River returned to its timeless routine.

"They won't come out here," said Ahma's husband. "There

is no road for their cars. The Japs have crooked legs. They don't like to walk."

The next morning, Moishe went to the field with Ahma's husband and son as usual. But the old farmer was wrong. At about noon, Moishe noticed the cranes and crows taking off from a far away field.

"Did you see that?" she asked in alarm.

"Someone is paying us a visit," Ahma's husband said worriedly. "Let's hurry back to the cottage."

They rushed back to the farmhouse to warn the family.

"Hide the *Yotahnings,*" said the farmer to his wife.

"In the bamboo thicket?" the wife asked.

"That is the first place anyone will search."

"Where else is safe?"

"The pig pen!"

"But the pig pen is widely exposed."

"I mean the cesspool underneath it," said the farmer. "People say the Japs are the cleanest people on earth. They say no Japs would even go near a cesspool. If they were right, that would be the best place to hide."

There was no time for debate. The Rabis went to hid under the cesspool as told.

"You two better get in there with them," Ahma said to her husband and son after she hustled the Rabis into the cesspool. "The Japs may recognize you."

"We will hide in the bamboos," the husband said.

"Didn't you just say that's the first place the Japs are going to search?"

"Let's hope they do that. It will divert their attention."

Only a lone Japanese soldier came. Just as the farmer had said, he did not come on foot. He came on a horse. No one was following him. At the farmhouse there was only Ahma to face him.

"Where is the *gaijin?*" the Japanese demanded half in Chinese and half in Japanese.

"What?" asked Ahma.

"*Yotahning.*"

"What *Yotahning?* There is no..." before Ahma could finish what she was saying, a whip hit her across her face, knocking her to the ground. The Japanese did not ask more questions. He got off his horse and went into the farmhouse. A moment later, he came out. He looked around and saw that there was no other place for anyone to hide. Then he saw the bamboo thicket by the river. Without hesitation he headed straight to it.

"The water is swift there!" Ahma yelled out after the soldier, trying to warn her husband and son. "You should not go by yourself!"

She got up and ran after the soldier, yelling continuously with each word louder than the previous one, "There is no one..."

Ahma's yelling was suddenly interrupted by a loud cry. Then a gunshot rocked the pastoral tranquility. Ahma hastened her pace toward the bank.

In front of the bamboo thicket by the river she saw two bodies lying on the ground, one motionless and one still twisting and moaning with his two hands grabbing on a thick bamboo pole sticking out of his abdomen. Ahma gave out a loud cry and collapsed onto the body that was not moving.

Standing by the uniformed body lying next to Li Wen on the ground was Ahma's husband. He had a heavy pickax in his hands. He was striking the uniformed body continuously with the pickax. The ground and the front of the farmer's body were colored red by the splashing of blood.

The Rabis could hear every sound that took place outside the cesspool. When the sound of pounding and moaning stopped, a single voice remained. It was high-pitched and prolonging. Someone was crying. No, it was singing, more like canting... It was Ahma wailing.

The Rabis got out. "You stay!" Rabi told his daughter. Then he turned to his wife and said, "Let's go take a look."

They rushed as quickly as they could toward where the sound came from. When they came to the edge of the bamboo thicket, they saw Ahma kneeling on a puddle of blood. In her arms was her son, Li Wen, with his head hanging limply over her forearm. Ahma's body was swaying back and forth like a mother rocking her baby to sleep. She was wailing and canting in tears. Her man was nearby. But he was not paying any attention to her. He was dragging a body toward the river.

The farmer finally reached the riverbank. He did not stop, he continued to drag the body. He waded into the cold muddy water with the limp body behind him. When his feet could not touch the bottom any more, he swam, still dragging the body. The swift current carried the couple down stream.

A short while later, Ahma's husband returned to where the Rabis were still standing in a trance. He walked past them and his wife as if they were not there and headed straight to the house.

The Japanese soldier's horse was still there, tied to the threshing bin with its neck stretching toward the haystack. Moishe was standing next to it. She pulled a handful of hay from the stack and fed it to the horse. The farmer untied the horse.

"Can we keep it?" she asked patting on the horse's broad muscular neck.

"No," said the farmer.

"Why not?"

"No," the farmer repeated.

Just then they saw Ahma come looking for them.

"What are you going to do with it?" she asked while trying to hold back her sobs.

"Let it go," the farmer said.

"It will go straight back to its stable."

"I know."

"Then those Japs will come looking for their soldier."

"You are right."

"They will find us and kill us all."

"Not before I kill a few more of those animals."

"What about Miss?"

He turned to look at Moishe. She was petting the horse and feeding it straws.

"What about her?" the farmer asked.

"They have already killed our boy. We can't let them kill her too."

"What do you want me to do?"

"I don't know. But we just can't let the horse go back," Ahma started to cry again.

Ahma's husband did not utter another word. He looked around his feet and picked up a large rock. Holding the rock in one hand he untied the horse with his free hand. With the rein in his hand he headed toward the river. He did not stop at the bank. He led the horse straight into the river. He waded to where the flow of the river was strong. Then he mounted the horseback and urged the horse to go further into the river by kicking it and patting it on the behind. As the horse headed deeper into the river, it was swept off its feet by the fast current. The rider continued to guide the horse into deeper water and swifter current. The horse obeyed. When the farmer saw that he was far enough away from shore, he raised the rock with both of his hands. It came down. The horse's head slumped into the water. It struggled and came back up momentarily. The rock came down again. The head slumped and never resurfaced.

The Rabis and the peasants spent the rest of the day digging out the bloodstained dirt and carrying it out to the river. They dumped the dirt into the river and cleaned themselves.

"Will the Japs come back when they find the bodies?" Mrs. Rabi asked.

"It is a big river," Ahma said. "It flows to the sea. Nothing comes back."

Mrs. Rabi must admit that the Chinese peasants were closer to nature than any other people she had known. They accepted death as an animal did. After she buried her son, Ahma never mentioned him again.

CHAPTER SIXTEEN

In China, peasants did not know the concept of holidays or days off. Their lives were dictated by the phases of the moon, the seasons, the weather and the crops. But Mrs. Rabi noticed that Ahma's family always took a day off each week. Most curiously, it always fell on Saturday. How did they figure it out that day? The Chinese did not have weeks. It had nothing to do with either the moon or the sun.

"Is there some religious significance to it?" she asked Ahma one day.

"I don't know," answered the peasant woman. "We have always been doing that."

"For how long?"

"I don't know. Our parents practiced that. They followed their parents' practices. I never asked them how this all had started."

"Only among the people around here?"

"No, only us from Kaifeng."

"Everyone in Kaifeng?"

"No, just us."

"Are there many people like you?"

"You mean in Kaifeng?"

"Yes."

"I have no idea. I have never been there."

"Why do you do it then?"

"To obey and revere our ancestors. Don't you think we should, Mrs?"

"Of course, of course. Where were your ancestors from?"

"Kaifeng."

"I mean originally, many generations ago."

"I don't know."

"What's your family name?"

"Li."

Could they have come from Palestine? Could these people be Jews? Could the name Levin have changed into the Chinese name Li over the years? Their boy did look more handsome than ordinary Chinese. Although his face was typically Chinese, his nose did seem a little bit higher and straighter than the ordinary Chinese if one looked closely. Or was it her imagination?

"Do you have some family books?" Mrs. Rabi asked.

"Books? We are peasants, Mrs. We are illiterate. All our ancestors were illiterate. What would we do with books even if we had them?"

"Do you eat pork?"

"No."

Ah ha! Mrs. Rabi thought she had found the clue. "Why don't you eat pork?" she pursued further.

"We don't eat any meat."

"Why do you raise pigs then?"

"We sell them. Good business."

"Don't you eat chicken?"

"No, they are more expensive than pork."

"But you did serve chicken to us."

"You are foreigners. You must have meat. We did not have enough to serve you everyday."

Seeing that she was getting nowhere, Mrs. Rabi decided to ask a direct question.

"Are you *Yotahning?*" she asked bluntly.

"*Yotahning?*" the peasant woman could not believe what she had heard. "Are you joking, Mrs? Do I look *Yotahning*? Do my husband or my son look *Yotahning*? On the contrary, I think

Miss looks more and more like a Chinese peasant girl. What a nice pair she would have made with my..." Ahma started to cry again.

Mrs. Rabi quickly changed the subject.

"Can you teach me how to weave a basket, Ahma?"

The farm returned to the tranquility of the Garden of Eden.

"Garden of Eden?" scoffed Rabi. "More like a purgatory invented by the Christians. I can't take this any more."

"Just be patient a little longer," his wife tried to conciliate him.

"It's not a matter of patience when you are in a void where you cannot feel either space nor time."

"At least we are living."

"What's the point of living when there is nothing to live for? The only difference between life on this farm and life in the wilderness is here they have a roof over their heads and they grow and cook their food. There is no civilization, not to mention activities; there is no necessity to communicate, not to mention reading and writing; they don't listen to music; they don't even hum or play *erhu*...."

"What do you mean no music? Can't you hear the birds singing during the day and the insects chirping during the night? Couldn't you hear music in Ahma's wailing when she mourned? We can't in synagogues. But do we cant when we are in mourning? No, we just cry. You don't hear any music in crying."

"That's about the only thing they have here: insects, mosquitoes, flies and ants. And that's also the limit of the so-called culture of these country bumpkins."

"They remind us that we are alive."

"Yes, we are alive but the world around us is dead. How is this different from the world being alive and we being dead?"

"The difference is in the first situation we knew the world

240

was dead, but in the second situation, we could not tell whether the world was dead or alive."

"This is worse than the Nazi labor camps. No water, no electricity, no toilet, no meat..."

"This may be worse than the Nazi labor camps. But what we have is the best. What our hosts have is far worse. There is no good or bad. There is only better and worse. Besides, I am my own master. No one tells me what to do. It was my own choice to come here. No one forced me. Moreover, I know I can walk out of this place any time I want."

"Let's go back to Shanghai, Mama."

"Don't you remember why we came out here for? Whether the King of the Jews is dead or alive, the Japanese could not have given up looking for us. You want to go back and get caught by Goya? We are not just talking about labor camp then. We are talking about the firing squad!"

"It's a choice between living a life in a world without culture and risking one's life in a world with some culture. I would choose the latter. At least I would know that after they killed me, the culture would continue on."

"Try to go back to sleep."

It had been four months since that Japanese on horseback visited Ahma's farm. No one came after that. Being extra careful, Ahma's husband had not gone to the village during this time. Now that he was going to harvest his crops in just one more week, he decided to go to the next market day to pick up whatever he needed for harvesting. Still being cautious, he went by himself.

The farmer was not away very long. He came running back all excited.

"The Japs are gone! I did not see a single one. Not just from the village, they told me that they had completely pulled out of Chongming Island."

Rabi decided to go into town to find out for himself. Since no one on the farm read Chinese except his daughter, he took Moishe along with him. Besides, she knew the way to the village. She had been there.

What Rabi had found out was unbelievable. He rushed back like the farmer did and said to his wife. "Pack up. We are going back to Shanghai!"

"What about Goya?" Mrs. Rabi asked in apprehension.

"Goya?" her husband's voice sounded almost like rejoicing. "I hope he is still there. This time it is my turn to look him up. Japan has surrendered."

"When?"

"Two months ago."

"What about that crazy man?"

"Hitler? Who gives a damn about him? Germany has also surrendered."

"When?"

"Several months before Japan did."

Ahma made some hardboiled eggs in tea and some steamed buns. Then she took the fattest of her chickens and tied up its legs. She put all of them in a basket and handed it to Mrs. Rabi.

"There might still be a shortage of food in Shanghai."

"What about you, Ahma? Aren't you coming with us?"

"Our son is not here any more. I hate to leave my man alone on the farm," Ahma said apologetically, "especially at the harvest time."

"Does our daughter know that you are not coming with us?"

"She's big enough to take care of herself. Besides, the Japanese are gone. No one will bother her. I will sure miss her though. But I will go visit you some day, perhaps after the harvest."

There was a ferry to Shanghai once a day. The Rabis got on the ferry the very next morning.

242

Hongkew had changed a lot in the Rabis' absence. The most obvious change was the disappearance of the barbed wire and the gate that separated Hongkew from the rest of the city. Everybody, including the Jewish refugees, could go anywhere without passes. In the Concessions, the change of guards was visible. The tall buildings at the Bund that used to fly the flags of the rising sun now flew the flags of stars. Instead of the radiating rays from the sun, the flag was lined with stripes around the stars. They were both in red. The Japanese battleship Izumo Maru that had used to anchor in the Whampoo off the Bund was now replaced by a bigger American battleship, the USS St. Paul. They both had guns on deck. Only those on the American ship were bigger. The Japanese military trucks that had used to roar all over the city were replaced by the American army vehicles. The only difference was one in the color of earth and one in the color of spinach. The green-uniformed ill-tempered Japanese soldiers with pea-pot hats had also disappeared. They were replaced by the white-uniformed carefree American sailors with flowerpot hats. The replacements were just as rowdy as the replaced.

Returning to Teelanchow gave the Rabis a bittersweet feeling of homecoming. They found their old residence. The quaint Little Vienna Café was still there. But the main drag along the waterfront was taken over by a row of bars that had not been there before. They strung all the way from Teelanchow to Garden Bridge. They were brightly lit on the outside and dark inside. They were jammed with noisy drunken American sailors on shore leave. Loud music, accompanied by wild laughter, shouting and swearing, spilled out of these bars and muffled the bells of the tramcars and the hollering of the street hawkers. It was painful to Rabi's ears. Was that supposed to be music? It was so loud and so heavy in beat that one could not tell whether the melody was following the beat or the beat following the melody. Its monotone sound even put the instruments players themselves to sleep. No wonder they all wore dark glasses when they played. Was this supposed to be a neo-renaissance or a regression? Rabi could not decide which was better, this or the murderous performance of "the King of the Jews". Perhaps his wife was right. The sounds of birds and insects were more beautiful. Suddenly he missed the sounds and the tranquility of the farm. Was that what the war had done to civilization and culture?

The Rabis found that the Polish family downstairs had taken over their rooms upstairs. Their belongings had been packed up and moved downstairs.

"Sorry," the landlord apologized to the Rabis. "I had no clue what had happened to you. The Japanese soldiers came right after you left. They turned this place upside down and beat me up. Then a few days later a short Japanese officer came asking for you."

"The King of the Jews?"

"I don't know his name. He's the one who used to play the fiddle on the street."

"That's him. How did he look?"

"I did not look at him. But even with one arm in a sling, he beat me up with a cane when I told him I had not seen you. I did not know where you had gone or when you would come back. This continued for a few days. After he and the soldiers stopped coming, I picked your things up and moved them downstairs. I hope you don't mind, Mrs. Rabi. I won't collect rent for the months you were not here."

Although this time they had to share the downstairs rooms with the landlord's family, the Rabis felt lucky just to have a home to return to. Now that everything was back to normal, the tailor knew that he should not have any difficulty picking up his business again.

CHAPTER SEVENTEEN

During the two months the Rabis were still thinking that they were hiding from the Japanese, Shanghai had sprung back to its pre-war bustling glory, neon signs, cars and people. Freedom of speech reappeared. Neighbors started to have shouting matches on the streets again. Democracy returned. Everyone reclaimed his right of way in the streets against the dictatorship of the traffic lights. But the look of the apparel on the streets could not match up with that of the old days. The nicely tailored suits on the pre-war colonialists were now replaced by the khaki uniforms on the American military personnel. Rabi immediately saw his opportunity.

On the second day of his return to Hongkew, the tailor made a visit to the Headquarters of the U.S. Navy on the Bund. Being properly dressed and having a clean shaved Western face, he had no trouble in passing the marine guards with his limited English. On this very first visit, he got two orders. When he went back to deliver the suits, he got more orders than he could handle.

He hired three Chinese tailors and turned his crowded apartment into a workshop. The Chinese tailors turned out excellent work and worked fast. They could actually sew better and faster than he did. Their only drawback, which became Rabi's advantage, was that they were slow to accept the new style. So Rabi did the cutting and they did the sewing. Before long, Rabi needed to hire more tailors. The Rabis' life suddenly took a big change. But the Teelanchow apartment was not big enough for his business.

Rabi thought, since he was setting the fashion for the post-war Shanghai, he might as well move into the most fashionable district of the city, the French Concession. With the recommendation of one of his influential customers, he rented an apartment on the 10th floor of the most prestigious residence hall in Shanghai, Grosvenor House. It was hidden in a secluded garden behind a row of expensive stores on the fashionable Rue Cardinal Mercier. Best of all, there was no more chanting of *Matin de Shanghai* in the morning and the hollering of the street vendors. His tailor shop occupied one of the slick-looking storefronts with a large display window. It was only a hundred meters from Avenue Joffre, the Champs-Elysées of Shanghai. Across the street was the French Tennis Club. A block south of this exclusive complex was Lyceum Theater, the home of Shanghai Symphony Orchestra, where Moishe had given her concert before they made their escape to Chongming Island.

As soon as the Rabis settled down in their trendy apartment, Mrs. Rabi went to Ohel Moishe Synagogue to look up her friends in the Kadimah group. She found the spirit among them soaring sky high. The Zionists of Shanghai realized for the first time that their dream could finally be realized. The philosophical discourse at Kadimah transformed into concrete planning. How to draft a constitution? How to negotiate with the British Empire? How should they go about it? What if the British said no? But first thing first. What kind of state did they want?

"A state for the Jews," was the basic understanding from the very beginning.

"For Jews only?" someone raised the question as an argument.

"Of course! Who else?" were the counter argument and the general consensus.

"Wait a minute," Mrs. Rabi raised her voice. "Let us not lose our heads. What all of us loathe most in our lives is that for generations after generations we have been excluded as foreigners by the countries we adopted wholeheartedly. We patriotically called them our homeland. What kind of home is it when our so-called 'countrymen' did not accept us? The truth is: we have never had a homeland. Because of that we want to have our own. Are you telling me that now we want to do exactly the same thing we loathed, to exclude people other than the Jews? I think this new state should set an example to the rest of the world that people of different races, different religions and different skin colors can live together equitably and peacefully. The city of Jerusalem is a good example."

"It's not that," Rabbi Meir Ashkenazi pointed out. "The purpose of a Jewish state is to fulfill a revelation in the Bible."

Mrs. Rabi was just a lone voice in an ocean of fanatic Zionists. She finally told her family, "If that is what they mean by Zionism, I want no part of it."

"Let's go home," suggested her husband as a comfort to his wife.

"Where is home?" she asked.

"Where our roots are. Where we can find our own culture."

"Where is that place?"

"Vienna, of course. Look at these people around us. They have, to put it politely, a totally *different* culture from ours. Take for instance; while impressionism has already become something in the past for our art, they are just beginning to argue whether or not nudity should be allowed in art. They've got a long way to catch up with the rest of the world. We can never blend in."

"At least we have made a living here. At least these people have accepted us. As a matter of fact, they have treated us as more than their equal."

"What do you mean *more than their equal?*"

"We can stay and become one of them while maintaining

247

our superiority. Our hosts will make sure that the life of the foreigners will always be above the average. Have you ever seen a foreign beggar or coolie on the street?"

"I'll say being less than equal in Europe is still better than being more than equal here."

"Do you really want to go back to that ghetto? Do you think that I could hire a cook, a laundrywoman, an ahma, let alone finding someone as faithful as Ahma? Do you think in Vienna we could move into an apartment like the Grosvenor House? Do you think I could join any social club as I wanted and find people there to argue about Zionism? Do you know where our old neighbors and friends are at this very moment? Do you believe that our so-called countrymen who kicked us out will now welcome us back with open arms? Here we are at least among friends."

"But look what kind of friends our own daughter makes here: a Gypsy, a flunky, an illiterate fisherman, an ignorant peasant and who knows what other Chinese without any culture. Do you see any nice Jewish boy?"

"Is that what you want, to have her meet only nice Jewish boys? Then go back to your ghetto!"

Moishe couldn't care less about Zionism, Vienna, Champs-Elysées, Maria-Theresa Strauss or the ghetto. All the places she knew were right here in Shanghai: Shanghai Jewish Youth Association School, the Fish Market, Ziegawei, the private tennis court and swimming pool at the Shens, Lyceum Theater, the Red House, the Russian food at Kavkaz and the gold-gilded interior of the movie house Cathay on Avenue Joffre. As far as she was concerned, this was her hometown, the place where she came to know about life. The first things Moishe did after returning to Shanghai was to look up her friends. She went to Ziegawei. To her disappointment, Jue's mother told her that Jue had gone to America.

"His father and I thought that if he was really serious about music and wanted to advance, he must go study in the West. There are not many activities here, not to mention great masters to take music lessons from. Western music is not a part of the culture of China," Jue's mother said. "We told him that music is for the ears. One cannot learn music by studying and practicing without listening. But he had kept dragging his feet until he gave up on your return. By the way, shortly after Jue left, your friend Lenduai came by one day. He said he had gone to your place and found out that you had moved out of town."

"Do you have his address?"

"He did not leave one with me. But from the way he talked, I had the impression that he was going somewhere far away."

"Why do you think so?"

"He said since he was not going to see you again, he asked me to give you something. Let me go get it."

It was the Stradivarius. Moishe found a note in the box, scribbled in ungrammatical German as the one he handed to the guard at Goya's French villa when he and Moishe went to retrieve the Stradivarius.

Moishe: Would you please give this back to Papa? It is too good for a Gypsy. It should be played only by a virtuoso. Also tell him that the band at Red House needs a violinist. Lenduai

Moishe was at a loss. Without Jue and Lenduai, Shanghai did not look the same as before. Out of desperation, she went to her old hangout, the Fish Market. She could hardly recognize the place. There were no shroud-less masts topped with the red square *Marco Polo* hats nor the big bulging eyeballs gawking over the muddy water. Yet the naked kids were still there. They were diving off the pier into the Whampoo River. But she could not recognize any of them.

There was a yacht tied alongside the dock. Her snow-white

hull was trimmed in red around the bulwark and the top of the cabin. It was a two-story cabin with curtained windows. There was a mast but no sails or bamboo battens. Instead of a Marco Polo hat, it had a bucket on its top that was large enough to hide a person. Moishe peeped through a window. The inside was painted in a sky blue color. There was a long table with benches around it. It was covered with a checkerboard tablecloth. On the table there were a tray of fruits and a cake. There were even electric lights. Someone was cooking on a large iron stove. The smell resembled her of her mother's cooking.

As Moishe was wondering what a yacht was doing at the Fish Market, someone stepped out of the cabin. It was a man with blond hair wearing a red and white checkerboard shirt. They looked at each other with puzzling expressions.

"What the hell is a lady like you doing here?" the man asked.

"What is a yacht doing at the Fish Market?"

"I don't see any yacht."

"This one you are on."

"Ha, ha, ha, ha!" the man broke out in a laugh that sounded like the barking of a sea lion. "You call this a yacht? I wish she were."

"What is she then?"

"A fishing boat, can't you see?"

"But there are no sails."

"Sails! Are you living in the Moby Dick time? We have a 300 horse power engine that will drag any fuckin net."

"Where are the others?" Moishe asked.

"What others?"

"The fishing junks."

"Oh, junks. I don't know. But I saw a whole bunch of them at Wusong."

"Where is that?"

"At the entrance of the Whampoo."

"How do you go there?"

"That's the first place you hit when coming into the river from the Yangtze."

"I know," said Moishe. "I mean how do you go there by land."

"That you've got me. Why do you want to know?"

"I want to go there."

"What for?"

"I want to look up someone on one of the junks."

"I can take you there."

"Will you?"

"After lunch."

"Shall I come back then?"

"Why don't you stay and have lunch with us?"

"You don't mind?"

"Why should I mind? Hop on board."

Moishe had long forgotten the smell of butter and the taste of bake potatoes, oven-fresh bread, roast beef, beets, onion, cake and pie. They brought back the good old days before they put up the barbwire fence in Hongkew or, more exactly, her childhood days in Vienna.

After lunch, the fishing boat took off and sailed downstream toward the entrance of the Whampoo. The sailing on a boat with an engine was so much different from that on a sailing junk. There was no tacking; there were no iron ships crossing their bow; there was no walking from one side of the boat to the other to push the tiller hard alee in tacking. One just stood there and turn a wheel. It looked so much easier.

"May I steer for a while?" she asked.

"Have you done it before?" the captain asked.

"No, but I have sailed on a junk."

"A junk! What the hell were you doing on a junk?"

"Fishing," Moishe answered with great pride.

"I'll be damned! But isn't steering the tiller on a junk a job for the laoda?"

"Yes, but the Laoda let me do it."

"You're not kidding? Okay, take over, Laoda."

The American could not believe his eyes when he saw how Moishe handled the boat in the jam-packed traffic of sampans with oars, junks under sails and the huge iron ships. They all behaved as if they owned the river.

When they reached Wusong, Moishe was flabbergasted to see so many junks crowded in the tiny harbor.

"You want me to take over the wheel?" asked the American skipper.

"I can handle it," Moishe said with great confidence. "It's much easier than handling a tiller."

"You read Chinese?" the American asked.

"Yes."

"What's the junk's name?"

"Junks don't usually have names. Those few that do have names don't display them."

"Then what's the use of having names?"

"For good luck."

"How are you going to recognize the junk your friend is on?"

"How do you recognize your wife, by her look or by her name?"

"These junky junks all look alike to me."

"That's what the Chinese say about us. All foreigners look alike."

"You've got to be kidding."

"Look at that one over there? She's cockeyed. And look at the one next to her. Her nose is broken."

"Holy Moses! They do look different. Do you see your friend's junk?"

"No."

Moishe was greatly disappointed. After looking at every one of them, she still could not spot Ah Bong's junk. Finally after an hour's search, she gave up.

"She must be at sea," Moishe concluded.

"Let's go home then," the American captain said.

Home for the American fishing boat did not look like any place in China. Moishe had been here before. It used to be a marshland separated from the bank by a narrow canal. Now in front of Moishe's eyes, there appeared a Norwegian fishing village! There was a long wooden pier on the waterfront that Moishe had never seen before. There must be over a hundred boats, that looked just like the one she was on, tied alongside the pier. The place had a smell of tar. On the pier, there were people working on nets. There were all Westerners.

"Where did these boats come from?" Moishe asked in puzzlement.

"America."

"What are they doing here?"

"Fishing."

"All of them?"

"Yeah."

"How does one find his boat? There are so many of them."

"They all have names."

"I don't see them," said Moishe.

"They are painted on their bows and their sterns."

"But they are all blocked by the other boats."

"Oh, don't worry. A fisherman can always recognize his own boat."

"They all look the same to me."

"Wait until you get to know one. You will see that she is totally different from all the others. Take our boat for example. See our mast? Then look at the other masts. See the difference?"

"Just like the junks then," Moishe said.

"There you go. By the way, you want to stay for dinner? Our cook is the best cook in the whole fleet. He even cooks Norwegian. He used to cook for the Consul General of Norway."

"I like his cooking."

Moishe Fantasy

Moishe not only stayed for dinner, she stayed after dinner talking to the crew. Half of them were Americans and half of them were Chinese from Ningpo. Moishe had picked up enough Ningpo dialect on her fishing expedition to thrill these Ningpo fishermen. She talked to both the Americans and the Chinese like natives of both places and laughed with them as one of them. By the time she realized that it was time for her to go home, the tramcar had long stopped running.

"I have an extra bunk in my cabin on topside," the captain said. "You can sleep in there tonight."

The "cabin on topside" was behind the wheelhouse. Besides the two bunks stacked on top of each other, there were all kinks of navigation instruments that bewildered Moishe. The one in which she was interested the most was the two-way radio. It was on when she walked into the cabin. She could hear fishermen at sea, all Americans, talking to each other. Listening to them talking about the condition of the sea and their catches. She suddenly felt that she was at sea herself.

Just as Moishe was climbing into the top bunk, her waist was grabbed by two strong arms. She turned around and found the captain's lips on hers. He smelled heavily of alcohol. It was repulsive. On top of that the captain had a strong body odor.

No one has ever kissed her on the lips, not even her mother. She pushed the captain away and said, "I am tired."

The American did not insist. He just climbed into the lower bunk with a sulk.

Moishe was really tired. She fell asleep right away. But in the middle of the night, she woke up gasping for air. She found her body pinned in the bunk by a naked hairy body and a hand caressing her breasts. The bunk was too narrow to push the body away. She tried to get up. She bumped her head on the cabin top.

When she gave up, to her amazement, she found the tickling sensation on her nipples quite pleasant. If she had known that, she thought, she wouldn't have pushed Ah Bong

254

away on the sampan. To get her mind off this American she barely knew, she tried to imagine that it was Lenduai.

The Shanghai Jewish Youth Association School was back in session. But Moishe did not go back. She did not even want to go near the place. Her last experience in the school auditorium was still haunting her. She was just half an academic year from graduation anyway. She wouldn't learn anything new in that time.

With the Japanese gone, the colonialists returned. It also brought the American military and the United Nations relief organization to Shanghai. That opened a new employment opportunity to the residents of this war-torn metropolis, particularly to the expatriates. The first priority in any employment was always given to the Europeans: foreign nationals, stateless or refugees from Europe. The Chinese accepted the practice as normal. To them it was just natural that every warm-blooded human being must take care of his own kind first.

Even though Moishe did not finish high school, it did not take her long to get a secretarial job at the United Nations headquarters. The place was located in the tallest building, the Broadway Mansion, on the north shore of the congested Soochow River. Having no working experience of any sort, she started at the bottom. However, she was quite content about it. For the Chinese, the same job would require a college degree. Besides, as an European, her starting pay was many times higher than that of the Chinese girl who was training her. Needless to say, it was many, many times more than what her mother paid to Ahma! Was it fair? The Chinese girl who was training her thought it was fair enough. She told Moishe that her pay was much higher than some of her friends who worked in some Chinese government offices. Moishe recalled what Ah Bong had said about catching the dolphin, that there was nothing fair in this world. "Everything has been predestined by fate." It looked like Ah Bong was right. In her world in Shanghai, her fate depended on what color her skin was, not on what she knew.

For the first time in her life, Moishe was on her own. Her father was busy in his tailoring business, her mother was busy with her social activities and Ahma was not there to listen to her or to tail her covertly when she went out. She had to watch out for herself when she went out at night. During the Japanese occupation she had to watch out for the drunken Japanese soldiers. Now she had to watch out for the drunken American sailors. The difference was: the Japanese soldiers grabbed girls on the streets by brute force whereas the American sailors grabbed them with their cigarettes, can food, nylon stockings and their American dollars. "Pom-pom, five bucks? No? Ten bucks?" The former were conquerors. The latter were liberators. With the Japanese soldiers, there was no escape. But with the American sailors, it depended on one's will power. Was that what Free Will was supposed to mean?

Now that Moishe did not have either Lenduai or Jue to go out with, she did not know how to spend her evenings. She found herself looking forward to the American fisherman to return from sea. The desire was purely physical though. He was not like Lenduai or Jue or even Ah Bong. With the American there was nothing to talk about or to do.

In the lonely evenings, all Moishe could think of doing was to go to the movies. After the war, the theaters in Shanghai were flooded with new American movies. But most moviegoers were Chinese who could not understand any English. They needed to have all the dialogues translated. Being proficient in many languages, Moishe found an evening job as a simultaneous translator in Roxy, a theater owned by an American motion picture company, Warner Brothers, on Nanking Road. Not only she could watch movies free of charge, she could also earn some extra money. On the nights she did not work, she would go to Red House to listen to the Gypsy music. It reminded her of Lenduai.

"Hey, why don't you ask your dad to come play with us?" the accordion player asked Moishe one day. "We need a violinist."

"What makes you think he will come?" she asked.

"Lenduai said he is a pretty good violinist."

"Why should any good violinist come to play with you?"

"For fun."

"Fun?"

"Lenduai said he likes to play."

"He's too busy with his business."

"You play the piano?"

"A little bit."

"Lenduai said you are a pretty good pianist. You want to come play with us?"

"Me?" Moishe was surprised to be asked.

"With just an accordion and a bass, we can't do much."

"What about Lenduai? Will he come back?"

"Maybe."

Hearing the word *maybe,* Moishe's heart rate shot up. Perhaps Lenduai might come back for her. Hadn't he sneaked on board the refugee ship just to be with her? Hadn't he come back to the school to look her up? Hadn't he come back to play in her concert? She could feel deep in her heart that Lenduai would come back for her. "All right," Moishe finally consented. Then she added, "Just for the time being, until Lenduai comes back."

CHAPTER EIGHTEEN

As Rabi returned to the Grosvenor House from his shop, the uniformed gateman tipped his hat and greeted him in English with a heavy Shanghai accent, "Good evening, Mr. Rabi," while pulling open the tall glass door framed in wrought iron. Rabi nodded to acknowledge the greeting and headed straight to the elevator. The elevator operator in white jacket greeted him in English, "Good evening, Mr. Rabi."

Rabi got off on the tenth floor. He rang the bell. Wang-sao opened the door and greeted him in Chinese,

"Ning huilai-le, lao-ye?"

Rabi was surprised to find the dining table covered with a fine Swatow laced tablecloth, delicate Jingdezheng china and patterned Indian sterling silverwares his wife had recently acquired.

"Is that you, Papa?" his wife's voice rang out from the kitchen.

He could never figure out that woman. When they were living in their crowded Hongkew apartment and had limited foodstuff available, she spent more time in that dirty kitchen shared by two other families, showing the cook how to cook on the tiny coal-burning firepot. Now that she had a roomy spic-and-span modern kitchen equipped with a white enamel gas range that had four burners and a full oven, she was rarely seen in the kitchen. During the war when the Jews in Europe were haunted by the Nazi and barred to enter the free world by all the allied countries, she was such a diehard in trying to create an independent state for the suppressed. Now that their suppressors had been put down, she dissociated herself completely from the Zionist movement. She spent most of her time mingling with the wives of the high society of Shanghai that was made up of former colonialists, the officers of the American occupying force and the Western business leaders. She even became a member of the French tennis club across the street.

"Whom are we expecting for dinner?" he asked.

"You've been complaining that your daughter was associating with the wrong people, Gypsies, fishermen, street kids and Chinese. Well, she has invited an American home for dinner tonight."

"A Jewish boy?"

"Who knows? There are so many Jews in America. Everyone in Hongkew can find a relative in America, the Lewinskis, the Schnepps, the Brownschwicks, the Ostroffs... Can you name one who has not applied for the American visa except us?"

"Did you do the cooking today?"

"What do you think I am doing in the kitchen now? Playing?"

"Where is Dahsifu?"

"He's helping me. Now that we have all the ingredients I can get my hands on, I am showing him how to cook a real Jewish dinner."

"What is a Jewish dinner?"

The Rabis' dinner guest showed up promptly at six. He dressed as a typical American, his jacket and pants were of different and mismatching colors. He was wearing a colored shirt and a tie in a loud color. How distasteful! But the tailor knew he should be the last one to complain. If these Americans were not so ignorant in fashion, his business couldn't have been so good. Every American, whether he was with the military, the United

Nations or the Red Cross, would have several fashionable suits made before returning home. But something about this American was bothering him. He did not look Jewish. The tailor finally figured out that it was the color of his hair. It was platinum blond. He had to look very hard to see that there were indeed eyebrows and long eyelashes on his face. He reminded the tailor of one of those Aryan people regarded by the Nazi as the superior race.

"This is for you, Mr. Rabi," the American handed to his host a package wrapped in newspaper. It was as large as a violin box.

"What is it?" the tailor asked.

"Open it."

Rabi unwrapped the package. It was a fish, with head and tail and scales! It was wet. It immediately reminded him of Ah Bong, the young Chinese fisherman who had used to bring them fresh fish wrapped in newspaper when food was so scarce in Shanghai during the Japanese occupation. Another fisherman? Why was his daughter always attracted to these people of little culture? Hadn't he and his wife provided her enough cultural environment?

"We caught this on our last drag before we returned to port. Nothing could be fresher than that," said the American.

"What kind of fish is that?" the tailor asked.

"A flounder."

"So big!"

"This is not big at all. You should have seen the halibut we caught in Alaska. This fish would be considered under size in America. It would have to be thrown back into the water. But here on these waters it is as big as they can come. These Chinamen have been raking the bottom of their coast in their junks long before our people had sea-going boats. There are so many of them junks that they have completely out-fished their waters. Pretty soon they won't have nothing left to fish for any more."

260

"With motorized fishing boats being brought into China after the war, you mean there are still fishing junks?" His daughter's fishing adventure came into his mind when he heard the word junks.

"You bet. There are more junks on the China coast than sea gulls."

"If fish is so plentiful in America, what brought you to China to fish?" asked Rabi.

"We were contracted by UNRRA to bring motorized fishing boats from America to China to modernize her fishery."

"What's UNRRA?"

"It stands for United Nations Relief and Rehabilitation Administration. We call it You Never Really Receive Anything from it. Ha, ha, ha, ha!"

"Where are you from?"

"Seattle."

"I mean where did your ancestors come from?"

"Oh, you mean where my old man came from? Norway."

Rabi suddenly felt relieved. "I heard that the Norwegians are very sympathetic to the Jews during the war," he said.

"Yeah, there are many Jews in Seattle. In fact, one of my neighbors is a Jew."

"I mean the Norwegians in Norway."

"That I wouldn't know beans about. I've never been to the old country. Come to think of it, it's rather strange. In America we have fishermen from everywhere in the world. Scandinavians, Slavs, Italians, Greeks, Japanese, you name it, but no Jewish fishermen."

"We were told that when the Nazi's ordered all the Jews in Norway to wear the Star of David, the King of Norway was the first one to pin one on his chest. Then the whole country followed suit."

"That ought to serve them Krauts right!"

"Krauts?"

"Sour Krauts."

"Sour Krauts?"

"I mean those God-damn Germans. Those Jews in Norway were sure lucky. They should have nothing to complain about. They should have seen those wretched live skeletons left in Germany."

"What live skeletons?"

"I was with the 55th battalion in Europe during the war. Shortly after the Krauts surrendered, we came upon this death camp. The only way we could tell that they were still alive was that they were standing on their own feet and their eyes were wide open."

"You mean the Nazi labor camp?"

"Labor camp? You've got to be kidding? What kind of work could the Krauts expect to get out of those skeletons? Let me tell you, there were no labor camps in Germany, only death camps."

"Where was this camp?"

"In this place called Dachau."

"Did you say death camp?" Rabi tried to confirm what he had just heard. Ever since the end of the war, there were rumors circulating among the refugees in Hongkew that the Nazis had set up many concentration camps to round up the Jews. Labor camps, he could believe. They provided free labor to help the Third Reich. Death camps? He could not imagine. He knew many Germans, as colleagues in music as well as his customers. They were no different from the Jews. Some might be arrogant, looking down on all non-Germans perhaps, but not inhuman. The rumor claimed that all the internees were sent to the gas chambers. What good would that do to the Germans? The Germans were practical people. He had challenged these rumor spreaders to show evidence to support their claim. So far no one could name any relatives or friends as victims or witness. Basing on that, Rabi discarded it as a Jewish anti-Nazi propaganda. There was a saying in Chinese, "The winners are called kings; the losers are called bandits." He knew his people too well. They like to cry and complain on every little pain to get sympathy. But now this American was telling him that he had actually seen face to face those "live skeletons"! He was not a Jew. There was no reason for him to make up the story. But if it was a death camp as he said, "How could you still find people alive?" the tailor asked.

"We found out later that they were waiting."

"Waiting for what?"

"To have their numbers called."

"For what?"

"For being put into the fuckin oven."

"What oven?"

"The incinerator."

"People say they were put to the gas chambers."

"What difference does it make? They all end up as ashes."

"Was that what these survivors told you?" the tailor asked in skepticism.

"No, they were so scared that they would not respond to any of our questions. Every time we asked a question, they huddled tighter together while glaring at us with fear. I guess it was our uniforms and the dark barrels of our rifles."

"Perhaps they could not understand what you said."

"Don't worry, they understood us plenty well. We had people in our battalion who spoke German, Polish, you name it. Even Yiddish and Navaho."

"What were the expressions on their faces when you told them they were freed?"

"Expressions? Even if they had expressions, what could they express on? There were no muscles on these skeletons. In fact, you couldn't even tell a child's face from that of an old man."

"Then how did you know what they were waiting for?"

"You had to be a moron not to. All you needed was to smell the air around you and to look at the smoke still coming out of the smokestacks. The fuckin place was filled with the smell of death. The only distinction between the dead and the living was the dead smelled and the living can smell. We opened the gate. No one moved. We even tore down the barbwire to show them that we meant what we said. Still no one moved. They just stared at us."

"Were they Jews?"

"Some, I imagine. How would I know? What does a Jew look like? I couldn't even tell women from men among them. But the Red Cross people, who came to take over the camp from us later, told us that they were the ones the Krauts considered scum and bad elements of the human race. There were Jews, Pollocks, Gypsies..."

Gypsies? The King and his family immediately came to the tailor's mind. He wondered if they had been caught and thrown into one of those camps. The evenings he had spent with the King drinking wine and playing the violins were the happiest time in his life. He recalled what the King had told him about Moses playing the Red Sea on harmonics. He remembered what the King had said about the rulers and the ruled. He was such a philosopher in his own right.

"How many of them were there?" he asked.

"No one knows," said the American. "They came in trainloads as animals and left in truckloads of dirt, I mean ashes. No one knows how to count ashes. It could be tens of thousands, hundreds of thousands... I wouldn't have any doubt if anyone told me that a million of them had gone through that place. Yet remember, that was not the only death camp. There were many more places like that in occupied Europe."

Just then Mrs. Rabi called out from the kitchen, "Dinner is ready."

After everybody sat down, Moishe went to get the menorah and started to light the candles.

"Why the candles?" asked the tailor. "Besides, it's your mother's job, not yours."

"Do you know what day it is today, Papa?"

"Not Friday, not Passover, not..."

"Do you remember what you have asked me to remind you when you get old and senile and forgetful?"

"I'm old but I'm not yet senile!"

"But you have become forgetful."

"What did I forget?" the tailor asked.

"You do not remember what day it is today?"

"What day?"

"It was ten years ago tonight when we had our last dinner in our apartment in Vienna."

"Oh, yes. Has it been that long?"

No one paid any attention to the tailor's question. Moishe lighted the candles one by one. Mrs. Rabi and her dinner guest watched in silence. The tailor's mind was somewhere else. Then suddenly, he broke the silence:

"*Baruch Ata Adonay. Yit-ga-dal ve-yit-ka-dash she-mei ra-ba be-al-ma de-ve-ra chi-re-utei...*"

"Papa, what are you reciting?" Moishe interrupted her father. But the tailor just ignored his daughter and kept on reciting,

"*Ve-yam-lich mal-chu-tei be-cha-yei-chon u-ve-yo-mei-chon u-ve-cha-yei de-chol beit yis-ra-iel, ba-a-ga-la u-ve-ze-man ka-riv, ve-i-me-ru: a-mein.*"

The American could not understand a word of it. He was staring at the tailor in fascination. He had had many dinners at his Jewish neighbor's home back in Seattle. But he had never seen them perform such a colorful ritual. Moishe, on the other hand, felt embarrassed by her father. He is really getting old, she thought. As the tailor went on, "*Ye-hei she-mei ra-ba me-va-rach...*" the daughter could not keep quiet any longer.

"Papa, you are saying the Kaddish!"

"Shut up!" said the tailor to his daughter. "Haven't you heard what your friend said about the truckloads of ashes that went out of the death camps?"

Suddenly he smelled food. Was that what his wife meant

by *Jewish food?* It did not matter. What mattered was that he could smell. As the American had said, he must be alive!

"Why should we bother to give thanks for our food when what we really must be thankful for is to have our lives?" the tailor asked. "The ashes cannot speak and have no one to say the Kaddish for them."

Then he raised his hands and cried out: "*Oh my God! Oh my God! Why did You let the few of us live and let so many others be butchered?*" But like those skeletons hurdled behind the barbwire, no voice came out of the tailor's mouth. Seeing pain and frustration on her father's face, Moishe stepped in to help out:

"Blessed be the lord of life, the righteous Judge for evermore..."

Then the tailor's voice came back. Halting at times, he joined his daughter,

"To the departed whom we now remember... may peace and bliss be granted in the world of eternal life... May they find grace and mercy before the Lord of heaven and earth... May their souls rejoice in that ineffable good which God has laid up for those that fear Him, and may their memory be a blessing unto those that cherish it... May the Father of peace send peace to all troubled souls..."

Peace? You call that peace? The tailor questioned in his mind while he was reciting the words. Why did God talk about peace on the one hand and allow it to be broken on the other hand? Is this a part of His grand design? Is sacrificing the innocent an ineffable good? Good for what? To teach the evil or to reward them?

He quickly ended his prayer,

"And comfort all the bereaved among us. Amen."

About the Author

Paul Chow grew up in the family of a government railroad manager. His father would have assignments that were constantly changing from one railroad line to another. As a result, he went to fourteen different schools for the eleven years of primary and secondary education he had received in China. During WWII, Chow quit school to join the Allied Forces in Burma to fight against the invading Japanese. After the war, he took up fishing and went to sea. But nine years of fishing turned out to be a boring life for him. In 1955, he bought a Chinese sailing junk to enter a trans-Atlantic yacht race. Without any sailing experience, he set out to cross the oceans with five of his friends. Having gone through a foul start, a typhoon on the China Sea and a strong gale along the coast of Japan, they arrived late for the race. At the age of 29, Chow went back to school. Ten years later, he obtained a PhD degree in physics from Northwestern University and went into teaching for the next 29 years. After retirement, Chow has devoted his time in writing. His work includes three novels, two biographies, two journeys and one physics book for non-science readers.

9399612R0017

Made in the USA
Charleston, SC
09 September 2011